BATTLE MOUNTAIN

ALSO BY C. J. BOX

BATTLE MOUNTAIN

A JOE PICKETT NOVEL

C. J. BOX

G. P. PUTNAM'S SONS
NEW YORK

PUTNAM
— EST. 1838 —

G. P. Putnam's Sons
Publishers Since 1838
An imprint of Penguin Random House LLC
1745 Broadway, New York, NY 10019
penguinrandomhouse.com

Title-page and section photograph by TPCImagery—Mike Jackson/Shutterstock

Library of Congress Cataloging-in-Publication Data

Names: Box, C. J., author.
Title: Battle mountain / C. J. Box.
Description: New York: G.P. Putnam's Sons, 2025. | Series: Joe Pickett novel
Identifiers: LCCN 2024050549 (print) | LCCN 2024050550 (ebook) |
ISBN 9780593851050 (hardcover) | ISBN 9780593851067 (epub)
Subjects: LCGFT: Detective and mystery fiction. | Thrillers (Fiction) | Novels.
Classification: LCC PS3552.O87658 B38 2025 (print) | LCC PS3552.O87658 (ebook) |
DDC 813/.54—dc23/eng/20241122
LC record available at https://lccn.loc.gov/2024050549
LC ebook record available at https://lccn.loc.gov/2024050550

Printed in the United States of America
1st Printing

The authorized representative in the EU for product safety and compliance is Penguin Random House
Ireland, Morrison Chambers, 32 Nassau Street, Dublin D02 YH68, Ireland,
https://eu-contact.penguin.ie.

For Olive
and Laurie, always

And for Daisy, RIP

"Time is measured by a clock of blood."

—J. A. Baker, *The Peregrine*

BATTLE MOUNTAIN

PART ONE

"He mounted like a rocket, curved over in splendid parabola, dived down through cumulus of pigeons. One bird fell back, gashed dead, looking astonished, like a man falling out of a tree. The ground came up and crushed it."

—J. A. Baker, *The Peregrine*

CHAPTER ONE

Seven Months Before

Nate Romanowski was thigh-high in the icy water of North Piney Creek under the craggy profile of the snow-covered Wyoming Range. He was there to kill a man named Axel Soledad, whom he'd pursued in a state of unhinged fury for months.

Soledad had left a trail of death and destruction behind him in his hunger for revenge against Nate and Joe Pickett. The cost had been catastrophic.

Liv. The blood, the body.

Nate blamed himself for his wife's death.

He blamed Axel Soledad more.

It was mid-April and the ice was finally breaking up. Large three-inch-thick platters of it bobbed along the surface, carried by the current. As he crossed the creek, he kept one eye upriver so he could spot the largest chunks floating his way and dodge them, lest they knock him off-balance. Even though he wore a pair of waders that he'd purchased at a fly-fishing shop in Pinedale, a

3

small town with a welcome sign that announced that it was All the Civilization You Need, the water was so cold that his legs had gone numb and he could barely feel his feet. The water in the freestone river was so clear he could see the rounded maroon and beige river rocks between his boots.

Nate was tall, blond, and rangy. His eyes were icy blue and piercing and they peered out from a high-altitude windburned face with high cheekbones and a hatchet-like nose. He wore his long hair tied back in a ponytail with a leather falcon's jess.

Under his parka was the weight of a Freedom Arms .454 Casull handgun loaded with five rounds. Half a box of spare cartridges was in his parka pocket. He doubted he'd need them. Five rounds meant five dead bodies, and from what he'd learned, there were only four people at his destination.

AT OVER SEVEN thousand feet in the mountains, it was still winter. Crusty snow clogged the pine tree–lined banks, and the first green shoots emerging from the snowpack were at least a month away. It was twenty-two degrees Fahrenheit and every breath he exhaled was in the form of a condensation cloud.

The night before, Nate had learned through a barroom conversation in Big Piney that a man matching Soledad's description had been holed up in a bizarre rental property on the west bank of Piney Creek. The property belonged to a marina owner from the Ozarks who was a Wild West aficionado. The Missourian had purchased a onetime line shack on a small private holding and transformed it into a mini frontier village with a two-story lodge, false-front outbuildings, and a serve-yourself saloon.

People would go crazy for it, the owner had announced. The locals in Big Piney and Pinedale had been less impressed. The property was so isolated that very few tourists ever booked it, and those who did were lucky to find it. It sounded like the perfect place for Soledad.

Soledad had shown up in the town of Big Piney a week ago with three others, Nate had learned—two men in their midthirties and a woman who appeared to be Soledad's girlfriend. They'd arrived in an older-model Honda Civic with Colorado plates.

While one of the men had retrieved the keys to the place from a local realtor who served as the owner's agent, the man behind the wheel had gotten out of the Honda and walked stiffly around on a pair of crutches. That was undoubtedly Soledad. Nate had no idea who the other three were, but one of Soledad's traits was collecting hangers-on. This certainly fit the pattern.

The drinks he had bought for the talkative realtor last night had been well worth it, Nate thought.

HE'D FOUND OUT during midnight reconnaissance that the remote lodge could be accessed off a county road and then a two-track that ended at the house. The only way to approach would be to drive his Jeep right up to the front door, which was not a good plan.

Rather, Nate stayed on a rough path that hugged the curves of North Piney Creek. He'd found a place to hide his vehicle off-road. Then he'd left it at three in the morning and worked his way downstream along the tangled bank of the creek. It had been hard going—there was no game trail or natural path—and he'd had to bushwhack through frozen brush and outstretched tree roots. For about half a mile, the creek had been frozen solid and he could slide his way along the top of it. But when he saw black openings in the ice ahead of him in the moonlight, and the surface began to crack under his weight, he realized that the only way he was going to be able to proceed was to get into the water.

When he did, the cold shocked him even through the waders, but Nate didn't mind. Like most prey, including big game, Soledad would never expect a threat to come from the water.

As THE SUN lit up the tops of the pine trees in a warm orange, the lodge came into view around a bend in the creek. The buildings were dark and squarish, and no artificial light shone from any of the windows.

Nate hugged the right bank, keeping the thick brush between him and the structures as he approached the enclave. It was as it had been described to him: a two-level wooden clapboard building and a small jumble of faux-Western businesses. A thin line of woodsmoke clung to the top of a chimney pipe and looked like a vaporous flag.

An older-model Honda sedan was parked on the side of the lodge.

Nate found himself shaking, and he stepped out of the creek onto the icy rocks to calm himself. He looked hard at the lodge, trying to guess which room Soledad would be in.

So, he thought. It has come down to this.

"Get ready, Axel," he whispered.

———

NATE ENTERED THE close-packed pines upstream from the enclave and slowly advanced toward the lodge. He tried to step on patches of snow that had seen the most shade during the day, so the surface would be hard and he wouldn't break through. As he moved toward the compound, he sized it up through gaps in the tree trunks.

In addition to the lodge, there was a line of small outbuildings extending to the side. Each was signed in frontier lettering: **SALOON, LIVERY STABLE, MARSHALL'S OFFICE, JAIL.** They all looked empty and forlorn.

A great horned owl watched his progress from its perch on top of a hitching-post rail. Its eyes were unblinking. Nate stared back, and for a second a connection was made. A beat after, the owl shuffled its talons on the rail, extended its wings, and flapped away. Nate nodded his approval. His message had been received: Trouble was on the way.

NATE WENT STILL when the front door of the lodge swung open and a man stepped outside.

Concealing himself behind a tree, Nate leaned to the right and peered around it. The figure was bearded and hugging himself against the cold. Tight black jeans, sneakers, a light leather jacket. It was not serious clothing for the location and the conditions. Where had Soledad picked him up?

The man walked across the hard-packed snow to what appeared to be an outhouse. Before going inside, he propped a semi-automatic rifle with an extended magazine next to the door.

The fact that the man had a weapon with him even for a trip to the outhouse made Nate smile. He was in the right place.

NATE WAS ON the move the second the outhouse door closed. He jogged to a space between the parked car and the side of the lodge, keeping his eyes open for movement behind any of the windows. There was none, and when he reached his destination he leaned his back against the siding of the house and removed his waders. Then he unzipped his parka. The grip of his revolver was warm from his body heat.

He bent over and looked inside the Honda through the side windows. There were fast-food wrappers on the floors and someone had left a coat on the back seat. He tried the driver's-side door and found it unlocked.

Nate leaned into the vehicle and opened the glove compartment and the console. The console revealed two cheap burner phones and a half-empty box of .410 shotgun shells. Then he backed out of the Honda and reached under the driver's seat. As he suspected, he found a gun and pulled it out.

It was a bruiser of a weapon: a Taurus Judge Public Defender, with a two-inch barrel and five .410 shotgun shells in the cylinder. They could be replaced with .45 rounds, but Nate was pleased with them. Unlike the rounds from his own .454 that could exit a body and punch through walls like they weren't even there, the Judge would be perfect for close-in work. Shotgun pellets couldn't be matched to a particular weapon like slugs could, they were devastating at close range, and the weapon wasn't tied to him in any way.

———

WITH THE .454 in his right hand and the Judge in his left, Nate shouldered the front door of the lodge open and swung inside.

The lobby was dark and jammed with overstuffed chairs and couches. Buckaroo prints hung on the pine-paneled walls, and an unlit wagon-wheel chandelier was suspended from the ceiling.

Past the lobby in the dimly lit kitchen, a doughy ginger-haired man with a growth of stubble looked up from a breakfast table in the kitchen. His eyes were red and unfocused, and he had a quizzical expression on his face that quickly morphed into anger.

"Who the fuck are you?" he asked in a phlegmy voice that suggested either illness or the effects of a hangover. He glanced down at a semiautomatic handgun on the tabletop next to his coffee mug. So did Nate.

"Where's Axel?" Nate said in a tense whisper. Then: "Don't do it."

But he did it and lunged for the gun.

Nate shot the man in the heart with the Judge. The impact of the blast flung him tumbling backward in his chair, and the sound of the shot was deafening.

But surprisingly, he wasn't dead. The ginger man scrambled on all fours on the floor out of Nate's line of vision, and his crablike hand reached up and appeared on the table, searching for the gun.

"Really?" Nate said as he blew a hole in the table with his new weapon, and the ginger man sprawled out and went still.

Nate strode across the room into an adjoining bedroom where the door was open. He peered inside at an unmade bed. There was meth paraphernalia on the bedside stand next to a half-full bottle of Fireball whiskey.

The window above the bed gave a clear view of the outhouse in the yard, where the occupant inside suddenly kicked the door open while buckling up his black jeans at the same time. When he reached around the opening for his rifle, Nate raised his .454 and aimed it through the glass. His revolver bucked hard and the window shattered and the man was hit center mass. He dropped like a stone. Illuminated by morning sunlight, Nate could see a round hole in the back of the outhouse wall where the bullet had passed through.

He backed out of the room and glanced through the open door of a second bedroom off the lobby. Like the first, the bed was unmade. Clothes were strewn across the floor.

Between the two bedrooms was a small bathroom. It was empty. Nate twisted the faucet and no water came out. That explained why the man had gone to the outhouse: The water pipes were frozen in the lodge.

There were no more rooms on the first level, and Nate eyed the staircase.

Two down, Nate said to himself as he ran up the stairs. *Go, go, go.*

SINCE THE LODGE had been built for guests, Nate expected to find several bedrooms on the top floor. In fact, there were four. Two closed doors on either side of the hallway were marked by hand-lettered signage inspired by historical Wyoming figures: **The Jim**

Bridger Room, The Buffalo Bill Room, The Chief Washakie Room, The
John Colter Suite.

Nate paused for a second at the top of the landing with both
weapons outstretched before him. It was quiet down the hallway
with no sign of activity from any of the rooms. He had no doubt
that Axel had heard the gunshots and was ready for the intruder.
Since the last door on the left was a suite, Nate made a calculated
guess that Axel had chosen the grandest for himself. He bypassed
the first three rooms and launched himself at the door of the John
Colter Suite, hitting it low with his shoulder, just below the doorknob latch.

The doorframe splintered as Nate bulled his way inside. He
rolled on the floor and came up on his knees at the foot of a four-
poster bed, both weapons aimed at a naked woman sitting bolt
upright in a maelstrom of covers. She had tousled brown hair, and
her face was smeared with eyeliner that had run across her cheeks,
making her look like a raccoon.

She was in her late twenties, thin and bony, and she screamed
as she scrambled away from him, clutching the tops of the sheets
and pulling them under her chin as if they would protect her.

Axel wasn't with her. There was no place in the bedroom for
him to hide and the window wasn't open. A pile of black clothing
lay on the floor beside the bed and a black bra was draped over a
lamp on the bedside desk. Black combat boots poked out from
under the bed. There was no other clothing in the room.

"Where is he?" Nate asked her.

"Where is who?" she asked back unconvincingly.

"Axel. Where is he?"

She seemed to be deciding whether to lie to Nate or tell the truth as she pulled the top of the sheets tighter to her chin.

Nate stood up, but kept both guns on her.

"He's gone," she said. "He left yesterday."

"Then why is his car outside?"

"Constantine took him to Jackson Hole. He was going to get a new car there. Constantine brought Axel's Honda back here so we wouldn't be completely stranded."

Nate thought that was possible. "Constantine was the city guy in the leather jacket?"

She vigorously nodded her head.

"Who was the other guy? The ginger?"

"J.R.," she said. Then she echoed the word "was," and it seemed to dawn on her what had happened downstairs. She looked up at Nate with horror.

"You killed them?" she asked. "Both of them?"

Nate asked, "When is Axel coming back?"

"I don't know. We're supposed to stay here until he contacts us."

"You don't have any idea? Are we talking hours? Days?"

"I don't know," she said again. Tears filled her eyes. "I got the impression he'd be back in a week or so. He left us a few hundred dollars to buy food and gas."

Then she shrugged and said, "Axel doesn't always explain things very well. He keeps a lot to himself."

"Who are you?"

Again she seemed to be thinking about whether to tell him the truth.

"I'm an activist," she said.

"I meant your name," Nate said through clenched teeth.

"Bethany," she said. "I knew Axel a long time ago, and he came back into my life and sweet-talked me into coming with him. No other dude I've ever known could do that, and I'm still a little surprised it happened. But I didn't know what kind of heavy shit he was into."

Nate believed that her name was Bethany and that she'd known Axel from before. And that Axel had the ability to talk Bethany into coming with him. He had that kind of charisma. But Nate didn't believe she was telling the truth. There was no way she didn't have a clue about what the man was involved in.

"Where did Axel find those two goons?" Nate asked, gesturing with the muzzle of his .454 to the first floor.

"Constantine and J.R.?" she said. "Denver. I really didn't know them very well," she added quickly. "I mean, I saw them around on the streets during rallies and shit like that, but we weren't close. They're not my type, you know? And I really didn't like it that Axel left me here with them. All they did was get high, shoot guns, and sleep all day. So what do you want with Axel?"

"I want to kill him," Nate said.

"Oh."

"You don't sound surprised."

"Axel has a lot of enemies," Bethany said.

Nate lowered both weapons and slid his .454 into its shoulder holster. "If he comes back, tell him Nate Romanowski was here. He'll know why."

Bethany indicated that she understood. "I've heard that name before. Probably from Axel."

"Probably."

Nate felt a little bad about scaring her. She was a dim bulb

13

from Axel's past and likely one of the street people Axel collected, but that was no reason to put her through more torment. As far as he knew, Bethany hadn't been part of Soledad's murder spree the previous months.

With a quick nod of his head, Nate indicated that they were done, and he turned for the open door.

That's when he heard the distinctive *snick-snick* of a revolver being cocked. Without hesitation, he threw himself to the left as she fired at him, and a bullet slammed into the opposite wall of the hallway where his head had just been.

In a single motion, he half spun and dropped and fired the Judge beneath his left armpit, taking off the top of Bethany's head and painting the wall behind her. But not before they locked eyes for a split second.

WITH HIS EARS ringing from the gunfire, Nate went back down the stairs. He found a plastic bottle of kerosene in a utility closet and emptied it on the hardwood floor. Then he lit the curtains on fire at each downstairs window and exited the building.

As he strode toward the river, the lodge behind him went up quickly. He could hear the fire popping as it consumed the pine paneling and climbed the staircase where Bethany's body lay. When he turned around near the bend of Piney Creek, the entire structure was engulfed in flames.

Nate didn't bother to pull on the waders when he entered the creek this time. The icy water stung him and soaked through his clothing. Almost as an afterthought, he tossed the Judge handgun to the side and let it sink to the smooth river rocks of the creek.

———

IT DIDN'T FEEL good. It didn't feel right. Three dead, including a woman by his own hand, and no Axel Soledad. They'd all been armed and dangerous, and the woman had fired at him. But he'd invaded their privacy, and a case could be made that each had responded in self-defense.

None of it would have happened if he hadn't forced the situation on them. He felt dirty, guilty, and bitterly confused.

And he felt inept and thug-like. He'd looked into Bethany's eyes and closely watched her emotions play out along with her words. Not once had he picked up the tell that she was gripping a handgun under the sheets and waiting for him to turn his back. Not until that last nanosecond when he looked back at her before pulling the trigger did he see true violence in her eyes.

Nate tried to hold himself together until he got back to his Jeep.

As he approached it, he saw the outlines of two of his falcons perched on top of the back seat. Despite the fact that they wore leather hoods, he could feel their contempt for him.

He was ashamed of himself, and he asked himself out loud what he'd become.

Before climbing into his Jeep, he reached into the breast pocket of his jacket and withdrew his cell phone. He'd left it turned off because he didn't want to be tracked and he didn't want to be reached by anyone, either. The device was his last real connection to the modern world.

Which was why he propped it up in the elbow branch of a nearby tree and obliterated it with two rounds from his .454.

He'd never been in such a dark place before. But he knew where he might seek out light.

FIVE DAYS LATER, FBI Special Agent Rick Orr walked through the compound accompanied by a sheriff's department deputy and the local coroner. The light snowfall created a hush and the flakes sifted through the tightly packed trees that bordered the buildings. His primary escort was Laurie Urbigkit, a local large-animal veterinarian who also served as the coroner for Sublette County, Wyoming. The deputy faded away back to his SUV to take a call on his cell phone.

Orr had often been told that he looked more like a studious, well-meaning college professor than a G-man, and he knew it was true. He was in his early sixties with wispy gray hair and round metal-framed glasses. He wore a thigh-length, belted beige trench coat, slacks that were not made for cold mountain weather, and slip-on leather shoes with smooth soles that provided no grip on the slick, snow-covered grass. He struggled to keep up with the coroner as she stepped under the yellow crime scene tape and strode toward the charred remains of the lodge.

Urbigkit was a slim and fidgety woman with long, silver-streaked hair braided into two lengths on each side of her head. They bobbed when she moved.

She'd been utterly shocked at Orr's arrival that morning and said that she'd never met an FBI agent before in her life and that she didn't know whether to be impressed or intimidated.

"Two of the victims were found in there," she said, gesturing toward the burned structure. "One male, one female. Those bodies were pretty crispy, I'll tell you. It took some time to figure out what happened to them, but I can say with confidence that the male was hit twice. Point-blank shotgun blasts. There must have been two dozen pellets in him, and of course shot like that is untraceable to the weapon that used it. Maybe the crime lab in Cheyenne can figure something out, but I sure couldn't.

"The female victim was shot once in the face, also by a shotgun blast."

With that, she paused. But before Orr could respond, Urbigkit continued. "I can ask the sheriff to let you see all the crime scene photos. I'd warn you, though, that if you've never seen burned bodies hit with shotgun blasts or high-powered rounds—"

"I've seen plenty," Orr said. Despite the cold and the days since the incident, Orr noted that the scene still smelled strongly of blood and ash.

He knew from talking to the sheriff that the crime scene had been discovered by a local trapper placing leghold traps along the river. If the man hadn't trespassed on the property, the sheriff said, it might have been weeks or months before the crimes were reported. There had been no missing-persons calls and no one had inquired about the well-being of the victims.

The coroner darted into the ash and snatched a singed, lint-covered stocking cap from the debris. She handed it to Orr. "Here, put this on. You look cold."

Orr took it reluctantly. He was used to being around forensics personnel who were meticulously anal about anyone besides them entering a crime scene. Even Orr, who had been with the bureau for over thirty years. Never before in his experience had a crime scene investigator cavalierly lent him an item of clothing from a victim. This, Orr said to himself, was amateur hour.

ORR SNIFFED THE cap. It smelled of both wood and stale marijuana smoke. When Urbigkit turned her back and headed toward the outhouse, Orr tossed the stocking cap aside and followed.

"This is where we found the third victim, the other male," she said, chinning toward the structure. He stepped under the crime scene tape and opened the door. It was a two-seater with a roll of toilet paper sitting on the plywood sheet between the holes. The coroner made a face and pointed toward the left hole.

"The body was found down there," she said. "Two days after the sheriff's department got here. One of the deputies went inside to take a dump and he looked down into the toilet vault and saw the body. It scared the shit out of him, so to speak. My opinion is that the killing took place in the yard where you're standing, and the shooters dumped the victim into the vault. Pulling that body out of there was no fun for anyone."

"I can't imagine that it was," Orr said. "So this victim was shot with a high-powered rifle instead of a shotgun?"

The coroner stepped into the outhouse and addressed Orr. As she did so, she placed her index finger on the coat fabric over her heart.

"He was hit right here," Urbigkit said. Then she turned and pointed to a clean hole in the back of the outhouse about shoulder high. "The round went straight through the victim and out through the back wall. And take a look at that hole."

She stepped aside so Orr could enter. He bent forward and looked through the large opening. He could see cottonwoods in the meadow.

"That bullet hole doesn't look like the results of any rifle round I've seen go through wood," she said. "It looks like it was done with a sharp drill bit. It went through the victim and through the outhouse and just kept going, probably to the next county. We'll never recover it. But whatever it was, it was a powerful weapon."

Orr recognized the features of the bullet hole, but he didn't reveal them to Urbigkit.

He asked, "Did you find anything else on the grounds? Fingerprints? Footprints? Hairs? Fibers?"

Urbigkit sighed and shook her head. She said, "You know, since I've been coroner in this county we've had exactly two murders in the last fifteen years. These three victims make five. What I'm trying to say is that none of our guys—including me—has a lot of experience in violent-crime forensics, you know? The two murders I mentioned were open-and-shut. The shooters were on the scene blubbering when the cops showed up. One was a guy who thought his wife was cheating on him—she was, by the way—and the other was between two Natives high on meth who got into a knife fight."

Orr remained silent.

"We don't do a lot of this," the coroner said.

"What's your theory?" Orr asked Urbigkit.

"The sheriff and I are on the same page here. You can ask him if you don't believe me. What we think is that the murders are gang-related and the shooters were sent to kill them. All three victims were from out of state, and so were the killers, we think.

When you look at the autopsy photos, you'll see that all three of 'em were tattooed hipster types from the city. Two of 'em had IDs from Denver, so they weren't from around here. I figure they found this place online and rented it out. Nobody around here knew any of them.

"Our preliminary conclusion, I guess, is that this was a horrible crime, but it doesn't have anything to do with us. As far as we know, there are no local connections with the victims, so this is random and frankly not a high priority. We're here to serve our constituents, not to get involved in gang-related activity from other states. I'm surprised the FBI sent you."

"Actually, I sent myself," Orr said. Then: "How many shooters did it? What is your professional judgment?"

"Two at the minimum," she said. "One with a shotgun and the other with that high-powered rifle. Maybe they had a lookout as well."

Urbigkit leaned in toward Orr as if to share a secret. "I think we're dealing with professional hit men," she said. "They were sent up here to take care of some targets. The shooters didn't take anything that we could figure out, and they did their work and left. I wish they wouldn't have burned the lodge down, because we might have learned more about the crimes, but they knew what they were doing."

"How did they get here and get away without leaving any trace of themselves, or tracks?" Orr asked.

Urbigkit shrugged. "That's what I'd like to know. Maybe you'll be able to figure something out when you read the reports and look at all the crime scene photos."

"I plan to do exactly that," Orr said.

The coroner looked at Orr closely. "You might want to buy some warmer clothes if you plan to stick around here for a while. Do you know what they used to call our county back in the day? Back when they did national weather reports?"

"No."

"They called us the 'Ice Box of the Nation,'" Urbigkit said. Then: "That's a hell of a thing to be known for, but it keeps the riffraff out."

"Until now," Orr said, gesturing toward the burned-out lodge.

PART TWO

"Like all hunters, the peregrine is inhibited by a code of behaviour."

—J. A. Baker, *The Peregrine*

CHAPTER TWO

Now

ON AN UNSEASONABLY warm early October day in the Sierra Madre range of south-central Wyoming, elk-hunting guides Joseph "Spike" Rankin and his new hired man, Mark Eisele, climbed out of Rankin's pickup and opened the rear doors to where their gear was stashed. When Rankin drew his binoculars from their case, Eisele did the same. Battle Mountain loomed over them and they quietly studied its timber and terrain before setting out on a scouting hike.

Neither man had any idea that what they would encounter that day would not only change their own lives but possibly alter the trajectory of the nation itself. Their conversation, conducted in tones barely above a whisper, was muted and all about the next few hours ahead of them.

"I think I see a bull moose up there in the aspen," Eisele said.

"That's a bull, all right. There's a couple of cows farther down that same mountain meadow."

Eisele lowered his binoculars to find them.

Rankin pointed with a gnarled finger. "Do you see that ridge about halfway up the mountain with the red buckbrush on top of it?"

"Yes."

"That's where we're going. From up there, you get a great view of the valley and meadows on the other side. It'll take about an hour of hard climbing to get there."

Eisele nodded. He knew to be completely deferential to the older man. Spike Rankin was a legend in this part of the state and he'd been guiding hunters in these mountains for over forty years. When Rankin had hired him two weeks before, he'd told Eisele that he "didn't want a lot of lip."

Eisele had responded that he'd get none from him.

"Especially in front of my clients," Rankin had said.

"Understood," Eisele had said.

BATTLE MOUNTAIN WAS massive and its unique conical outline could be seen from forty miles away in any direction. It was one of many mountains in the Sierra Madres of south-central Wyoming, but it was by far the most prominent. Its southeastern face was veined with sharp arroyos that stretched from the valley floor toward the summit, which was nearly ten thousand feet in elevation. The peak emerged from the dark timber at around nine thousand feet and formed a bald, snow-dusted knob that was stark against the cloudless blue sky. From the summit to the foothills held a world of diverse ecosystems. Dark, old-growth pines covered the face of the entire mountain except for open meadows that looked like errant punctuation. Splashes of yellowed aspen broke up the sea of timber. Halfway up the mountain was a slash of gold exposed granite where a piece of the mountain had fallen away years before, leaving the scar and a huge hillock of broken scree at its base.

Eisele vaguely recalled learning about the mountain and where it had gotten its name in his third-grade Wyoming history class in Cheyenne. There had been a frontier battle there, obviously. He couldn't recall the details.

But, he thought, it probably looked the same now as it did then. No road scars across its face, no fencing, no power lines, no structures of any kind. It was excellent habitat for mule deer and elk. Moose apparently liked it, too.

"Take water, lunch, your optics, and a first-aid kit in your day-pack," Rankin said. "Do you have protection?"

"Protection?" Eisele asked with a sly smile.

"I'm not talking about rubbers," Rankin said with irritation. "I mean bear spray and a handgun."

"I've got bear spray and a .357 Magnum," Eisele said as he clipped both to his belt.

"I'd rather it was a ten-millimeter or a .44 Mag," Rankin said. "I don't expect to run into any grizzly bears around here, but when it comes to those beasts, the bigger, the better. You heard what happened a year ago."

"Of course," Eisele said. Everybody knew about the murderous grizzly attacks that had occurred across the state the previous fall.

"Them bears can move fast," Rankin said. "Maybe faster than you can draw your weapon if it isn't handy."

"Maybe I can get a bigger handgun before we come back with

our hunters," Eisele said. "I think I can borrow one from my father-in-law."

Rankin indicated his approval.

"Did you bring mountain money?" he asked.

"Mountain money?" Eisele said, puzzled. He had about fifty dollars in his wallet.

"Toilet paper," Rankin said. "It's more valuable up here than dollar bills."

"I'll remember it next time," Eisele said.

"Do that," Rankin said. "I can share mine if you need to take a shit."

Eisele was dressed head to foot in Kuiu high-tech hunting clothing and Zamberlan Italian hunting boots that he'd spent a small fortune on. Rankin wore weathered jeans with a sagging butt, a Wyoming Cowboys football T-shirt, a bloodstained camo vest, and ancient Red Wing hunting boots.

When they were ready, both men eased the doors shut on Rankin's pickup as quietly as possible and started up the mountain.

EISELE TRIED TO keep up with Rankin as the older guide led the way. Rankin was short and stocky and in his midfifties with a salt-and-pepper beard and close-cropped hair. He moved in a relentless and deliberate pace that was as sure-footed as a mountain goat, Eisele thought. And he did it almost silently. It was as if he were gliding a few inches above the loose rocks, dry twigs, and haphazard pine cones that Eisele seemed to find with every other step.

At one point halfway to the buckbrush ridge, Rankin stopped, turned around, and glared at him.

"Look ahead of you before you step," Rankin said. "Then place your foot on something that won't make noise. You'll spook the elk away long before you can get to where you're going. You make as much noise as a bunch of drunk monkeys trying to fuck a football."

Rankin's colorful language and occasional bad grammar belied the fact that he'd graduated from Stanford and that, prior to becoming an outfitter, he'd both built and divested himself of a very successful pharmaceutical company. Eisele's father-in-law said that very few of Rankin's clients had any idea that the guide could likely buy and sell them if he chose and that the man liked to play up his facade.

His nickname, Spike, apparently had come from the fact that his mother was sure he'd been conceived in the temporary shelter known as a spike camp while she was elk-hunting with his father.

"Sorry," Eisele said, using the break to catch his breath. There was a sheen of sweat across his entire upper body and he'd wiped it from his face several times already with the sleeve of his jacket.

"It's okay to pause," Rankin said. "Stop, look around, sniff the air, and just *listen*. The last thing you want to do is walk up on a bunch of elk with your hunter huffing and puffing so hard you can't set him up for a shot. Besides, he'll likely be even more out of shape than you are, if that's possible."

Eisele leaned forward and placed his hands on his knees. His lungs burned and his calves and thighs ached. The higher they climbed and the thinner the air, the worse it got. The exertion didn't seem to affect Rankin, which was annoying.

———

THE ELK-HUNTING SEASON on Battle Mountain was on pause, Rankin had explained. Archery season had taken place from the first of September through the thirtieth. Antlered-elk season for rifles started up October 15, followed by "any elk" season through October 31. Antlerless elk season went from November 1 through November 12.

Since all of Rankin's clients were rifle hunters, he was booked solid from mid-October through mid-November. He used the two weeks between the end of archery season and the beginning of rifle season to set up his elk camp and horse corrals, scout the area so thoroughly that he knew where most of the trophy animals hung out, note where any other elk camps might be located, and hire a camp cook and an assistant, which this year was Mark Eisele. The aim was to provide the highest-quality elk-hunting experience possible, given the limitations of hunting on a roadless mountain located largely in the Medicine Bow National Forest.

Eisele didn't know much about the first group of hunting clients coming the next week, other than Rankin's description of them as "well-heeled fellows from North Carolina."

WHEN EISELE HAD complained the previous summer at a gathering with his wife's family in Cheyenne that he was getting bored working remotely in his basement for the Silicon Valley high-tech company that employed him, his father-in-law had overheard the conversation.

"You need to get outside and challenge yourself," the man had said. "Life is more than a keyboard and a monitor. You need to get some calluses on those baby-soft hands of yours.

"I need to hook you up with Spike Rankin," he had added while patting his pockets for the location of his cell phone. "Spike's a good friend of mine."

Eisele had agreed, and later blamed the three Coors beers he'd had prior to the conversation. He'd been both surprised and dismayed that his wife, Megan, had encouraged him to do it, even though it meant he'd be gone for much of the fall.

"What about my job?" he'd asked her.

Megan had laughed. "You always say that nobody reads your reports anyway," she'd said. "Just send in the same reports you did last year and see if anyone notices."

So far, they hadn't. Working remotely did have its advantages.

EISELE WAS BREATHING hard again when they breached the line of brilliant red buckbrush that marked the edge of a flat overlooking the distant valley below. He pushed through it, trying not to snag his clothing on the branches. He wished it was cooler and he thought he'd probably overdressed for the hike. Time to peel off a layer, he thought.

As he was reaching for the zipper on his new outer shell, Rankin stopped midway through the brush and turned around.

"We'll cross this flat and drop over," he whispered. "There's a great place on the other side where we can hunker down and scope the entire valley all the way to the river. This is where I've seen more big six-by-six bulls than anywhere else in this country. Sometimes, I've seen three or four of them at the same time. The trick is to note where they are and not let them see *you*. We want them to stick around until our hunters show up."

"Got it," Eisele said.

"Stay low when you go over the edge so you don't skyline yourself. And when we get to our scouting location, don't stand up so the elk can notice you."

Eisele nodded.

Rankin indicated with a jerk of his chin that he wanted Eisele to follow him. They cleared the bank of buckbrush and crab-walked across the grassy clearing. Eisele stayed about four feet behind Rankin. The high-altitude sun warmed his back as he followed.

When Rankin reached the edge of the flat, he stopped again, then stood up to full height. To Eisele, it seemed as if Rankin had suddenly given up on the hunt.

"Shit," he snorted. "It looks like somebody's got our spot."

"What?"

"Somebody's in our goddamned scouting location. I've *never* seen anybody up here before."

Eisele shouldered around Rankin and stood next to him on the rim. The view was absolutely magnificent. Far below the massive sloping hills was a single ribbon of silver snaking through the valley floor: the North Platte River. A distant ranch complex with a slew of outbuildings hugged its banks and Eisele could make out a bridge across the river and a network of roads between the structures. Several corrals held large herds of horses. In the center of the outbuildings was a three-story dark lodge of some kind with a green roof.

"Man, that place looks fancy," Eisele said.

"It is," Rankin grumbled. "It's the B-Lazy-U Ranch. Have you ever heard of it?"

Eisele said, "I've heard of it, but I never thought I'd actually see it, much less spend a night there. It's like two thousand dollars a night or something."

"More than that," Rankin said brusquely. "This is the closest you'll probably ever get to it. But the ranch isn't our problem."

He pointed directly below them down the slope. "*That* is our problem."

Eisele followed Rankin's finger to see movement behind a breastwork of fallen spruce trees about a hundred yards below them. As he focused on the movement, five figures became clear. They were dressed all in camo and they blended into the terrain so well that, for a moment, it looked like the ground was undulating. To the side of the breastwork were two ATVs partially hidden beneath cut pine branches.

One of the figures abruptly turned and stared right at them. The man wore green and black face paint and his eyes looked sharply white as they widened with the discovery of the two guides standing on top of the ridge. The man said something and the other four quickly turned as well. Eisele could make out four men and a woman, all in their late twenties or early thirties, all brandishing what looked like semiautomatic rifles. Spotting scopes mounted on short tripods extended above the breastwork and were aimed at the ranch below.

There was something in their movements that suggested military training, Eisele thought. They moved with precision and had an ease with their weapons and gear that Eisele knew he couldn't replicate. What kind of elk hunters were these?

33

The man who'd seen them first swung his weapon up and shouldered it and threw the bolt back with a metallic click. Eisele felt his stomach clutch and his eyes widen.

"Whoa there," Rankin called down. "No need for that. We didn't know you were up here and we didn't mean to surprise you. I use this place to scout elk every season, and I didn't see a vehicle parked down on the road. We didn't know anyone was up here."

Rankin was trying to sound friendly, but Eisele noted the alarm in his voice.

"Like I said, we're just up here scouting elk," Rankin said. "We can easily move to the other side of the mountain, since you folks got here first. It's a big mountain and we can all share it."

The man with the rifle looked to two of his companions, said something too low to hear, then turned his attention back to Rankin and Eisele.

"Drop your weapons," the man said.

"How about we just back away?" Rankin said. "I've got clients coming next week and we can hunt on the other side of the range. Plus, you wouldn't want to leave a man up here without protection."

That word again, Eisele thought.

"I said, drop your weapons," the man repeated. As he did so, the four others squared up and raised their rifles as well. Eisele fought against a sudden explosive bowel movement. He couldn't move. All he could see were five tiny black dots, the muzzles of the firearms.

"Look," Rankin said, showing the people below the palms of his hands, "I don't know what you've got going on here, but it isn't our intention to crash the party. We'll back away and move along.

This is a public national forest, after all. We all have a right to be on this mountain, but we respect giving you some distance."

Eisele's hand twitched near the butt of his holstered .357 Magnum. His inclination was to pull it out very slowly and drop it at his feet. And then turn and run like he'd never run before.

One of the other men in the group said something to the lead gunman. To Eisele, it sounded harsh and definitive, although he couldn't make out the words.

"Maybe you folks could tell me what you're doing up here," Rankin said. "Does the Forest Service know you're up here? Does the local game warden?"

Eisele wished his boss would just hand over his weapons and shut up. This wasn't worth a confrontation, he thought.

Then Eisele clearly heard the woman say, "Sarge, they've seen us."

And suddenly, the morning was split open with booming gunfire. Rankin was thrown backward by the impact of bullets as if kicked by a horse. Eisele dropped and spun as rounds sizzled through the air above him, but as he started to run, he was hit, and the velocity of the bullet sent him sprawling face-first into the grass.

For a few seconds, he lay there, his arms at his sides and his mouth gaping open. He couldn't move and he couldn't quite locate his arms and legs to crawl away. There was a severe burning sensation in his right shoulder and from the left cheek of his buttocks.

He struggled to keep his eyes open, and he could hear the scrambling of the gunmen as they ran up the slope to where he lay. As his revolver was roughly pulled out of his holster, someone said, "This one's still alive."

"The old man is, too, but he doesn't have long to go," someone else said. "We're gonna have to strap his body on the ATV and take him back."

Eisele felt someone grip his right shoulder to turn him over. The pain was sharp, and he gasped as he was rolled onto his back.

A foot above him were the faces of Sarge, the lead shooter, and a woman with green eyes and a full mouth. Both of their faces were smeared with paint. Both leaned over him, partially blocking the sky.

"What are we gonna do with these two?" the woman asked.

Eisele felt absolutely hopeless. His fate was up to them, and he couldn't find the words to try to convince them otherwise. He wished his wife and father-in-law were there so he could say to them, "Look what you got me into."

As the woman spoke, Eisele noticed something over her shoulder that seemed remarkably out of place. It was a sleek small jet airplane streaking across the sky toward the north. It was descending, and its landing gear was deployed.

The scream of the jet distracted the woman and she looked up.

"Here they come," she said. "Right on time."

CHAPTER THREE

A T THE SAME time, two hundred and fifty-two miles to the north-northeast at the confluence of Buffalo Creek and Spring Creek within the steep red rock walls of Hole in the Wall Canyon, Nate Romanowski eased around a truck-sized boulder and peered up at his falcons in the sky. There were two of them, a prairie falcon hovering almost still in a thermal current and a peregrine hundreds of feet above it doing a slow rotation. Both were tiny specks within the massive light blue sky, although the high-flying peregrine occasionally intersected the wispy tail of a lone cirrus cloud.

Nate was in the act of hunting, but here he wasn't the hunter. Although he was armed with his revolver in a shoulder holster and his falconry bag was looped over his shoulder, his role in this hunt was that of a human bird dog, whose sole purpose was to flush game birds and small creatures that hunkered within the jumble of broken rocks and tangled brush that covered the wide canyon floor.

That's when he felt it: a tingle that washed through him from scalp to toes. Someone was coming.

He froze, squinted to sharpen his vision, and carefully scanned the length of the switchback trail that was cut into the side of the canyon wall to his right. The trail was wide enough to accommodate a hiker—or, in years past, outlaws on horseback—and it was the only approach from the top.

There was no movement on it at the moment. No interlopers.

But still, Nate had come to once again trust that feeling, the tingle. If someone wasn't sneaking down the trail—and they weren't—there was still a disturbance in the natural order of things. Maybe it was hunters or ranch hands on the surface above, and they'd back off.

Or maybe not.

The only sounds were the tinkling of the icy stream through the river rocks and the murmur of a slight wind that blew east to west across the opening mouth of the canyon four hundred feet above him. Those sounds, and the sudden loud grumble of his stomach.

He was hungry, and so were his birds. Interloper or not, they had to eat.

Nate checked the loads of his handgun and slid the weapon back into its holster. Then, with a quick scan along the trail to confirm that he hadn't missed anything or anyone, he continued the hunt.

NATE ROMANOWSKI'S MOUTH was obscured by months of an untrimmed mustache. He sported a beard bound by a leather string. A dirty-blond ponytail, streaked with silver, hung down from the back of his neck like a horse's tail. Both his beard and his ponytail contained feathers knotted in place by strands of hair.

His clothing—a faded green canvas long-sleeved shirt and Carhartt carpenter jeans—had been ripped and repaired so many times that only a few stretches of fabric remained that didn't show stitches. The soles of his boots had been worn paper-thin, so he'd replaced them with moccasins fashioned from elk hide that laced up to just below his knees.

Even his shoulder holster had been replaced because the old one had become waterlogged at one point and had stiffened into the texture of wood. The holster he'd thought out and constructed was of both mule deer and elk hide, and it was beaded and fringed. His .454 Casull fit snugly into the new version.

Nate had not had a conversation with another human being for months. In his mind and in the state he was in, that hadn't been long enough to get to where he needed to be.

IF HE WAS stalking game himself, Nate never would have taken the route along the right bank of Spring Creek. Instead of moving quietly from boulder to boulder and stopping often to listen for the footfalls or snorts of deer, bighorn sheep, pronghorn antelope, or elk, he deliberately stepped on dry twigs and loudly kicked his way through piles of loose rocks. His loud approach was intended to drive and then flush out game, even though he had yet to see any signs of life. Although his falcons appeared oblivious to his presence, he knew both were carefully observing him and were aware of his noisy progress down the canyon floor.

When he shouldered around the thick reddish-brown trunk of an ancient ponderosa pine, he could see the confluence of the creeks ahead of him. The two streams met in a crux of a V and flowed north, doubling the flow of Buffalo Creek. The grass was ankle-high and thick and studded with skull-like river rocks that protruded from it. As he neared the V, he could detect a shimmering in the grass ahead of him and he smiled.

"Get ready," he said to his falcons as much as to himself.

The covey of chukars busted out of the grass at the point of the confluence because they couldn't run ahead of him any longer and not go into the water. They lifted off in a percussive flurry of flapping wings. At least a dozen of them, he thought, shooting through the air like errant fireworks all launched at once in different directions.

The chukars—sometimes called "devil birds" due to their speed and the zigzagging ascent that made them extremely difficult to hit with a shotgun—never saw what was coming from the sky. The prairie falcon intercepted the highest-flying chukar and sent it tumbling to the ground in a puff of feathers. The peregrine descended like a missile between the canyon walls and hit two additional chukars in rapid succession and clipped a third. The two lifeless targets thumped to the surface next to the creek, and the third chukar spiraled down like a crippled fighter plane and smacked headfirst into the top of a boulder behind Nate before bouncing to the ground.

The peregrine continued its dive through the covey until it did a graceful U-turn several feet from the stream. Nate watched the prairie falcon pursue a chukar that was skimming along the creek. His raptor dipped down and grasped the target in its talons, driving it down to the ground in a death grip that killed the prey on contact.

Then it was over and Nate whispered his thanks to his falcons, to his luck, and to God for providing a meal for them all.

NATE COLLECTED THE downed chukars into a pouch he formed from the loose front tails of his shirt. The birds were still warm and he could feel them through the fabric on his skin. Chukars were beautiful birds, he thought. They were the size of a large partridge or small chickens, with small heads and plump bodies lined with creamy gray feathers. Their beaks were blood-red and a bold black stripe that looked like sloppy eyeliner extended across their faces and curled to their breasts.

While holding the bounty of birds in place with his left hand, he pulled on a thick leather glove with an extended cuff over his right hand and secured it by gripping the end of the cuff in his teeth. Then he whistled and extended his right arm. The peregrine landed on it gracefully with a flare of its wings.

"Here you go," he said, lowering the bird and giving it one of the chukars. After eyeing him for a second, the falcon pinned the carcass to the ground and dipped its head and tore out the throat of the chukar and proceeded to eat it, feathers, bones, and all.

Although he would have preferred the prairie falcon come to him the way the peregrine had—through the air—he found the smaller falcon thirty yards down the stream consuming the bird it had chased and driven to the ground. Its beak was bloody red and covered with downy feathers.

"You get a pass this time," he said to the less-experienced prairie falcon. "Good hunting."

Nate noted the metallic smell of spilled blood that wafted through the canyon.

He loved it.

When his birds were sated and lethargic and happy, he placed them on top of his shoulders for his hike back to his dwelling, which was a deep cave in the side of a sandstone canyon wall. The peregrine rode on his right shoulder and the prairie falcon rode on his left.

On the footpath that serpentined up from the floor through boulders and heavy brush, Nate stopped suddenly and didn't move. He again sensed a presence in the area.

When it materialized, he'd be ready.

That evening, while two chukars roasted on a stick over an open firepit at the mouth of his cave on the eastern wall of the canyon, Nate peered into the darkness beyond and waited. Drips of fat from the birds sizzled and flamed on the coals and the orange light from the fire danced on the walls of the cave and the caragana brush just outside the opening.

Nate was reminded once again that the natural advantage of the outlaw caves within the canyon was their location in relation to the footpath on the opposite wall. The caves afforded a clear view of the length of the trail, but from the trail itself, the limestone formations were shrouded with brush that concealed their mouths. Butch Cassidy, the Sundance Kid, and the rest of the Wild Bunch had chosen well. A few of the best-hidden caves still had hitching posts for horses and Nate had found an ancient cast-iron frying pan in the back of his that he'd cleaned up for his own use. In fact, he'd used the pan to fry up six medium-sized brook trout that he kept warm by placing the skillet next to the hot rocks of the firepit.

Earlier, Nate had watched as a single form moved down the trail as the sun set. The man was too far away to see clearly, but he was large and moved with a graceful stealth. Nate assumed more men would follow, but they didn't. He'd lost sight of the intruder when full darkness enveloped the canyon, but he could occasionally hear the click of rock on rock after the man forded the stream on the canyon floor and started his climb to Nate's cave.

As the fire crackled and smoked and the skin of the chukars turned golden-brown, Nate slipped out of the cave and shinnied along a path to his left until he was behind a boulder that gave him a clear view of the opening. He held his revolver loose and at his right side, ready to raise it up and fire at any second.

"Nate? Did I find you?"

The voice was low, rumbling, and familiar.

"Nate? I saw the fire and came to the light. Is that you, buddy?"

Nate's shoulders relaxed as he slipped his gun into its holster and he stepped out from behind the boulder.

"It's Geronimo, man."

And it was.

"Are you hungry?" Nate asked. His own voice sounded weak and unfamiliar to him, the result of not using it regularly.

Geronimo said, "You know me. Of *course* I'm hungry. And whatever you're cooking smells damned good."

GERONIMO JONES SQUATTED next to Nate in front of the fire and watched the skin blacken and crack on the outside of both chukars. They'd just completed a greeting where Nate had extended his hand and Geronimo had swept it aside so he could embrace Nate in a bear hug. Geronimo was six feet tall and 240 pounds, with ebony skin and heavy ropes of dreadlocks that extended to his shoulders. His hug was ferocious. Nate had winced. He wasn't a hugger.

"What's that? Chicken?" Geronimo asked.

"Chukar," Nate said. "Fried trout on the side."

"Sounds damned good. Looks damned good."

"How did you find me?" Nate asked.

"A little bird told me."

"Was this little bird named Joe Pickett?" Nate asked.

Geronimo smiled. "Nope."

"Sheridan, then?"

Sheridan Pickett was Joe and Marybeth Pickett's oldest daughter of three. She'd been Nate's apprentice in falconry and had grown so skilled and mature that he'd left his falconry company to her to manage on her own. Not that she'd had any say in it.

"Sheridan said you used to hang out here before you went straight," Geronimo said. "Back in the day."

Nate smiled. Sheridan was smart.

"She said to tell you Kestrel is doing well," Geronimo said. Kestrel was Nate's three-year-old daughter. He'd left her with Mary-beth because he knew she'd be safe and well taken care of.

"That's good to hear."

"I've been looking for you for a while," Geronimo said. "You're a hard man to find when you don't want to be found."

"That was the idea," Nate said. "That's why I shot my cell phone in the heart. But now you've screwed it all up."

THEY SAT BACK after they'd devoured the chukars and trout in silence and burned the bones in the fire. The temperature outside had dropped significantly and the stars had come out hard. The moon had not yet appeared in the opening between the walls of the canyon.

Like Nate, Geronimo was a dedicated master falconer with a Special Forces background. Unlike Nate, he was closely tied to like-minded loners throughout the country via encrypted apps and message boards. The network was composed of falconers who respected their calling and who'd pledged to follow their own un-written code. Members respected each other's territory—Nate was associated with northern Wyoming and Geronimo's territory in-cluded the city of Denver and the nearby mountain towns—and they spread the word about falconers who encroached on their sense of order or demeaned their collective honor.

It was through this network that Geronimo had first heard of a man named Axel Soledad, and allied himself with a warrior named Romanowski and a game warden named Pickett to hunt him down. They thought they'd been successful in neutralizing him after a firefight that'd left Soledad bleeding out on the streets of Portland.

Unfortunately, they'd been wrong.

"I SHOULD HAVE figured that an outlaw like you would chose an outlaw canyon," Geronimo said.

Nate shrugged.

"I couldn't help but notice that there aren't a lot of Black folks around here."

"Nope. There aren't a lot of folks of any hue, in fact."

Geronimo had soft brown eyes and they swept slowly over Nate, who was illuminated by the fire. "Damn, you look pretty raggedy-assed," he said. "When's the last time you shaved?"

"It's been a while."

"You look like you've lost weight."

"Probably."

"Maybe I should hole up in a cave and eat nothing but what I can catch or kill like you," Geronimo said, patting his belly. "Jacinda is a hell of a cook and she keeps me fat and happy, unfortunately. And the little one, Pearl . . ."

Nate sharply looked away.

"Sorry," Geronimo said. "I didn't mean to bring back memories."

THE PREVIOUS YEAR, Nate had lost Liv when she'd been brutally murdered at their home in front of their daughter, Kestrel. He'd taken revenge on three of the four murderers, but Axel Soledad was still out there, his trail gone cold. It ate at him, his failure to track Soledad down.

God, he missed Liv.

NATE HAD REALIZED too late that his years of normalcy on the grid with a wife, a daughter, and a successful business had dulled his primal instincts and abilities. Where he had once been able to intuit the direction of his quarry by entering into a state of what falconers referred to as *yarak*, he'd found himself lost and fumbling and feeling like a vagabond in a strange world instead of being part of it. His predatory nature had receded, to be replaced by guilt, regret, and anger at his own bad decisions the night Liv was murdered.

So he'd abandoned the hunt and retreated to Hole in the Wall, which was familiar territory.

There, with only his two falcons to keep him company, Nate had tried to strip himself down to his core—to once again tune in to the natural world around him and become a part of it, not an observer. To once again see, hear, smell, and touch with alarming sharpness.

This vision quest was designed to once again enter the state of *yarak*, where his actions were swift and brutal and amoral and instinctual.

He couldn't bring Liv back or fix what had been taken. He felt nothing but shame when he realized recently that a day had gone by and he hadn't thought of her. Was he healing or becoming even more self-absorbed?

Nate wasn't sure. He wasn't sure about anything anymore.

———

AFTER A LONG, uncomfortable silence, Geronimo asked Nate how long he'd been living in the Hole in the Wall Canyon.

"Seven months, two days," Nate said.

"Jesus, that's a crazy long time to be off the grid."

"Not long enough," Nate said.

"You can't stay much longer, I'd guess. Your Wyoming winter is coming. You've got your falcons to think about, even if you don't think about your own welfare."

Nate reluctantly agreed. As the days got shorter and the nights longer, he'd been thinking about that. Game in the canyon was getting harder to find, and soon the creek would freeze over. It had already snowed a couple of times.

"Will you go home?" Geronimo asked.

Nate shook his head. "I'm not ready yet. I may never be."

"Why not?"

"I can't be near anyone who could get hurt. Not again."

Geronimo said, "If things were normal in my world, I'd offer to let you stay at my place in Colorado. You know we have a couple of guest rooms."

"I remember," Nate said.

"But my circumstances have changed." As he said it, Geronimo's expression darkened. "I'm on the run like you are, just for different reasons. That's why I'm here."

"What are the circumstances?" Nate asked.

"For one thing, I've heard through some friends that the FBI is looking into us. Some agent named Orr has been asking questions."

"It wouldn't be the first time," Nate said. "But I'm not familiar with Agent Orr. What else made you go on the run?"

It was Geronimo's turn to look away. "I'll tell you all about it, but not right now. You need to shake free of all of this and come with me. I need you at your best."

"What if I'm not there yet?" Nate asked.

"Then I'll go it alone. But I'd rather not."

WHEN HE'D ARRIVED, Geronimo had unslung a shotgun and propped it against the cave wall behind him. Nate now eyed it and asked, "New shotgun?"

Geronimo's previous weapon of choice had been a unique triple-barrel 12-gauge. He said, "It's a Benelli M1014 semiauto. It'll hold six in the tube and one more in the receiver with that extension on it."

Nate raised his eyebrows.

"I figured I'd need more firepower for what comes next," Geronimo said.

"What comes next?"

"That's what I'm here to talk to you about," Geronimo said.

"Axel?"

Geronimo nodded. "He came after me and my family, too. Or at least his goons did."

Nate felt a sharp twinge of fear. "Is Jacinda . . ."

"She's all right. I packed her and Pearl up and drove them to her mother's house in Detroit. But it was a close call, and the only reason I'm here today is pure luck."

"What happened?" Nate asked.

"I'll tell you all about it," Geronimo said. "We'll have plenty of time together now that I've found you."

Nate didn't reply.

Geronimo glared at him. "So let's get you off your skinny grieving ass and go after that son of a bitch and his pack of animals, since you missed him the last time."

CHAPTER FOUR

THE NEXT MORNING, Wyoming game warden Joe Pickett drove slowly on a corduroy county road northeast of Saddlestring until he could locate an enclave of ramshackle structures a few hundred yards from the shore of a shimmering prairie lake. The clapboard buildings had no glass in the windows or shingles on the roofs, and several potbellied goats roamed among them. The single-wide trailer located within the enclave was the last-known address of Matt Theriault and his partner. Joe's task was to see if he could find evidence on the property that Theriault had poached a mule deer out of season. And arrest him for it.

Theriault—pronounced "Terry-O"—was a longtime local miscreant known for wearing tie-dyed T-shirts and cargo shorts even in subzero temperatures. To Joe, cargo shorts plus winter equaled "moron." Theriault was also known for his hair-trigger temper and the fistfights that had led to his being banished from most of the local bars. He was said to be a nice guy when he was sober, but that was rare.

Someone in the area had sent an anonymous message to Joe via the Wyoming Stop Poaching Now web hotline the night before. Within the message was a link that led Joe to Theriault's Facebook page. After consulting with his wife, Marybeth, and his youngest daughter, Lucy, about how to use the social network, Joe had found several day-old photos of Theriault in full camo posing over the body of a five-by-five mule deer with Eagle Mountain clearly in the background. That area had been closed for deer hunting for two weeks, and a quick check of the state database showed that Theriault hadn't purchased a deer license, either.

In the photos, the treeless summit of Eagle Mountain was dusted with snow, with the heaviest accumulation on its west slope. Joe compared it to what he could clearly see outside on the eastern horizon, and the images matched up. The photo had been taken a day or two before.

Joe was constantly astounded at what people posted on the internet about themselves. He'd apprehended a half dozen people over the years based on what the violators had uploaded for the world to see.

He took the turnoff to the enclave and parked his Game and Fish Ford F-150 between two of the shacks with a clear view of a trailer house. A decade-old Ram pickup was backed up to an ancient icehouse on the side of the trailer, but no one was inside the vehicle. A wisp of smoke rose out of the chimney pipe on top of the trailer before the wind jerked it away, suggesting it was occupied.

Joe called in the plate number to dispatch in Cheyenne and the dispatcher confirmed that the vehicle was registered to Amy Ehrlich of Twelve Sleep County, Wyoming. Ehrlich was Theriault's partner.

"Stay here," Joe said to Biscuit, their new one-year-old black Lab puppy. Biscuit took the place of Daisy, Joe's longtime companion who had been diagnosed with cancer the previous winter and had to be put down. It was a traumatic decision, and Joe had cradled his Lab in his arms as she was sedated for the last time. He hoped that Biscuit would be half the dog Daisy had been. Biscuit was jet-black, lean, and surprisingly calm for her age. So far, so good.

To Joe, a Game and Fish pickup without a Labrador inside was a sad vehicle.

HE COULDN'T TELL if anyone within the trailer had seen him out there. He'd deliberately approached from the county road and spent several minutes inside his pickup before getting out. There was no reason to panic Theriault or Ehrlich with a macho entrance and takedown. Especially someone as volatile as Theriault.

While he ambled his way to the Ram truck, Joe stayed in the open. They couldn't mistake the distinctive pickup and his red uniform shirt from inside, he thought. He went through a mental checklist of his gear: digital recorder, cell phone, handheld radio, handcuffs, bear spray, .40 Glock, ticket book. *Check, check, check, check, check, check, check.*

He considered calling for backup from the county sheriff, but decided not to do it. Sheriff Jackson Bishop and his new deputies liked to come on strong, and several excessive-force complaints had recently been filed against them. That wasn't Joe's style.

Joe glanced into the bed of the pickup as he passed it. There were smears of blood on the metal floor as well as several tufts of bristly deer hair. He didn't doubt that a forensics test would confirm it was deer blood.

He guessed that if he threw open the door of the old icehouse that the vehicle was backed up to, he'd find the hanging carcass of the buck deer he'd seen on Theriault's Facebook page. But to do so legally, he'd need a search warrant that he didn't have.

Due to the very tough winter, the mule deer population in his district had declined upward of sixty percent. That was the reason Joe had foregone using his own license for deer. Although he never faulted hunters for harvesting game for meat, he had no patience with trophy antler hunters, especially poachers who ignored the regulations. If Theriault had done it, Joe planned to charge him with every violation he could. A conviction would result in a hefty fine, loss of all hunting and fishing privileges for several years, and the confiscation of Theriault's hunting rifles and gear.

Since the state agency didn't issue body cams to game wardens, Joe activated his digital recorder and placed it in his breast pocket as he climbed the three wooden steps to the metal front door of the trailer. With his right hand on the grip of his Glock, he rapped softly on the thin metal of the structure with his left.

"Hello? This is Joe Pickett, the game warden. I need to talk to Matt Theriault."

Nothing. No response.

Then he knocked again, harder.

"Hello? Is anyone inside?"

Joe quickly looked over his shoulder toward the icehouse. If they were in there instead of the trailer, they were close enough to see and hear him.

He balled his fist and pounded on the door. It shook the trailer.

"Hey—is anyone home?" he shouted while he identified himself once again.

Finally, there were stumbling footfalls from inside. He could feel from the vibration on the aluminum skin of the trailer that someone was approaching the door.

"Who is it? What do you want?"

A woman's voice. It sounded weak, shaky, and slightly terrified.

Joe again identified himself. Then: "Hey—are you okay in there?"

The bolt was fumbled with a couple of times, then finally thrown back. The door opened a few inches and Joe stepped back so it wouldn't hit him in the head and knock his hat off. The smell of woodsmoke, stale fried food, and something else hit him from inside. It smelled like vomit.

Amy Ehrlich shakily placed her face between the side of the open door and the doorjamb and leaned against the interior wall to keep herself standing. She was dark-haired and heavyset and wearing a thin yellow bathrobe. Her eyes were half-open and her skin was gray and sallow.

"I guess you know why I'm here," Joe said. He was prepared for whatever came next, knowing it might be a threat, a confession, a statement of total innocence, or the admission to a crime he knew nothing about.

On this occasion, it was none of those. Ehrlich's eyes rolled back into her head and her mouth flopped open and she collapsed like a rag doll. Her weight made the door fly open and Joe barely retreated in time to not be swept off the steps by it.

She fell in a heap and then stretched out, her arms up above her head and her now-exposed white legs lying inside the trailer on the dirty vinyl flooring. Then, after a beat, she began to convulse. Her arms and legs twitched, and white foam covered her mouth.

"What is happening?" Joe asked himself aloud. He quickly mounted the stairs and stepped over her.

Matt Theriault was on his side next to a cluttered table as if he'd just slid out of it. He appeared to be either sleeping or dead.

Ehrlich's convulsions became more violent, and her naked heels bounced off the floor like a drumbeat. She was gagging, and Joe pulled her into the trailer by her ankles and flopped her over onto her belly. She was heavy and hard to roll over. Although the gagging stopped, her convulsions continued.

He called 911 and requested an ambulance as quickly as possible. When the local dispatcher asked him what he thought the problem was, he said, "I think they OD'd, but I can't be sure."

"We're sending the EMTs now," the dispatcher said.

"Tell them to hurry."

"FUCKING FENTANYL," SHERIFF Bishop said to Joe. He held up a small Ziploc bag of pure white powder that he'd snatched from a mirror on the tabletop. "These folks are the third and fourth victims this week. They probably thought it was cocaine they bought. Some asshat came through town selling this poison. I'd like to find whoever it was and mess him up for good."

An evidence tech who had been taking photographs of the scene strode over and impatiently grabbed the bag from the sheriff's hand and dropped it into an evidence envelope. Bishop shrugged.

"Please let me do my job," the tech pleaded.

"Sorry," Bishop said with a dismissive wave of his hand.

"Four victims?" Joe asked, stepping aside to clear the way for the EMTs to work. They'd already wheeled Ehrlich outside because she was still breathing, but Theriault had been pronounced dead on the scene. The EMTs had tried to revive him with a portable defibrillator, but they were unsuccessful, and their efforts had produced an acrid odor of burned flesh that contributed to the stale smells already inside the trailer. There was no reason to transport his body to the hospital.

Joe needed fresh air and he turned toward the door, when Bishop said, "Three fatalities. Maybe four if Theriault's girlfriend doesn't make it."

"Her name is Amy Ehrlich," Joe said.

"Whatever."

Bishop *looked* like a no-nonsense western sheriff, Joe thought. He was in his early forties with broad shoulders, a bushy cowboy mustache, a square jaw, and a staccato way of speaking that made him sound authoritative on many subjects even if he wasn't. A former deputy from Park County and the son-in-law of newly retired Judge Hewitt, Bishop had been elected in a landslide and had immediately rehired two former deputies, Ryan Steck and Justin Woods, who had quit because the department had become such a feckless mess under former sheriff Scott Tibbs. They joined Deputy "Fearless" Frank Carroll, the only LEO who'd survived the purge when Bishop arrived. Carroll had confided to Joe that Bishop's first words of instruction were to "kick ass and take names." Hence the allegations of excessive force.

Bishop roamed through the trailer, obviously not impressed with it. He called out and described further drug paraphernalia and the weapons he found stashed in drawers and closets through-out the structure, then returned to Joe.

He was fuming. "Both of them were on welfare," he said. "But somehow they could afford weed, meth, and fentanyl they thought was cocaine. Plus five guns running from a .38 snub-nose to an AK in the closet. Not to mention that seventy-two-inch TV on the wall with probably every streaming service that exists."

Joe had noticed the huge screen as well. He fought back nausea and nodded to the door to indicate that's where he wanted to go.

Bishop didn't pick up on the gesture. "Let's hope Theriault's girlfriend recovers enough to tell us who sold them the fentanyl," he said. "Otherwise, there will be more bodies piling up and the voters will start calling for my head. But I'm not the problem.

"Folks say to blame the Chinese government for the fentanyl epidemic," Bishop continued. "The Chicoms supply the Mexican drug cartels with the precursor chemicals to make fentanyl. They're deliberately killing our kids, and losers like Theriault and his girlfriend here. But do you know who I blame?"

Joe said he didn't.

"*Our own government*," Bishop said, dropping his voice to a whisper and leaning close to Joe. "The deep state on the East Coast. They allow this all to happen and they encourage it."

"Why would they do that?" Joe asked.

"They want to eradicate us rural folks," Bishop said. "It's part of the plan. Wipe out the white rural class and replace us with all those people coming over the southern border who will vote for them."

Joe didn't know how to respond. He hadn't heard Bishop make

conspiratorial statements like that before, and it certainly hadn't been a platform in his bid for sheriff.

As if realizing he'd said too much, Bishop quickly changed the subject. "Did the governor's office get ahold of you?" he asked Joe.

"When?" Joe asked. "Do you mean today?"

"This morning. They called our office asking if we knew where to find you."

Joe drew his phone out of his breast pocket and looked at the screen. He'd missed three calls that morning from Ann Byrnes, who was chief of staff for Governor Rulon.

"Uh-oh," Joe said.

"Why didn't you answer?"

"I was busy and cell service is bad out here, I guess."

"It's bad everywhere in my county," Bishop said. "That's something I hope to do something about." The sheriff was back in campaign mode after a dark little side trip, Joe thought.

Then: "What were you so busy doing?" Bishop asked.

"I was going to arrest Theriault for poaching a deer. I found it a few minutes ago hanging in his ice cooler outside." The mule deer buck was hanging next to a pronghorn antelope carcass that had the backstraps cut off. Theriault was obviously a habitual poacher, Joe had concluded.

"I'm not surprised," Bishop said. "He seems like the type. But I guess you don't have to worry about him anymore."

"I guess not."

Joe used the moment when the EMTs rolled Theriault into a body bag to shoulder around Bishop and head for the open door to return the call to the governor's office.

"Oh, Joe," Bishop called after him.

"Yup?"

"How's Sheridan doing? Now that she's running the falconry business on her own?"

Joe hesitated before answering. Everyone in the area knew Sheridan's single status since her fiancé-to-be had been killed by a grizzly bear the year before, but Joe recalled Sheridan telling her mother that the sheriff's interest in her was off-putting and odd. He was also a married man.

"She's fine," Joe said.

"She sure is," Bishop countered.

Rather than confront the sheriff at that moment, Joe turned his back on him and went outside.

JOE HAD ONLY one bar of cell reception on his phone in the yard, but a second appeared when he climbed into the bed of his pickup and stood on top of the large toolbox behind the cab. He punched the last recent call on his call log.

Ann Byrnes answered after one ring. There was a substantial amount of whooshing background noise that Joe recognized as belonging to an aircraft.

"This is Joe Pickett. I'm sorry I missed your previous messages. Can you hear me?"

"Yes I can. The governor would like to know where you've been all morning," Byrnes said without any kind of salutary greeting.

I'm not at his beck and call, Joe wanted to say—but didn't. "Game warden business," he said instead. "In and out of cell phone range, I'm afraid."

"Where are you now?"

"I'm at a rural residence east of Saddlestring. We're in the middle of investigating a couple of drug overdoses and a poached—"

"Can you get to the airport in fifteen minutes?" she asked, cutting him off. "We're flying from Gillette back to Cheyenne in the state plane, but we can divert to Saddlestring."

Joe transferred the phone to where he could pinch it between his cheek and shoulder and shot out his arm and looked at his watch. "I can be there in twenty if there aren't too many cows on the road," he said.

"The governor will meet you in fifteen minutes," Byrnes said, and disconnected the call.

JOE ARRIVED AT the Twelve Sleep County Municipal Airport as the state plane touched down on the runway and taxied toward the small terminal. He parked his truck in front of the lobby doors, where he wasn't supposed to park, and went inside.

Saddlestring had only two commercial flights a day, both to and from Denver. One was early in the morning and the second was midafternoon. Since he was there between them, Joe was the only living soul in the airport except for a cat that was curled up on the United Airlines Express ticket counter. Not even the six TSA agents, who often outnumbered the passengers, were present.

His boot heels clicked on the granite floor and echoed in the lobby. He crossed the room and ducked under the belt of the TSA retractable crowd-control stanchions, bypassed the metal detector, and pushed his way through the double back doors. As the state plane approached and flared to its side, Joe reached up and grabbed his hat so the exhaust from the twin jets wouldn't blow it off.

Rulon One was the unofficial name of the state airplane, named after Spencer Rulon, the current *and* former governor. Joe was achingly familiar with the plane, and he hated to ride in it. Not only was he a nervous flier, but the only reason he was ever in the aircraft was because of unusual and uncomfortable circumstances.

Governor Rulon had been elected—again—the previous November after a truncated campaign following the previous governor Colter Allen's sudden announcement that he wanted to "spend more time with his family" and wouldn't seek reelection. Joe had been there, on the plane now in front of him, when it all happened.

At that time, Joe had disabled Allen's aircraft from taking off by firing several bullets into the right engine. It had been the most expensive act of destruction of state property in his career, and that was saying something. When the costs for repairing the jet were added to the list of wrecked vehicles Joe had been responsible for, it was very possible that no state employee would ever break his record. That fact had been pointed out to him several times by agency budget officers, and he tried to ignore it or change the subject.

JOE AND RULON had a long history that Joe had thought was concluded four years before, when Rulon had completed his second term as a Democrat in an eighty percent Republican state. Governor Allen, a Republican rancher from Sublette County, had proved to be impulsive, unpopular, and corrupt. He'd since moved to California, and Joe had heard rumors that the ex-governor was trying to revive his dormant acting career to no avail.

Rulon was once again proving that he was a unique politician. So unique, in fact, that the voters of Wyoming looked past the (D) behind his name.

He'd hit the ground running by stating during his first week in office that he was going after federal agencies that had, in his opinion, overplayed their hands and exceeded their constitutional powers in recent years in the state. Therefore, he would sue them all. Those agencies included the Environmental Protection Agency, the Department of Homeland Security, the Department of Energy, the Department of Agriculture, the Department of Education, and the Centers for Disease Control. No sitting governor had ever sued six federal agencies all at once. He also challenged the vice president to a duel with pistols unless the feds promised to "leave my state the hell alone."

Why the vice president and not the president himself? Because, Rulon declared, the president couldn't be trusted with a firearm.

It had been a wildly popular debut.

In his first stint as governor, Rulon had asked Joe to be his agent on various assignments. Rulon had said he liked the fact that Joe could go anywhere in the state and embed himself in all kinds of situations as a game warden and not be suspected of having an alternative agenda.

Rulon always made sure he himself had plausible deniability, and he'd made it clear that if Joe screwed up, he couldn't expect to be bailed out. Reluctantly, Joe had agreed to those conditions because he felt he had no choice. Rulon had called Joe his "range rider."

Joe had speculated to Marybeth that perhaps with all of those legal initiatives going on at once that Rulon might have forgotten about him. That was fine with Joe.

But apparently not.

CHAPTER FIVE

T HE STAIRS TO *Rulon One*, a Cessna Citation Encore jet with the Wyoming Cowboys bucking horse logo on the tail, were folded down to the tarmac. Joe climbed them, and the copilot nodded a greeting and stepped aside so he could retract the steps and close the door behind him.

Governor Rulon sat grinning behind a small desk at the back of the plane and Ann Byrnes sat a row in front of him with an iPad on her lap. The other six seats in the aircraft were unoccupied.

"Ah, Joe," Rulon said as he struggled out from behind the desk. "Thanks for meeting with me." The "meeting area" on the aircraft was cramped for space.

When he was in the aisle, Rulon placed his meaty hands on both of Joe's shoulders. It was a familiar gesture from an instinctively tactile man. Rulon chuckled and said, "Well, now—together again." Then: "Why aren't you wearing that fine hat I got for you?"

Years before, Rulon had presented Joe a nine-hundred-dollar

Resistol Cattle Baron cowboy hat with his name inscribed on the sweat brim.

"This is my work hat," Joe said, touching the brim. "I save your hat for special occasions."

Ann Byrnes cleared her throat and sniffed. "One might think that meeting with the governor *was* a special occasion."

"Give him a break, Ann," Rulon said while he wedged himself back behind the desk and shot her a side-eye. "We called him out of the field."

Byrnes looked at her watch and said to Rulon, "We have ten minutes if you want to be on time for the Wyoming Stock Growers reception this afternoon."

"Oh, those guys will wait a few minutes," Rulon said. "We both know they love me." Then: "Sit down, Joe."

Joe did so. Byrnes occupied the seat next to Joe and, despite her arch tone, he thought Rulon absolutely needed a chief of staff like her. The governor was notoriously exuberant, easily distracted, and often late. Past chiefs of staff had not always been good choices, including ones with secret agendas of their own, and once, an attractive female chief who was known to sometimes answer the phone while sitting on the governor's lap.

Byrnes fixed her eyes on Joe and mouthed, "*Ten minutes.*"

Joe indicated that he understood.

RULON HAD GAINED weight since the last time Joe had seen him, and his ruddy complexion seemed to have paled. Joe wondered if the job was more daunting than Rulon had expected it to be in his second stint.

As if reading Joe's mind, Rulon patted his belly behind his desk and said, "Reception after reception after reception. Speech after speech after speech. All involve vast quantities of food that I'm expected to eat. And we aren't even to the cursed legislative session yet."

Wyoming's legislature met for only forty days every other year, and only twenty days in between. Many people in the state thought even that was too much. Rulon was on record saying he agreed with them.

"You know," Rulon began, "I'm not real sure why I'm doing this again. I think I can tell you that in confidence, can't I?"

"You can," Joe said.

"I've had a very good life, and in my first go-round, I left as a much-beloved ex-governor," Rulon said matter-of-factly. "When I termed out the first time, I made a hell of a lot more money as a lawyer than I ever did as a public servant. Plus, I could represent whomever I wanted to represent and do some good without always looking over my shoulder to see who in the Cowboy Congress was trying to stab me in the back.

"So here I am, right back in the thick of it again. What's wrong with me, Joe?"

Rulon seemed to be sincere when he asked the question, but Joe wasn't so sure. Rulon was the most natural political animal Joe had ever been around. The man thrived in the limelight and seemed to revel in picking fights and taking on anyone who the governor thought was working to harm or belittle the state of Wyoming. Voters thought of Rulon as a man who would fight, and Rulon rarely disappointed them.

"I don't know how to answer that," Joe said. "Except that I

think most folks are glad you're back in there. Governor Allen was—"

"A feckless little faux-rancher asshole," Rulon said, finishing Joe's sentence with words Joe wouldn't have said. "I tried to warn people about him, but no one believed me."

Joe nodded. He knew that was partly accurate. Rulon had had concerns about Allen, but he'd kept them mostly to himself. But like every politician Joe had ever encountered, Rulon was much more comfortable with his own version of the truth.

"Anyway, water under the bridge," Rulon said with a dismissive wave of his arm. "To the matter at hand."

"To the matter at hand," Joe repeated.

"Are you still gonna be my guy? My trusted range rider?"

Joe frowned. "I guess it depends on what you need."

Rulon threw his head back and laughed. "You haven't changed, Joe. You're still the guy who arrested a governor for fishing without a license way back in the day."

"Yup. And I'm still a guy who won't do politics. I wouldn't do it for Governor Allen and I won't do it for you."

"I assure you this isn't politics," Rulon said. "It's personal."

Joe looked at him warily. For men like Rulon, Joe had learned, *everything* was politics.

"Did you ever meet my son-in-law, Mark?"

"I don't think so."

"Mark Eisele?"

"Nope."

"He's married to my daughter, Megan, who, as a modern-type woman, goes by her given last name. So I understand if you've never heard of the Eiseles. Anyway, they have a little one—a girl—and more on the way, I hope. Megan takes little Charlotte to work every day, and Mark works for some Silicon Valley tech firm out of their home in Cheyenne. I have no earthly idea what in the hell he does for them. He tried to tell me once, but I fell asleep."

"Charlotte is your granddaughter?" Joe asked.

Rulon lit up at hearing her name. "Grandchildren are an absolute blessing," Rulon said. "Don't let anyone ever tell you otherwise. They are the greatest gift there is. You'll find out someday."

"I hope so," Joe said. He and Marybeth had a bet on which of their three daughters would have a child first. Marybeth thought it would be Lucy, their youngest, because, unlike her older sisters, she'd always been gentle, maternal, and openly pined for a family of her own. Middle daughter April, the maverick, was focused on her work for a private detective agency in Montana. Joe's bet was on April, since April always seemed to do what was least expected of her. Both agreed that it wouldn't be Sheridan, who was all-consumed with running Yarak, Inc. in Nate's absence.

"Do you know why grandparents and grandchildren get along so well, Joe?" Rulon asked him.

Joe shook his head. As he did so, Ann Byrnes sighed and rolled her eyes. She'd obviously heard the anecdote a million times.

"It's because they share a common enemy," Rulon deadpanned. Then: "It's not that I don't like Mark. I don't want it to sound that way at all. But, well, Mark's a nerd, you know? He grew up on the East Coast, and the only thing he's ever looked at—besides my daughter, I mean—is a series of screens. He's never hunted, never fished, never played organized sports, never camped, never, well, you get the idea."

"He's an indoor person," Joe said.

"That's being very charitable, yes," Rulon said. "I'd describe him as half a man, but I get in trouble with my wife and daughter when I say that."

"I can imagine," Joe said.

Rulon suddenly gestured toward the Bighorn Mountains through the airplane's portal window. "I mean, why live out here when your existence is no different than it would be if you were in downtown San Francisco or the D.C. Beltway? People need to get out there and experience life, you know? My Charlotte, and future grandkids, need to know there is a natural world out there beyond their iPads. Charlotte needs to know so she can turn out to be a well-rounded and well-adjusted human being. But her parents need to show her the way, you know?"

Joe didn't interrupt, but he wasn't sure where Rulon was going or how long the journey was going to take. In his peripheral vision, he noted that Byrnes was checking her watch.

"Our kids went outside, you know?" Rulon said. "Even Megan. She used to love to turn over rocks while I was fishing to see what was under them. She had pet worms in a jar, for goodness' sake. And a salamander named Ashcroft. We let her get actual dirt on herself. I think if Mark had his way, he'd bubble-wrap Charlotte and never let her go outside. He just doesn't know any better, I guess."

Byrnes softly cleared her throat. It got the attention of the pilots, as well as Joe and the governor. Time was running out.

"Sir, I'm sorry, but we'll need to wrap this up," she said.

Rulon glared at her, and for a moment his neck flushed pink. Then he sighed, temporarily defeated. Byrnes was no doubt doing exactly what Rulon had asked her to do: keep him focused and on time.

"Joe," Rulon said, "I hooked Mark up with an elk-hunting guide and encouraged him to get out of his home office this fall and learn about the outdoors firsthand. He was reluctant to do it, but Megan supported the idea, much to my surprise."

"Okay," Joe said, urging the governor to get to the point.

"Mark agreed to do it. I'm proud of him. I wanted him to experience the great outdoors and learn some skills. In all honesty, I might have pressured him more than I should have."

"Okay. Who is the guide?"

"Spike Rankin. Do you know him?"

"Yup," Joe said. "He hunts in southern Wyoming, down around the Battle Mountain area."

Joe smiled to himself as he recalled meeting Rankin over the back of a pickup once. Rankin was a tough nut, an opinionated curmudgeon, but one of the best outfitters in the state. Rankin didn't suffer fools, and poor Mark would have to toe the line or he'd be humiliated.

"Well," Rulon said, leaning into Joe and lowering his voice, "it seems that Spike Rankin and my son-in-law have been missing since yesterday."

"Probably scouting," Joe said. "That isn't very unusual."

Rulon shot a glance to Byrnes, then turned back to Joe. Joe got the impression that Byrnes didn't approve of what was coming next.

"Spike Rankin is an old buddy of mine," Rulon said. "I asked him on the sly to text me a progress report on Mark every day, and he agreed. I wanted to keep track of the father of my grandchild, you know? Well, Rankin texted me saying Mark was doing better than he thought he would do, and that they were going to do a scouting recon in the mountains, just like you said."

"Okay."

"Then yesterday—nothing. Megan is starting to get a little bit worried that she hasn't heard from Mark, either. I assured her that it's not unusual at all for Rankin to be out of cell signal range, and I told her not to fret about it. But I'm starting to worry now, too."

"Have you contacted the sheriff down there?" Joe asked.

"No," Rulon said emphatically. "And I won't. I can't."

"Why not?"

"Sheriff Regan Haswell is not only crooked, he's one of my longtime enemies," Rulon said. "He's one of those crazy ultra-right wingers who thinks everyone in state government is corrupt. He answers to no one, including the governor."

Joe was aware of the ideology of the sovereign nation and their odd beliefs. The sovereigns believed that the duly-elected local sheriff was the only legitimate authority they had to answer to in the nation. Therefore, they paid no federal income taxes and ignored federal regulations in general—as well as most state laws.

"If Haswell knew about Mark, he'd make a huge issue of it and embarrass the hell out of me if he could," Rulon said. "And if I asked him, he sure as hell wouldn't go out there and discreetly find Mark and Rankin. That's for sure."

"What about highway patrol or DCI? Are they involved at all at this point?"

Both agencies, like the Game and Fish Department, were within the executive branch and therefore answered to the governor.

"No," Rulon said. "Why would I send DCI cops or troopers

into the mountains looking for elk hunters? Does that make sense to you?"

"Probably not," Joe conceded.

"The fewer people know about this, the better."

Joe was puzzled for a moment, then he got it. "Megan and your wife don't know Mark is missing yet, do they?"

Rulon shook his head.

"They don't know that Rankin had agreed to check in with you every day?"

"That's correct," Rulon said.

"And you're worried that all hell will break loose in your immediate family if something has happened to Mark, since you pressured him to go with Rankin. It's all your doing."

"That about sums it up," Rulon said.

"This isn't a good situation for you," Joe said.

"You think?" Rulon emphasized the importance of that by widening his eyes and thrusting his chin toward Joe.

"Governor," Byrnes interrupted. "We really need to go."

Joe felt the aircraft hum and shake as the pilots fired up the jets. The copilot removed his headphones and started the procedure to unlock the door and extend the steps back to the tarmac so Joe could leave.

"Can you go south to that Battle Mountain country and see if you can find him?" Rulon asked Joe. "Like I said, this is personal. It might be nothing at all—Rankin and Mark might be high in the mountains setting up their elk camp out of cell signal range. Or Rankin might be preoccupied and he's forgotten to text. Or something unfortunate happened to the both of them. Either way, I'd owe you a big one if you could find out."

Joe didn't respond. Governor Rulon had rescued him from trouble countless times, and he'd used his influence to free Nate Romanowski from the grip of rogue federal agents. More than once.

"I'll see what I can do," Joe said.

He was surprised when Rulon leapt from his seat and grasped Joe by the sides of his head and kissed him on the top of the crown of his hat. "Thank you, Joe. Thank you."

Byrnes stood in the aisle, glaring down at Joe to move. *Rulon One* began to tremble as the jet engines powered up.

"Call or text me your progress," Rulon called out to Joe as he straightened his just-jostled hat and moved toward the open door. "Bless you, son! Bless you! Go find Mark and bring him back to me in one piece."

As THE EASTERN mountains turned electric pink with the last gasp of dusk, Joe packed clean clothing into a duffel bag in his bedroom. Downstairs, he heard Marybeth enter the house and call out to him. Joe had called Marybeth after his meeting with the governor and gotten her out of her board meeting to brief her. Even though the governor didn't want anyone but Joe and Ann Byrnes to know about the pickle he was in, Joe told his wife everything, like he always did.

He found her in the kitchen holding a take-out box of pizza in her right hand while balancing Kestrel Romanowski on her left hip. Marybeth was still dressed in a dark suit and white blouse from her library board meeting that day. For the past year, Marybeth had taken the child to work with her. Kestrel spent her time in a library-sponsored day care for part of the day and the rest in

Marybeth's office playing with toys and reading children's books in a kid's corner Marybeth had set up.

Their three dogs—Bisquit, Tube, and Bert's Dog—converged on Marybeth and the pizza smells from various places in the house.

"Here, I'll take her," Joe said.

Marybeth swung her hips and Joe plucked the toddler out of Marybeth's grip.

"Unka Joe," Kestrel said as she beamed. "Throw me, Unka Joe." Her eyes sparkled with devilry.

Like he did every night now, Joe launched Kestrel into the air almost to ceiling height and caught her on the way down. And like she did every night, Kestrel squealed.

The three of them sat at the table eating pizza, and Joe realized how natural the situation had become. Years after their three daughters had left them an empty nest, they were caretakers of a toddler once again. He told Marybeth what the governor had said about why grandparents and grandchildren got along so well.

"But Kestrel isn't our grandchild," Marybeth said.

"She sort of seems like one. She's our *practice* grandchild. I think Liv would approve and Nate would be pleased."

"And speaking of our common enemy," Marybeth said with a sly grin, "I spoke to Sheridan today. She said Geronimo Jones came by looking for him yesterday. She steered him in the direction of Hole in the Wall Canyon."

"Smart," Joe said. "That's where I'd look."

"So why haven't you?"

"You know why."

It was a sore subject between them. Marybeth didn't dispute the fact that she felt both safer and more comfortable when Nate was around. It had nothing to do with the added responsibility of seeing to Kestrel's well-being, which Marybeth had taken to easily and naturally. Joe quietly bristled at the fact that Marybeth felt that way, even though he knew she had a point. After all, it was his duty to keep his family safe and secure, not Nate's.

"Tell me again why you haven't gone after him," Marybeth said.

"I know Nate," Joe said. "He's gone to ground for a reason. He'll come back when he's ready."

Just as Joe had conceded Marybeth's point, Marybeth quietly conceded Joe's.

She turned to Kestrel, who was in the process of removing each round of pepperoni from her pizza and eating them individually. "I'll miss this little one when he does come back for her."

"I think we both will," Joe said.

"And if for some reason he never shows up, I can see her becoming part of the family."

Joe had been waiting for Marybeth to voice it. April had become a part of their family in roughly similar circumstances.

"He'll come back," he said.

"How LONG DO you expect to be away?" she asked.

"A few days, I think. If it takes longer than that, we'll have to start up a full-fledged search and rescue operation. The governor doesn't want that to happen because if it goes public then his family would have to know. But it might be unavoidable."

"I hope you don't plan to try and do this all on your own," she said. "I know how you are."

He smiled and said, "I'll need some help down there. I spent some time in the Sierra Madres, as you know, but I'm not familiar enough with the country to do this solo."

Tube, their half-Lab and half-Corgi mix, had come from Joe's brief assignment to southern Wyoming years before.

"Who is the game warden down there?" she asked.

"Susan Kany. I met her last year at the Wyoming Game Wardens Association meeting. She's a rookie."

"Does she know the district well enough to help you?"

"I hope so. She seemed pretty with-it," Joe said. "No doubt she's met Spike Rankin at some point, so she might know where his camp is and where he hunts elk."

"Are you going to tell her why you're down there? The real reason?"

"I'm not sure yet. I think I can massage it so I don't necessarily have to mention the governor's name."

"Let's hope it's as easy as that," Marybeth said. "What about the sheriff?"

"Rulon doesn't trust him. But that doesn't mean that I probably won't meet with him and let him know what's going on if I have to. It's professional courtesy. Local law enforcement usually doesn't like it when someone from the outside starts operating in their county. And from what the governor said, Sheriff Haswell definitely wouldn't welcome me with open arms if I didn't reach out to him at some point."

"He sounds like our sheriff," Marybeth said. Then to Kestrel: "You can't just eat pepperoni, sweetie. You have to eat the whole slice, or at least try it."

Kestrel sat back in frustration for a few seconds, then reluctantly reached for the pizza slice.

"While you're gone, I might ask Sheridan to stay with me," Marybeth said. "I can use the companionship, and she likes it when she doesn't have to cook for herself."

"I was going to suggest that," Joe said.

"Plus, with not having Nate around . . ."

"Yes, I know," Joe said more sharply than he intended to.

An hour and a half later, after Joe had secured all of the gear he thought he'd need for the mission and put it into the large toolbox in the bed of his pickup, Marybeth opened the door to the detached garage and leaned against the open doorframe with her arms crossed. She was wearing the oversized barn coat she wore to feed her horses and do other corral chores.

"You're leaving tonight instead of tomorrow morning?"

"Yup. I thought I'd get a jump on it. This way, I can be in Warm Springs first thing in the morning."

The town of Warm Springs was in south-central Wyoming and it was the closest village to Battle Mountain and the Sierra Madre range, where Rankin and Eisele had disappeared. The game warden station for the district was also located there.

"Are you taking Biscuit with you?"

"Nope. I'm leaving her here. She's a better watchdog than Tube or Bert's Dog. I mean, as you constantly remind me, since Nate isn't around . . ."

"He's done it again, hasn't he?" Marybeth asked.

"Who? Nate?"

"Governor Rulon. He's put you in a tough situation, where if you succeed he can skate without anyone being aware of what might have happened, and if you fail he'll blame you for the loss of his son-in-law."

"That's harsh," Joe said. But it was partly true.

"I had a choice," he said. "I could have said no."

"But you didn't because ultimately Rulon is your boss. And the boss of your boss. He could make our lives miserable if he wanted to."

"Of course. But don't forget how many times and ways he's helped us out," Joe said. "Times he didn't have to step up."

She said, "Promise me you'll do what you can—but stop before you get yourself into a life-threatening situation. The governor got himself into this dilemma. It's his problem, not yours. And not ours."

"I'll do my job and not cross the line," Joe said.

"You've said that before."

Joe draped his arms over the top of the wall of his pickup and looked her over. Marybeth appeared quite provocative to him, the slinky way she was framed in the doorway.

"Did you already read Kestrel a story and put her to bed?"

"Yes. She fell asleep faster than usual."

"So we once again have the house to ourselves?"

Marybeth's eyes widened for a beat when she realized what he was suggesting, then she gently shook her head. "Not with a toddler down the hall, Joe."

"Why not?" he said. "She's our practice grandchild. We need to work on sneaking around again."

Which made her laugh. But instead of retreating back to the house, Marybeth came into the garage and extended her hand and said, "Follow me."

A HALF HOUR later, Joe's cell phone burred when he backed his pickup out of the garage. He saw on the screen that the call was coming from Ann Byrnes.

"Joe Pickett."

"Joe, this is Ann Byrnes, Governor Rulon's chief of staff."

"I know who you are. You don't have to say that every time."

"Are you in Warm Springs?"

"I got delayed, but I'm on the way."

He smiled to himself as he said it. The delay was more than worth it.

"I was hoping you'd be there by now," Byrnes said with obvious irritation.

He sighed. "It's a four-and-a-half-hour drive from Saddlestring, you know. Not everyone has a state plane."

"I'm well aware of that," she said. "Well, I hope you're successful—and quick."

"Me too."

"Because until we can get this situation resolved, the governor will be beside himself. He's not very productive when he's in the state he's in."

"I get that," Joe said. "I'll do my best."

"Quickly and efficiently," she said. "And undercover, so to speak."

"Yup."

"Please keep me informed of your progress. Even if it's bad news."

"Do you think it might be bad news?" Joe asked.

"Well, it's about to be two days if we don't hear from him tonight. What do they always say about the first forty-eight hours of a law enforcement investigation?"

"They say if you don't solve the crime within that time, it's unlikely you ever will."

"Let's hope that's not the case here. That would be extremely unfortunate, not to mention unacceptable."

"I'll keep you informed," Joe said, punching off.

CHAPTER SIX

MARK EISELE HAD slipped in and out of consciousness so many times that he wasn't sure where he was, how long he'd been there, and what was or wasn't real. His dreams had been turbulent and elaborate and vivid, and several times he'd awakened with his sheets soaked through with sweat from fever dreams.

In one of them, he had chased his father-in-law down a long hallway of a creepy old resort hotel in the mountains, à la the Overlook Hotel in *The Shining*. While he trundled away from Eisele, Rulon kept glancing over his shoulder, imploring his son-in-law to stop pursuing him. The man was winded and flushed. But when Eisele finally cornered Rulon near the elevator and tackled him to the carpet, he was pulled off his father-in-law by massive bodyguards as well as his wife, Megan—*and* his mother-in-law. For the purposes of his dream, they were heavily muscled and extremely strong. And he was easy to subdue.

In another, he slowly came to in a gleaming white hospital room. In it, Eisele was propped up slightly in bed and covered with clean sheets. An empty tray of hospital food was moved to the side of the bed. There was a football game on the overhead television and he could see the gold dome of the state capitol though the window. Snow fell, even though the sun was out. He felt no pain, even though he was heavily bandaged and he couldn't move his legs or arms. He didn't know how he'd managed to eat his meal.

Two nurses entered the room and he greeted them. One had Megan's face and the other his mother-in-law's, but neither woman *was* his wife or mother-in-law, and they were clearly puzzled when he insisted they were.

The nurse with Megan's face said they had come to check up on him, as they did every couple of hours. When he asked why, the two women shared a glance between them that was ominous and it filled Eisele with dread.

"You really don't know why?" the Megan-faced nurse asked him.

He looked back at her blankly.

"Should we tell him?" she asked the mother-in-law-faced nurse.

"Show him."

Which was followed by another ominous glance.

Then the Megan-faced nurse reached out and peeled the top sheets off of Eisele. He felt cool air on his bare legs, and when he looked down there was a mass of bloody bandages covering his genitals, and he let out a shriek.

"They got shot off," the Megan-faced nurse explained. "We're hoping to find you some new ones."

"Which might be tough," the mother in law faced nurse said. "We might have to use some skin from your thigh to rebuild a penis and install an air pump in case you ever want to try to be, you know, *intimate* again . . ."

———

BUT WHEN HE woke up this time the room he was in was dark and there was no view of the capitol, and no nurses with familiar faces. The room smelled slightly of old smoke. His fever had abated and he wasn't covered in sweat. His sheets were dry.

He tried to sit up, but couldn't, and he realized he was restrained. A one-inch-wide nylon strap, like the kind used to keep a tarp secure over a trailer bed filled with garbage on the way to the dump, stretched tightly across his chest and held him down. He could see no release on it, and he assumed the ratchet mechanism was located under his cot, where he was unable to reach for it.

Despite the strap, Eisele was able to pull down the top blanket inch by inch with his hands by grasping the folds of the material and tugging it toward his feet. Eventually, the top of it slipped under the strap and the blanket gathered around his waist.

By pinching the sheets between his knees and then kicking his feet, he managed to work the blanket down the length of his body, where it piled over his ankles. Then, after closing his eyes for a moment and whispering a prayer to a God he'd never spoken to before, he raised his head and looked down at his groin.

It was fine. There was no mass of bloody bandages. Only a pair of light blue, urine-stained scrub pants.

His head flopped back and he blew out his breath with relief. As he did so, he realized that his activity had set off sharp bolts of pain in his right shoulder and left buttocks.

That's right, he thought. *They shot me.*

———

EISELE COULD ONLY recall snippets of what had happened after he went down. He remembered the two painted faces above him, and the jet airplane that screamed through the icy blue sky as it descended. Then being strapped face up on the back of an ATV as it bounced along a rough trail, the impact of each pothole or rock sending sharp stabs of pain through him that plummeted him back into darkness.

Then there was the sight of a dowdy Old West town with a wide street, a smattering of buildings in different stages of disrepair, close dark pine trees hemming in the village framed by snowy mountains, and the rough handling of several people carrying him through the lobby of one of the structures as if he were a sack of potatoes. They swung him from side to side as they carried him, and he got a good look at the tin-stamped ceiling. The people carrying him wore camo clothing.

Was there really an Old West town, he wondered, or was that something that had come from a movie or television series? He couldn't be certain whether he'd seen it or if it had been in one of his dreams.

EISELE CAME TO the realization that he wasn't alone in the dark room. Ragged breathing punctuated the silence to his right and he turned his head in that direction.

In the dull orange light of a portable heater plugged in between their cots, he could see a blanketed form. The heater rattled and hummed as it cranked out warmth in the dark. An aluminum IV stand was above the other cot and a plastic tube extended from a bag of clear liquid to within the sheets. He couldn't see the face of the person in the cot, but he assumed it was Rankin. He *hoped* it was Rankin.

"Spike, is that you?" Eisele asked. His voice was hoarse and phlegmy.

"Spike, can you hear me?"

No response.

"Spike, if it's you, I need you to be strong, because I'm not much help to you. In fact, I don't know what in the hell is going on."

Again, there was no response.

A FEW MINUTES later, Eisele heard muffled voices on the other side of the closed door. Several of them, at least two men and a woman. They seemed to be casually conversing. There was a band of light under the door, and someone walked close enough to it to cast shadows.

"Hey!" he shouted.

The voices stopped.

"Hey, I need some help in here. There's two of us."

There was the sound of a squeaky doorknob being turned, and for a quick moment Eisele was blinded by light from the other room. He involuntarily closed his eyes and turned away.

Someone entered and closed the door behind them. When he opened his eyes he saw that the beam of a headlamp was illuminating his torso. The beam moved down from his chest to his groin.

"You pissed yourself again," a female said sourly. He recognized the voice as the woman who had bent over him after he was shot. The woman with camo paint and a full mouth.

"I'm sorry," Eisele said. "I wasn't awake to know what I was doing."

"Yeah, yeah," the woman said.

"I'm strapped down. I can't move."

"Like I didn't know that."

"Untie me so I can use the bathroom."

She ignored him. The beam on her headlamp was now on the form in the next cot.

"Is that Spike?" Eisele asked. "Is he okay? Because he doesn't respond, and it doesn't seem like he's okay."

The beam contracted as she leaned over the person. She pulled the top cover of the blanket up and the light probed beneath it. She held up the corner of the material so it blocked Eisele's view.

After a few seconds, she draped the blanket back over the form.

"Is that my hunting companion?" Eisele asked.

"I guess so," she said. "He's the older guy you were with. He doesn't seem to be doing so hot," she said matter-of-factly.

"We need a doctor," Eisele said.

She scoffed at that. "We're doing what we can do. This is field medicine at its best. It saved the lives of a lot of good soldiers."

"We need to get to a hospital. Spike sounds really bad, and I'm in a lot of pain."

As he spoke to her and became more lucid, he was filled with more and more questions.

"Are you here to rescue us, or are you holding us captive?"

"What do you think?" she asked with a harsh laugh.

"What's your name?" he asked. "I'm Mark Eisele, and the other guy is Spike Rankin."

"We know that."

"So what's your name?"

"We don't use our real names here. Only our call signs. I'm known as Double-A," she said. It came out reluctantly, and Eisele wasn't sure that she hadn't just made it up on the spot.

"Where in the hell are we?" he asked.

She turned to him and doused her headlamp while she did it. He couldn't see her clearly, but he could feel her presence just a few feet away.

"This old town used to be called Summit," she said. "Now we call it Soledad City."

PART THREE

"Terror seeks out the odd, and the sick, and
the lost."

—J. A. Baker, *The Peregrine*

CHAPTER SEVEN

NATE ROMANOWSKI SAT in the passenger seat of Geronimo Jones's matte-black 2015 Chevy Suburban 2500 as they sped along the almost empty roads of Yellowstone National Park en route to Gardiner, Montana. Most of the park's accommodations had already been closed for the season. They'd entered the park via the East Entrance and were working their way up the right side of the figure-eight road system hugging the contours of the Yellowstone River. Geronimo drove much faster than the park-imposed forty-five miles per hour, and as he did so, he cursed at occasional recreational vehicles poking along and a herd of bison, who lazily crossed the blacktop and created a one-car traffic jam.

Geronimo had explained to Nate that he'd purchased the massive vehicle the month before at a Denver Police Department impound auction. It had previously belonged to a gangbanger who had installed smoked bulletproof glass in the windows and steel plates in the front passenger and driver's doors. The gangbanger had also replaced the inflatable tires with pure rubber ones that could absorb bullets and power over road spikes without going flat. There were secret compartments in the doors, floorboard, and cargo area for weapons, gear, and, most likely, drugs.

Geronimo said, "It ain't subtle." Nate agreed.

GERONIMO HAD REMOVED the second row of seats in the Suburban and replaced them with a latticework topped by a thick horizontal dowel rod. Balanced on the rod were Nate's peregrine and red-tailed hawk. Both were hooded and they learned quickly to lean into turns and brace themselves when Geronimo slowed down or sped up. Next to Nate's falcons was Geronimo's huge white and black mottled white gyrfalcon, which was also hooded. Geronimo had spread a bedsheet over the floor to catch splashes of excrement that made the inside of the vehicle smell like a combination of musk and ammonia.

They stopped the vehicle periodically to retrieve fresh roadkill on the side of the road, including, in one instance, a mule deer fawn. While Geronimo drove, Nate fed the falcons in the back and then climbed into the passenger seat.

AT CANYON VILLAGE, Geronimo took a left and gunned it on the road that cut across the middle of the figure eight to Norris Junction. The road existed simply to connect the loops and featured no special attractions—no geysers, mud pots, fumaroles, or waterfalls. The most interesting thing on the drive to Nate was the ability to judge how tall the pine trees had grown since the devastating fires of 1988, which had collectively formed the largest wildfire in the history of the massive park and scorched nearly eight hundred thousand acres. The once-burned landscape was covered with young pine trees again.

"You could slow down a little," Nate said as they topped a steep rise going seventy-five.

"We're in a hurry," Geronimo replied.

"Remember when I told you I couldn't invite you to stay with us in Colorado?" Geronimo asked.

"Yes," Nate said. His eyes stayed on the road ahead in case a wandering buffalo or elk suddenly appeared.

"I didn't tell you why."

"No, you didn't."

"It's because my house was burned to the ground."

Nate looked over. He recalled the million-dollar home set on ten acres on a mountainside with a magnificent view of the Denver city lights. He'd stayed in a guest bedroom and had breakfast the next morning with a then-pregnant Jacinda and Geronimo. Pearl wasn't in the picture yet.

"If it wasn't for a child's broken necklace," Geronimo said, "I'd have burned up with it, along with my wife and child."

"Explain."

"It happened a month ago, in September," Geronimo said. "Pearl was playing with a cheap bead necklace some friend of hers had given her as a party favor. Can you believe two-year-old girls get invited to organized birthday parties these days? Anyway, my Pearl-girl loves her jewelry, which doesn't bode well for me in the future.

"So, like with all of Pearl's toys, she broke it. The beads went everywhere, and Jacinda told her to pick them up. I helped her, which meant crawling around on my hands and knees and fishing them out from under the couch and such. Somehow, one of those beads went straight up into Pearl's nose."

"That sounds like something Kestrel would do," Nate said. He recalled his daughter inserting a Barbie shoe into her ear once, and the wailing she did as Liv removed it.

"I don't mean perched in a nostril," Geronimo said. "I mean straight up her nose so far we couldn't see it. She really shoved it up there. Don't ask me why. I guess to see how far it would go.

"So, Jacinda called our clinic and they said to pinch her other nostril and hold her mouth open and blow in it. They thought the bead would come shooting out like a bullet."

"But it didn't work," Nate said.

"It didn't work. So even though it was dark out and time to eat dinner, we had to bundle up Pearl and take her to the nearest emergency room. I guess we left the lights on when we left because we were shaken up by the whole ordeal."

"Go on," Nate said.

"We saw the glow up in the trees when we drove back from the clinic two hours later," Geronimo said. "I knew it was our house, and it was like a kick in the gut. I mean, everything was in that house. Paintings, jewelry, cash, family photos, *everything*. My triple-barrel shotgun. Thank God my gyrfalcon was in its mews out back and it didn't get burned up.

"Jacinda and I accused each other of being careless and causing the fire to start. She thought I left a lit cigar in my man cave and I thought she'd forgotten to turn off the stove or something.

"But it turns out," Geronimo said, "that our neighbors saw a car on our road fifteen minutes after we'd left. They described it as a muddy four-by-four with no license plates. There were two men in it, but it was too dark to see them clearly enough to get a description that's worth anything. Those guys torched our house. The fire department's arson investigator confirmed it. The guy said a fast-acting accelerant caused the fire and was put on all the outside doors and triggered at once."

"Sounds professional."

"It does. And get this: The arson investigator said the accelerant was likely diethylene glycol gel packs adhered to the doors."

"Diethylene glycol?" Nate said. "That stuff will stick to anything and burn really hot, even on wet wood in the rain. I remember using them in the military."

"Yeah, me too. I guess you can buy them commercially, but you'd need to know what to buy, you know? My assumption is that the arsonists have a military background."

"Uh-oh."

"And because we'd left all the lights on when we left with Pearl, I'm pretty sure they thought we were inside."

"Any idea who did it?" Nate asked.

"Not at first," Geronimo said. "But after I sent Jacinda and Pearl to Detroit to stay with her mother, I did some digging."

"Axel Soledad's thugs," Nate said.

Geronimo nodded. "And if it weren't for that bead up Pearl's nose that made us leave the house unexpectedly, he would have killed us all."

Nate continued to look ahead.

"I should have finished off that dude when I had the chance," Geronimo said. "He was down and I should have gotten close and blown his head off."

"I wish you would have," Nate said.

Both men went silent until they descended into Norris Junction, where steam from the geyser basin wafted up through the heavy pines. Nate thought about how different his life would have turned out if Geronimo and Joe Pickett hadn't left Soledad to bleed out in a lot in downtown Portland. How they'd assumed, incorrectly as it turned out, that the man they'd chased across half the country was gone for good.

He had no doubt that Geronimo was thinking the same thing.

"How DID YOU figure out that Soledad was behind the attack?" Nate asked as Geronimo turned north at Norris Junction for Mammoth Hot Springs.

"A few ways," Geronimo said. "First, when I found out that Soledad survived, I knew he'd come after me just like he came after you. I mean, I've made some enemies in my time, but only one of them would send goons to my house to burn it down with me and my family inside.

"Second was what I learned on Bal-Chatri," he said.

"Ah."

Bal-Chatri was a special portal within a crude retail website that sold falconry gear like hoods, jesses, nets, traps, and other paraphernalia. The name of the portal came from an especially effective trap for capturing wild raptors. Most users scrolled right past the tiny button on the site with the strange foreign-sounding name. But when the button was clicked, it took the user to an encrypted other world on the dark web. Bal-Chatri was used by authorized falconers to communicate, exchange best practices and tips, and to call out unscrupulous falconers who had violated the unwritten rules that had been agreed upon within the small but fervent universe.

The community with access to Bal-Chatri was highly specialized, and the members could only access it with a series of passwords and prompts. The members were limited to outlaw falconers with a libertarian bent, most with military backgrounds like Geronimo, Nate, and, for a time, Axel Soledad. The discussions within the portal were candid. Names were named.

Most falconers hunted a great deal on public lands, which were largely undeveloped and comprised half or more of the surface area of the western states. Federal land managers, depending on the administration and the whims of bureaucrats two thousand miles away in Washington, D.C., could make life miserable for falconers who wanted to hunt their birds on public lands. Many of the falconers on the Bal-Chatri site thought their freedom and liberty were under attack as new rules and regulations were handed down and administered. The group was largely pro–Second Amendment and profoundly anti-fed. One of the longest and best-documented threads was of the many encounters members had had with agents of the federal law enforcement community who suspected them of being traitorous insurgents.

But they also policed themselves. Members within Bel-Chatri insisted on maintaining a strict code of conduct among falconers, which included not encroaching on one another's backyards and not trapping birds strictly for commercial sale to foreign customers.

Axel Soledad had been kicked out of the group long before for breaking most of its rules. He had targeted other falconers to trespass on their private nesting sites and steal their birds outright. Soledad then sold the birds to unscrupulous buyers, who were the representatives and officials for corrupt and criminal regimes, primarily in the Middle East. Soledad then used the money— hundreds of thousands of dollars' worth—to finance anarchists in the U.S. and to foment riots and violence in cities throughout the country.

Since Geronimo was one of the administrators on the site, he monitored it closely and had special access to the actual identity of nearly all of the members. He referred the site as "BC."

He said to Nate, "For being a bunch of cranky individualist paranoid types, many of our fellow outlaw falconers on BC are outright gossips. They want to know what's going on with other members of the group, and they like to engage in too many conspiracy theories for my taste."

"That's why I don't go there much," Nate said. "I like to keep my conspiracy theories to myself."

Geronimo chuckled at that. Then he said, "There was one thread I found after my house burned down that I found especially interesting. One of the guys, named C. W. Reese, said he'd been approached by an ex–BC member about joining his group. The ex-BCer was pretty cagey, but this group had something to do with taking serious action against the government. This ex-BCer knew that Reese is a hothead. Like us, he's ex-military and he had bad experiences with his superiors. So he must have seemed like a good recruit."

"How so? What's C. W. Reese like?" Nate asked.

"He's extreme," Geronimo said. "There's no doubt about that. He hates all politicians equally and he describes himself as an 'armed anarchist.' I can't tell you if he's really serious about that or just blowing smoke."

"Who approached him?"

"His name was never spelled out on the thread, but I read between the lines."

"Your Reese guy wasn't specific as to what Soledad is up to?"

"No. I'm not even sure he knows. All he said was that even though he likes the idea of making some bureaucrats accountable, he got a weird vibe from the guy. And before he made a decision to join Soledad or reject him, some crazy lawyer showed up at his house and demanded to know all about the exchange. Some big Amazon-type woman, is the way my guy described the lawyer. It spooked him, knowing that this lawyer was investigating him."

"Does she have a name?"

"He calls her the Giantess. But he never said her actual name. Two other BCers weighed in and said a woman lawyer of the same description had contacted *them*. Of course, these guys are all worked up and they think it might be a setup by the feds to entrap them."

"Of course they think that," Nate said. "I would, too." Then: "How did the Giantess get access to the site?"

"I wish I knew," Geronimo said. "The possibility that an outsider has access to Bal-Chatri has everyone on it even more paranoid than usual. Especially if it's the feds who penetrated it and are sending the Giantess out on their behalf to entrap guys."

"Does Reese trust you enough to talk?"

"I'm not so sure," Geronimo said. "That's why we're going to

Gardiner. I contacted Reese, and he'll only talk in person. I *think* he trusts me, but he wants to look me in the eye."

Nate squinted. "So you think that if we find out the actual identity of the Giantess, it could help lead us to Soledad?"

"I hope so," Geronimo said. "And this time when we find him, we finish the job. We don't leave him in some alley bleeding out. We finish him with a kill shot."

Nate didn't need to agree in words. He hoped he'd be the one to perform the act.

C. W. REESE lived in a tiny tree-shrouded house on Vista Street in Gardiner, Montana. The back of his home looked out over Yellowstone River Canyon, and the river, even in October, emitted a hushed roar as it flowed north.

Geronimo passed the house and pointed out the yellow Don't Tread on Me Gadsden flag hanging limp from a pole and the corner of a falcon mews jutting out from around the back corner of the building.

"That looks like him," he said as he proceeded along Vista and parked on the next block, out of sight of Reese's home.

"No need to spook him," he said as he climbed out.

"We probably already have," Nate said. "Not much gets by the residents here. Especially when we show up in the tank we're driving in."

Gardiner was a small ramshackle unincorporated community of less than nine hundred residents. It was located hard against the North Entrance to Yellowstone. The Roosevelt Arch, which was constructed in 1903, bore a plaque that read FOR THE BENEFIT

AND ENJOYMENT OF THE PEOPLE. Most of the full-time residents worked for concessionaires and contractors within the park, or were hunting, fishing, or whitewater-rafting businesses. Or, in the case of C. W. Reese, a small-time bird abatement specialist who bought and sold guns and gold on the side.

Nate and Geronimo noted the No Solicitors and No Trespassing signs near the gate of the white picket fence and they walked up the cracked sidewalk to the front door and knocked on it. When several dogs barked inside but no one came to the door, they walked around the house into the backyard, where the mews was located.

As Nate came around the corner, he turned his head and looked straight into the gaping black O of a large handgun muzzle. An arms-length behind it was a gaunt, bearded man in a torn green army parka standing close to the exterior wall of the home. At the gunman's feet was an open paper sack filled with frozen dead pigeons. He'd obviously been out feeding his falcons in the mews in the backyard when they'd arrived.

"C. W. Reese?" Nate asked softly. "I'd suggest you put that down."

"Who are you and how do you know my name?"

As Reese asked it, Geronimo came around the corner and quickly stopped.

"Nate Romanowski," Nate said. "And this is Geronimo Jones."

Reese's mouth dropped open and his eyes got wide.

"Seriously?" he asked.

"We're not armed at the moment," Nate said. "We left our weapons in the car. So, if you don't holster that handgun, I'll take it off you and pound your head with it."

"Do what he says," Geronimo said to Reese. "If you've heard of Nate Romanowski, you know what he's capable of."

Reese slowly opened his army jacket with his left hand and slid the .50 Desert Eagle into a long black holster. "I like powerful handguns, too," he said to Nate. To Geronimo, Reese said, "Welcome to my humble home."

"Can we sit down inside?" Geronimo asked him.

"Absolutely," Reese said. His demeanor had completely changed. "Let me kennel my dogs and then you can come on in. I can make another pot of coffee."

"That would be nice," Geronimo said.

Reese paused at the back door before going in. "I never thought Geronimo Jones and Nate Romanowski would show up here."

After Reese went inside, Geronimo leaned into Nate and said, "You're quite the celebrity, it seems."

"You too."

"Did you really leave your weapon inside the truck?"

"Of course not," Nate said.

REESE'S KITCHEN WAS unkempt, with dishes piled high in the sink and unopened mail and flyers covering the countertops. While a pot of coffee brewed, Reese opened his refrigerator door and showed them a display of two dozen handguns and compact submachine pistols sitting next to each other on the racks. The only non-gun item inside was a six-pack of Moose Drool beer. He explained that his basement had recently flooded, so he had to relocate his inventory to the top floor.

"I don't have a proper gun safe," Reese said. "But if you're interested in any of these pieces, I'll make you a hell of a deal."

"We're not here to buy guns," Nate said.

"What's in the freezer?" Geronimo asked.

Reese opened the door and stepped aside to reveal hundreds of small paper bags crammed into it that fit into the space like a puzzle. Both Nate and Geronimo knew instantly that the bags were filled with frozen roadkill, pigeons, and rodents to feed his falcons.

"Pickings are slim here in the winter," Reese said. "Sometimes we can grab up a few ducks on the river, but I have to stockpile falcon food."

"Understood," Geronimo said.

The place reminded Nate of a half dozen homes of falconers that he'd either lived in or visited over the years. Serious falconers didn't care about entertaining guests or the overall decor. Houses were simply places to store gear, food, and weapons between trips out into the field with their birds.

"So tell me about Axel Soledad and the Giantess," Geronimo said.

AN HOUR LATER, after recounting the approach by Axel Soledad and the follow-up from the woman Reese referred to as the Giantess, he said, "I'd like to come with you guys if you're going after him. That guy not only stiffed me on twenty-five thousand dollars' worth of rifles and shotguns, he's a dangerous liar who is misrepresenting the cause. He needs to be dealt with."

Nate and Geronimo exchanged a glance. "What guns?" Geronimo asked.

"Oh—I didn't tell you how I met Soledad in the first place."

"No, you didn't," Geronimo said with a scowl. "You seemed to have left that part out."

Reese ignored the dig. "He showed up here last October driving a 2012 Honda Civic with Colorado plates. He parked right out front on the street and came to the front door on crutches. He said he'd heard about me through some friends and he wanted to do business. Did you know Soledad has to use crutches to get around?"

"Yes," Geronimo said. "He got his legs blown out in Portland a few years back. Now, go on."

"Yeah, well," Reese said. "He didn't identify himself as Axel Soledad. He gave me a fake name, Dallas Cates, or something like that. It was only later that I put two and two together."

Nate didn't react, even though Cates, an ex-con with a bottomless grudge against Nate and Joe, and who had allied himself with Soledad, had been directly responsible for Liv's murder. And Nate had dealt with him the best way he knew how.

"Anyway, he seemed like a good guy," Reese said. "Friendly, capable. One of us, you know? He asked me about my military service, and he did it in a way that suggested he was a vet. I told him about feeling completely betrayed by the U.S. government, and especially by the higher-ups. About how they sent us into harm's way in Afghanistan and then betrayed us. He said he had a similar story—"

"You don't need to go into all of that," Geronimo said. "I've read the threads. Tell us what Soledad did when he was here in this house."

"He was casing me out, is what he did," Reese said. "The whole time, he was probing me to see where I stood. He got me to like and trust him, and I'm not an easy mark. I showed him my inventory and then I helped load up that Civic with seven semiauto long guns and six combat shotguns. It was my biggest sales to a single individual ever. Then he gave me a check inside an envelope and said he'd be in touch."

Reese paused and spat out a series of curses before continuing: "Only after he left did I open the envelope and look at the check to see it belonged to someone named Katy Cotton of Walden, Colorado. And when I tried to cash it I found out the account had all of two hundred and twenty-five dollars in it. That son of a bitch stole somebody's checkbook and screwed me."

"Katy Cotton?" Geronimo asked Nate.

"Joe Pickett's birth mother," Nate said. "It's a long story, but he hadn't seen her for years until her body was found less than a mile from his house a year ago. She'd been murdered by a carjacker who disappeared. Now we know it was Axel and he drove straight up here to arm up."

"He's a son of a bitch," Reese said. "He got me to trust him and then he screwed me."

"When did he contact you again?" Geronimo asked.

"End of summer," Reese said. "He sent me an encrypted message on Bal-Chatri. He said he liked my posts and he said he was assembling some guys to get revenge on people who betrayed us overseas. At that point, I didn't realize that Soledad and the guy who screwed me out of my inventory were one and the same."

Geronimo moaned. "Axel must have figured out how to get back on the site after we locked him out. I don't know how he did it."

"He's diabolical, is what he is," Reese said, his eyes bulging. "And he strung me along and said all the right things about reclaiming our country from those bastards. I was ready to sign up with him and join him, if you want to know the truth."

"Why didn't you?" Nate asked.

"Because he tripped up," Reese said with a satisfied leer. "He mentioned that he could send a couple of his guys to Gardiner to pick me up. But I had never revealed on the site where I lived. Not even the state. My profile on the site is anonymous, like most of the members. I've never mentioned it in my profile or on the threads, have I, Geronimo?"

Geronimo agreed. "No. It wasn't until I spoke to you directly that you told me where you lived."

"But Axel knew, that bastard," Reese said. "Because he'd been to my house and had stolen twenty-five thousand dollars of my inventory. Now he wanted me to join up with him. He must have thought I was really stupid not to figure out that this Dallas Cates, whoever he is, and Axel Soledad were the same guy. That's when I bolted and refused to respond to any of his messages. He must have known he fucked up."

"That's where the Giantess comes in," Geronimo prompted.

"Yes. She contacted me through BC as well."

"Damn it," Geronimo spat. "How many impostors do we have on my site?"

"She wanted to meet me and hear all about Axel," Reese said. "She wanted to come here, but I didn't want anyone else knowing where I lived. Finally, we agreed to meet in Billings at a little restaurant there. I hoped she'd help me find Axel, and she seemed to know a lot about him."

"What is she like?" Geronimo asked.

Reese's eyes widened again and he stood up and reached high above his head. "She's really tall," he said, indicating with his hand her height of about seven feet. "Really tall, and blond. But proportional, you know? She made me feel like some kind of midget. To be honest, I was kind of scared of her."

"What kinds of questions did she ask you?" Geronimo said.

"It was mainly about what Axel was up to. I had to tell her I didn't know any specifics, because I don't. I only know the general outline, you know? She kept pressing, but I held firm. She said she was following up with people across the country who had been contacted by Soledad, trying to put some kind of lawsuit or case together. She was vague about that."

"Who does she represent?" Nate asked.

Reese shrugged. "Not me. I asked her to go after him to get my inventory back at least, but she said she didn't want to get involved with a large weapons transaction."

As he said it, Reese looked away and Nate noticed.

"You sold him the guns without a background check, didn't you? The sale is technically illegal."

"This is Gardiner," Reese said sheepishly. "We kind of do our own thing here."

Nate narrowed his eyes. "How many of the guns you sold were left with you on consignment?"

Reese's face turned red. "Most of them," he said in a near-whisper. "The guys who consigned them to me are really putting the pressure on. They want their guns back or they want the money that was paid for them. Obviously, I don't have either, so I'm really in a jam."

Geronimo said with scorn, "You sound like a hell of a busi-nessman."

"I'm not a businessman," Reese said. "I'm a falconer. You know how it is. We do what we can so we can take our birds out."

"Back to something you said," Nate pressed. "You said you wanted to go after Soledad because he is misrepresenting the cause. What do you mean by that?"

Reese became solemn. "There are a lot of us disaffected mili-tary veterans out here. We feel like we got played and that the people in charge used us to advance their own careers or because they had their own agendas. They sold us a line of bullshit about serving our country and then threw us under the bus. None of them have been accountable for it. I thought Axel understood. But I think he's using some of us, just like we got used before.

"I don't know what his game is, or what his target is. I just know he needs to be stopped. So can I come with you boys?"

Geronimo and Nate again exchanged a look. Then Nate said, "No."

"Come on," Reese pleaded. "I can hold my own."

"You're a loose cannon," Nate said. "You don't deserve to be a master falconer and you hurt the reputation of falconers in gen-eral. You defrauded your business partners, you're impulsive, and you talk too much."

"I have to agree," Geronimo said, standing up. "Thank you for the coffee."

"Oh, come on," Reese said. "I can follow orders. You'll see."

"We can't take that chance," Nate said, turning his back on the man. Then: "Get some help. You need it."

As Nate and Geronimo were leaving the house through the

front door, Reese followed a few steps behind. He seemed desperate.

He said, "Did I mention I have the business card the Giantess gave me?"

Nate paused on the pathway and turned around. "You do?"

"I'll share it with you if you'll take me along," Reese said. "Here, let me go get it."

While he disappeared into his back bedroom or office, Nate said. "I don't trust him."

"We might need some bodies to take on Axel," Geronimo said. "But this guy seems like trouble."

"He just wants his money or his guns back," Nate said. "I don't blame him, but that's not a good reason to bring him in. And I don't think he's mentally stable."

"You mean like you?" Geronimo said with a grin.

Reese returned and handed Nate a semi-battered gold card inscribed with black lettering. The card read:

CHERYL TUCK-SMITH

Attorney-at-Law

314 N. Reed Ave.

Cheyenne, WY 82001

To Reese, Nate said, "We'll call you if we need you."

They left him disappointed, but hopeful.

B-Lazy-U Ranch Interlude

The Waitress

THE NEW WAITRESS stood shoulder to shoulder with other B-Lazy-U Ranch employees on the loading dock behind the towering and magnificent central lodge. They'd been called to assemble there because the refrigerated semitrailer filled with food for Centurions Week had arrived. It was a cool but sunny morning, and the air smelled sharply of pine and woodsmoke. Breath condensation puffed from the mouths and nostrils of the assembled as they waited. The new waitress stood in the second row and didn't engage in small talk with the others.

She'd learned that the lodge was built in the 1920s by a silver baron who had struck it rich on the eastern slope of Battle Mountain. The massive logs used for the construction of the central lodge had been harvested from the Encampment River Canyon and floated downstream by tie hacks. From where the logs had piled up near the confluence of the Encampment and Upper North Platte Rivers, teamsters transported them through a mountain pass to where the ranch was now located.

The B-Lazy-U Ranch, which had once been frequented by railroad tycoons, New York financial titans, Chicago gangsters, and politicians, had been the most modern and extravagant dude ranch in the Rocky Mountains at the time. Because of the long airstrip constructed through the sagebrush two miles away from the ranch, the B-Lazy-U was a frequent destination for pilots and guests who owned private planes. There were black-and-white photos of biplanes landing in the early years, as well as "borrowed" military fighters in the 1940s and '50s.

As the years went by, the luster faded somewhat as the elites moved on to other more accessible resorts, and guests were now primarily extended families from the Eastern Seaboard and Deep South who came every year and bequeathed their annual week-long stays to their next generation of faux-cowboys and -cowgirls.

Now, over a century since the B-Lazy-U had been founded, the place had been restored to its former glory. Although the lodge itself had been fully renovated, while maintaining its character—big-game animals from the area adorned its interior walls, all the hanging chandeliers were made of intertwined antlers or wagon wheels, the rooms and public spaces were still dark and clubby—everything else had been thoroughly modernized. The many guest cabins throughout the property were individual pods of luxury, with high-speed broadband internet, twenty-four-hour room service, and ranch staff on call to accommodate every request a guest could make.

Not everything had been upgraded, though. The only television available for guests was a small one located on the wall above the backbar in the saloon, where the Weather Channel, without volume, played nonstop.

The waitress had recently learned all about the history of the ranch—as well as the expectations the management demanded of its staff—at a mandatory two-day new-hire orientation conducted by the general manager.

There had been fewer than thirty "tenderfoots" in the room, which was the name they gave to new employees. She was a tenderfoot, and as the GM had informed them all, she was damned lucky to have been hired.

Any warm body could find a job in the hospitality industry, he'd said. There were more jobs available than people who would take them. But very few applicants could make the cut to become a team member of the B-Lazy-U Ranch.

"So consider yourself one of the chosen ones," he'd said as he passed out nondisclosure agreements that required every tenderfoot's signature.

She did consider herself one of the chosen ones, and she readily signed the NDA. The new waitress had been confident she'd be hired for Centurions Week. She not only had experience in the high-end luxury resort business, but her entire résumé just *sang*. There was never a doubt she'd get the job.

Eighty-five percent of the staff were longtime employees. Many of them came from three specific universities in the Deep South, where the ranch owners had long before established relationships, and others were the offspring of longtime guests. It was a very inbred atmosphere, and it was hard for new people to break into. Not that befriending the rest of the staff was her goal.

The staff was huge, she'd learned. They outnumbered the guests, six to one. It was more like working on a super-exclusive private yacht than a ranch. In addition to food and beverage, housekeeping, maintenance, groundskeeping, and transportation staff, there were horse wranglers, fishing guides, yoga instructors, hiking and climbing guides, shooting instructors, and personal concierges assigned to every cabin.

LIKE EVERY RESORT with longtime staff, there was a well-established hierarchy and a social structure that was byzantine and often cruel. HR would be of little help if new employees complained, because they had so much on their plate already. The new waitress knew to listen, observe, say little, keep her head down, and work hard.

She'd learned from experience how important it was to establish good rapport with the host, the head of food and beverage, and the chief bartender. Others, despite how much seniority or self-importance they had, simply didn't matter that much.

But as always, there was an exception to that rule. In this case, it was a waitress named Peaches Tyrell. Peaches, originally from somewhere in rural Georgia, was stout, but surprisingly nimble and quick. Now in her late sixties, she was the longest-serving employee on the ranch, and she knew everything and everybody. Guests hugged her first when they arrived, and she doted on them.

Peaches could also get an employee fired on the spot with a quick word to the F&B director.

Stay close to Peaches, the new waitress had told herself. *Be kind to her. Respect her.*

THE HOURS WERE brutal for the staff at the B-Lazy-U. Everyone was expected to work sixteen-hour shifts, followed by downtime in the middle of nowhere. It wasn't like the ranch staff could go clubbing or shopping on their days off, because there were no actual clubs except for cowboy bars in the tiny towns of Riverside and Encampment.

Although some team members made forays across the border to Steamboat Springs or beyond that to Fort Collins or even Denver on their off days, the new waitress had yet to join them.

She had places to go, but she didn't speak of them to anyone. Especially not to Peaches.

But the pay was good, employee housing and food was decent, and there were real advantages to interacting with well-heeled guests from around the country and the world. Relationships, both business and personal, were fostered in the close-in environment. Ranch employees on the make shared success stores late at night in the employee bar.

The new waitress had no stories to tell yet.

But she would.

So, she stood on the loading dock in a group of servers, bussers, and several sous-chefs. The sous-chefs were allowed out of the kitchen to do manual labor because the actual chefs were crazy and paranoid, and they never left except to go on multiday benders.

Everyone was dressed in street clothes, or what could be referred to as street clothes at a mountain ranch resort. There were lots of fleece vests and ball caps, as they weren't required to don their uniforms of snap-button, red-checked western-style shirts, tight jeans, cowboy hats, and aprons until the guests began to arrive.

The semitruck and refrigerated trailer maneuvered on a narrow circular path that cut through a grass meadow. Team members from the transportation department walked alongside the cab and shouted to the driver to stay on the pavement and not veer off into the grass. It would *not* do to have tire tracks in the turf when the guests arrived.

It took a while. The new waitress was patient, unlike others on the dock.

Tension was high.

"I heard the first jets arrived in Warm Springs this morning," someone said. "We can expect the first Centurions to show up at dinnertime."

"Then we better get this goddamn truck unloaded," another team member groused.

"Language," Peaches cautioned sweetly from the back. "Language."

AT LAST, THE trailer of the vehicle inched up to the dock and blocked the new waitress's view of Battle Mountain. The driver of the truck swung out and directed the transportation guys how to open the back doors so they wouldn't damage the dock when they swung open.

"It'd be nice if they had a forklift for all of this stuff," a busser standing next to the new waitress complained. "But no, we have to carry every box in one by one."

"Ridiculous," someone else said. "This is fucked up."

"It's the way we do things around here," Peaches said in a honey-coated southern accent. Her comment quieted the complainers because they realized who she was, and that there was no advantage to pissing her off.

The trailer was full. Each box was cold. There were boxes of steaks, seafood, chicken, ice cream, and every other kind of frozen food imaginable. The boxes were stacked from the floor of the trailer to the ceiling.

The new waitress joined the line and slowly advanced forward. When she was in the cold trailer, she lifted a box of steaks and turned and carried it into the lodge to where the walk-in freezers were. The chefs were there to direct her where to place it.

She made dozens of trips. There was no break, and she didn't need one. The waitress had no doubt she was more fit than anyone else on the loading dock.

THE UNLOADING TOOK two hours. She made a point of being one of the last employees to enter the trailer for the few remaining containers. It was cold inside, and cavernous, by the time she did it.

One of the other servers trudged behind her, breathing heavily. It was Peaches. Sweat beaded on the woman's forehead and wetted the armpits of her smock.

The new waitress turned to her and said, "Don't worry about this. I've got it."

"Are you sure?" Peaches asked. There was no doubt she was relieved.

"There's only three boxes left," the new waitress said. "I can handle it."

"Bless you," Peaches said. She turned and trudged toward the loading dock.

THE THREE REMAINING boxes were unmarked except for an *X* on the side of them in black marker. They were in the left corner of the trailer. Each was no bigger than the food boxes she'd already carried.

As she approached them, the driver swung up into the trailer behind her. She turned and nodded to him. He curtly nodded back. The driver was fit and young with dark eyes and a prominent handlebar mustache. A jagged scar marked his right cheek.

"They're heavy," he said.

"I know," she said. "Was there any problem getting through security at the gate?"

"I'm here, aren't I?" the driver said.

"You are."

"I'll help you."

"Good. That way we can get them out of here."

"Do you have a place for them?"

She said she did, but it wasn't in the lodge. "I found an old vegetable cellar back in the woods. No one uses it for anything."

"Perfect," he said. He grunted as he lifted the first box.

"Follow me," she said.

CHAPTER EIGHT

J OE WAS SOUTHBOUND three miles north of Warm Springs on
Wyoming State Highway 130, when he flinched involuntarily as
a very large shadow passed over his entire pickup. It was an oddly
similar sensation to an eagle flying overhead in front of the sun
when he was in the field. But when he glanced up through the top
of the windshield, he saw the gleaming underside of the fuselage
and wings of a white corporate jet streaking toward town with its
wheels down at low elevation.

A second later, the roar of twin jet engines made his steering
wheel vibrate. The jet descended farther and touched down on a
long runway on the south end of Warm Springs, and then it vanished and gradually taxied over a rise in the terrain on the other
side.

He'd been to Warm Springs years before when the sagebrush
flats on either side of the highway were covered with snow. That
instance was also at the behest of a governor—although the previous one. The case involved the disappearance of a female British
CEO of a public relations firm who had last been seen on one of

the most exclusive guest ranches in the nation. The incident of the missing woman threatened to become an international incident if she wasn't found.

That winter Sheridan had been employed as the head wrangler on the Silver Creek Ranch, where the CEO had vanished. Joe and Sheridan had been joined by Nate Romanowski in the investigation.

As often happened with Joe, the fairly straightforward investigation had gone pear-shaped. It had all ended well, though.

MOUNTAINS BORDERED THE valley on three sides: the Snowy Range to the east, the Sierra Madres to the west, and Battle Mountain to the south. The treeless summits of the peaks were dusted with snow, but nothing like it had been that January when Joe was there.

The layout of the river valley town was familiar to him, with its smoking lumber mill, distant twin water towers, and the wide North Platte River flowing through it. As he entered the town limits, he once again caught the slight whiff of sulfur from the public hot springs that gave the place its name.

WHEN HE ENTERED the diner that hugged the left bank of the river, Wyoming game warden Susan Kany bounded up from her seat to greet him. She beamed and shook his hand with both of hers and led him to her booth.

A table of five middle-aged men in the center of the diner eyed Joe with bemused interest and watched him slide in across from

Kany. Joe recognized them, even if he didn't actually know them. They were the city fathers, and they met every day at the same table in the same restaurant to report on what had happened the day before and to make decisions on behalf of the town. A similar breakfast group met at the Burg-O-Pardner every morning in Saddlestring, and Joe felt like he had never left.

Joe knew *them*, but he wondered what the group thought of him and Susan Kany together. Communities in Wyoming kept close track of their local law enforcement officers.

Two game wardens, each in red uniform shirts with pronghorn antelope shoulder patches, bronze name tags over pinned badges, Wrangler jeans and cowboy boots, and holstered handguns on their belts. Joe in his early fifties, lean and of medium height and build, with threads of silver permeating his short sideburns. Kany was a compact young woman in her late twenties, athletic and attractive, with large brown eyes and a quick smile.

Joe ordered coffee. Kany ordered a Diet Coke.

When the waitress delivered their drinks and took lunch orders, she said, "The word will get out to all the poachers in the valley that the game wardens are here having lunch."

It was meant as a joke, and a couple of the men at the center table chuckled.

"Believe it or not, I've heard that one before," Joe said to her.

"This is Joe Pickett, Yvette," Kany said to the waitress. "He's one of our more . . . *well-known* game wardens."

"Thanks for not saying infamous," Joe said.

"Welcome back," the waitress said. "The last time you were here, you stayed at the Hotel Wolf. Room number nine, right?"

Joe eyed her with suspicion.

"I worked there in housekeeping at the time," Yvette said with a wink. "I made your bed and left you clean towels. You were a pretty civilized guest. I appreciated that you didn't leave me a messy room, and you left me a tip. Not many guests do both."

"Ah," Joe said. "Thank you."

After Yvette left with the orders of a cheeseburger for Joe and a Cobb salad for Kany, Kany said, "Small towns, eh?"

"Small towns," Joe echoed.

Kany leaned forward across the table and kept her voice low so she wouldn't be overheard by the town fathers. "Now you can tell me why you're here," she said more than asked. "Please keep in mind that our friends over there are mighty curious as well, so keep your voice down."

"I understand."

WHILE JOE EXPLAINED the reason he had come, he purposefully withheld several pieces of information. He told her he'd been asked to help locate outfitter Spike Rankin and his employee, but Joe didn't say who had asked him and he didn't reveal the relationship between Governor Rulon and his son-in-law.

"I'm hoping you know where Rankin's elk camp is located and we can find him," Joe said to Kany.

Her expression showed skepticism while Joe spoke.

"I don't get it," she said. "Why didn't they just ask me to go find him? Why did they send you all the way down here from Twelve Sleep County?"

121

"That's how bureaucracy works sometimes," he said with a shrug. "Don't take it personally. I quit trying to figure out the logic in state government a long time ago."

Kany sat back and eyed Joe with suspicion. He didn't blame her. She was sharp, he thought, and even if she didn't outwardly question his story, he knew it didn't completely add up. Joe's badge indicated that he was number twelve in the game warden hierarchy within the state—the twelfth in seniority out of fifty. Kany's badge revealed that she was number forty-eight. So she deferred.

Joe wasn't comfortable thinking of himself as one of the good old boys within the agency, but he understood it if Kany felt that way. From what he'd revealed, there was no good reason why she hadn't been asked to locate the outfitter in her own district.

"I've met Spike Rankin a few times," she said. "He's a crusty old guy, but he seems straight as an arrow, and he didn't give me any crap at all when I asked him for his camp permit or when I checked out his hunters. There was a time last elk-hunting season when one of his clients wanted to mess with me a little by pretending he couldn't find his license and inviting me to search his tent with him, and Rankin shot that guy down real fast and told him to comply. I appreciated that."

"That's good to hear," Joe said. "I've only heard good things about him as well. He's an ethical hunting guide."

"He showed me respect," Kany said. "He didn't treat me like the new-girl game warden. That doesn't always happen around here."

"I was the new game warden once," Joe said. "I know the feeling."

"But I sure got the vibe that he'd call me out in a heartbeat if he thought I was doing something wrong or being heavy-handed," Kany said. "So I played things by the book. I always do."

"That's always a good idea," Joe said. "Even when it isn't the easiest way to go."

She smiled shyly at that, Joe noticed. No doubt, she knew much more about him than he knew about her. Although he was proud of his Dudley Do-Right reputation for the most part, he still wasn't used to being a man whom younger wardens looked up to and shared stories about. He didn't think he'd ever get used to it. In Joe's mind, nearly twenty years later, he was still a rookie and in over his head.

"Maybe we should go talk to Sheriff Haswell," Kany said. "That guy has been here for a hundred years and he knows everyone. He might have an idea where Rankin is."

Joe sucked in his breath and held it a moment. The governor expressly said he didn't want to involve Haswell, but Joe couldn't tell her that. Yet.

"How about we check out Rankin's elk camp first?" Joe said. "Because if he's been there all along, there's no reason to involve the sheriff at all, and I can get out of your hair."

"You're not in my hair," Kany said as her Cobb salad arrived. "It's a pleasure to host you here in my district."

As Joe picked up his cheeseburger, Kany said, "I went to school with your daughter, you know."

"My daughter? At UW?"

"Sheridan," Kany said. "I was in a couple of classes with her. I talked to her once at a party. She was sweet and smart."

Joe contemplated that for a moment. It meant Susan Kany was

around twenty-six, like Sheridan. And it made him feel suddenly very, very old.

"I didn't tell her I was coming down here to work with you," Joe said finally. "I'll ask her if she remembers meeting you."

"We were on different tracks," Kany said. "We hung with different crowds. I was interested in criminal justice and aviation. She was more into wildlife biology, I think."

"That's right," Joe said.

"She was into falconry," Kany said. "I thought that was pretty cool."

Joe swallowed and said, "She's running a bird abatement company now up in Saddlestring. She has lots of falcons to fly and hunt."

"Good for her," Kany said. "Please tell her I said hello. You must be proud."

"I am."

"Should we take my truck?" she asked.

For a second, Joe didn't follow what she was saying.

"We can leave your truck at the Wolf and you can get in with me and ride shotgun," Kany said. "Believe me, if the two of us both drive out of town in the same direction the rumors will start that we're involved in some kind of big investigation. Then the gossip will start."

Joe agreed.

"Small towns," she repeated. Then: "I assume we want to keep this all on the down-low, right?"

"Yup." Without Joe saying it explicitly, Kany intuited Joe's intent to keep the search for Rankin looking as innocuous as possible. She *was* sharp.

"Let me get the check," Joe said when they'd eaten. But she quickly snatched it from Yvette.

"The State of Wyoming pays either way," she said. "I'll handle this one."

"Thank you, taxpayers," Joe said as he stood up and clamped on his hat.

"You're welcome," said one of the town fathers from the adjacent table.

AFTER LEAVING HIS pickup parked in the lot behind the Hotel Wolf and throwing his gear bag into the bed of Kany's truck, Joe paused at her passenger door while she made room for him inside. Game and Fish pickups served as mobile business offices, and Kany's vehicle was no different. The cab was filled with clothing, optics, boots for every occasion, ticket and regulation books, weapons, shed antlers, and other detritus picked up along the way in the field. She cleared the passenger seat and pulled a sleepy Jack Russell terrier toward her so Joe could climb inside.

"This is Ginger," Kany said. "Don't let her climb all over you."

"Hi, Ginger."

Joe found it charming that, unlike every other (male) game warden with a dog aboard, Kany had a Jack Russell instead of a Labrador. He scratched the dog on the head and closed the door. Ginger leaned into him and stared up into his eyes.

"She seems to be quite taken with you," Kany said. "But she's a pretty cheap date, to be honest."

"I like dogs," Joe said. "We have too many of them at home."

"Being single, one is all I can handle." Then, looking south toward the range that looked like a blue-black battleship on the sea: "Rankin's main elk camp is at the base of Battle Mountain. I figure we should start there."

Joe said that made sense to him.

Kany took WYO 130 south through Warm Springs. Joe looked around. As the highway climbed up a hill toward the outskirts of the community, he said, "There are a few more houses than I remember." He particularly noted a new subdivision under construction in the flats to the west.

"They can't build them fast enough," Kany said. "We've had an influx in population since the pandemic, like lots of places in the Mountain West. Last I heard, there were fewer than ten houses for sale in the whole valley. It's a real problem for the businesses here—they can't hire new people because there's no place for them to live."

"Just like Saddlestring," Joe said.

"If I didn't have the state game warden station, I couldn't afford it myself," she said.

"Where are the newcomers from?"

"Cities."

As THEY DROVE by the airport on the top of the hill, Joe noted the private jet he'd seen earlier when he'd approached Warm Springs. The jet was parked to the side of the runway. The aircraft looked even bigger on the tarmac now that it was still.

Next to the large corporate jet were two others just as large.

"Wow," Joe said. "What's going on around here?"

"Have you ever heard of the Centurions?" she asked.

"No."

"I hadn't either until I moved here. It's a big-time secret gathering of muckety-mucks from all over the country. They fly in every October and meet at a real fancy dude ranch about forty-five minutes away called the B-Lazy-U. Few people know this, but the Warm Springs airport is the third-largest airport in Wyoming when it comes to the length of the runways. It can accommodate aircraft all the way up to a 737. And we don't have a single commercial flight. Do you see all those rental cars?"

They were hard to miss, Joe thought. Three rows of black SUVs were lined up between the highway and the small private airport terminal. He guessed there were eighty to ninety vehicles.

Kany pulled off the road onto the shoulder and gestured toward the parked jets.

"That first one is a Bombardier Global Express," she said. "It holds twelve to sixteen passengers, depending on the interior configuration. The one in the middle is a Gulfstream G500. It's a beauty that holds up to thirteen, I believe. The one that just landed, the biggest one, is an Embraer Lineage 1000. Nineteen passengers. But none of these jets are ever full. Often, it's just one or two passengers."

Joe looked over at her with astonishment.

"I told you I studied avionics," she said. "I used to want to fly one of these private jets, so I learned all about them. I never thought I'd see them all in one place, much less a place like Warm Springs."

"How did I not know about this?" Joe asked rhetorically.

"Hardly anyone does," she said. "Just the pilots and the locals."

"Are there more jets on the way, then?" Joe asked.

She took her hand off the wheel and swept it across the horizon from right to left, indicating the entire airport. "By the end of the week, the tarmac will be covered with them," she said. "They'll park small jets under the wings of the big jets. Believe me, you've never seen anything like it before."

"Crazy," Joe said.

"Like I said, it's a big deal that no one knows about," Kany said. "The folks here are more than aware of the event, but they're encouraged to keep their mouths shut while the Centurions are here. It's all kind of mysterious, and it took me a while to finally learn what goes on. As you can imagine, the event is quite the cash cow for the local economy, and it bridges the gap between summer tourism season and full-blown hunting season in the valley."

Joe recalled that when he was there before he'd been surprised by how many well-known celebrities, politicians, and business tycoons frequented the location. On the exclusive guest ranch Sheridan had worked on, she'd had to sign nondisclosure agreements to keep the identity of many of the guests private. She'd been annoyed when her father wasn't familiar with several of the names she leaked to him, even though Marybeth was aware of them. They included country music stars, famous actors, billionaire rappers, and real estate moguls. Sheridan had also explained to her father that the locals were used to celebrities in their midst and they were largely not impressed with them. Warm Springs residents just went on about their business, she said. It was one of the reasons famous people liked to visit.

"So what goes on at this big event?" Joe asked Kany, intrigued.

"Apparently, they meet annually at the B-Lazy-U Ranch and do all the traditional cowboy stuff: horseback riding, fly-fishing, skeet shooting, hiking, all that. Then they have a couple of formal meetings and initiate new members, then they all fly home. In a week, there won't be a single aircraft at this airport.

"From what I understand, the Centurions have been around for sixty or seventy years. I've never been to the ranch they gather at, but I've talked to a couple of people who have been."

Joe whistled. He watched as one of the black SUVs left the front line of vehicles and turned toward the airport exit. He could see that behind the driver there were two passengers in the back seat, who had probably arrived on the Embraer Lineage that had passed over his pickup on the way into town.

"So who are these big muckety-mucks?" Joe asked.

CHAPTER NINE

MARK EISELE WASN'T sure what time he awoke, but he thought it was midmorning. There were thin bands of light at the edges of the blacked-out window. His night had once again been fitful and hallucinatory, filled with dreams that included Megan and his in-laws, but there'd been something else that kept startling him into consciousness: the sound of gunshots.

On the street or grounds just outside the structure he was kept in, there had been rapid-fire, high-pitched *cracks*, deep *booms*, and snapping small-arms fire, along with the revving of engines and occasional shouts. It sounded like the people outside were involved in a skirmish or playing war games not far from his cabin. He wished he could get up from the bed, tear the taped cardboard from the glass of the windows, and look outside.

Then there were the pitiful sounds coming from Spike Rankin in the next cot. Rankin had yet to regain consciousness at any point, as far as Eisele knew, but he seemed to be weakening as the hours and days went on. Rankin didn't weep or moan from pain, but he issued soft reactive grunts as if someone were applying sudden pressure to his chest. Eisele had called out to him several times, but Rankin hadn't answered in any way.

No one had brought them anything to eat, for how long? Two days? Three days? Eisele tried to recall how long a human could live without nutrition of any kind, and he couldn't remember the answer. He knew it was much longer than three days. Eisele wished he could simply google "How long can a human survive without food?" It struck him how vulnerable he felt that he simply couldn't look at his phone and ask it that question. He hadn't been without a working smartphone since middle school.

WHILE HE WAS hearing gunshots early that morning, Eisele had discovered that he could access water to drink. Someone— Double-A?—had placed a water bladder of some kind on the pillow next to his head. He found that he could turn his head and suck in room-temperature water through a flexible tube. It tasted brackish, but he could feel himself healing from the inside out as the fluid replenished his body. He'd consumed half the bladder, but not enough yet to have to urinate. That would come, and he would welcome it as another step in his recovery. He didn't want to wet his scrubs that had finally dried out. The pungent odor from his clothing hung in the air within the still, dark room.

Someone—Double-A?—came into the room with their headlamp every four to six hours, and he'd feel a sharp prick on his right forearm. Then he'd drift away. They were drugging him. He assumed it was to keep him quiet and out of it.

He'd only awaken when he'd hear either muted conversations through the door in the next room, Rankin's animal-like grunts, or gunshots.

How many of them were there? And what were their plans for him? For Rankin?

THE DOOR OPENED and the light from the next room hit him in the eyes, making him wince. He hadn't heard anyone approaching the door, but he recognized Double-A by her silhouette.

She said, "The younger one is awake right now" to someone behind her in the other room. Then, to Eisele, "Good morning. It's time for your medication."

"Please—I don't want any. I think I might be hungry, though."

"Are you, now?" she asked without kindness.

"I think Mr. Rankin is dying," Eisele said. "You've got to help him."

Double-A ignored him. She seemed preoccupied by something going on behind her in the lit room. Then she stepped to the side and a lean figure glided into the room as if he were walking on air. It was otherworldly, and Eisele thought he might be seeing things that weren't there. The man was outside the room one moment, and then he was standing right next to his cot as if he had floated there. Eisele could feel his presence.

"Can we have a little light?" the man asked Double-A over his shoulder. She responded by twisting the lens of a headlamp until it shone into the room. The beam danced up the length of Eisele in the cot, but there was enough ambient glow that he could see more of the man standing next to him.

Eisele realized the man hadn't been floating after all, but had deftly propelled himself into the room using crutches. Like Double-A, he was dressed in rumpled camo.

"Thank you, Double-A," the man said to her in a kind voice.

The figure at his cot was in his early thirties; his thin, gaunt, craggy face with sharp facial features was shadowed by the beam of the headlamp. He had high cheekbones, sunken cheeks, and a buzz cut with a growth of beard approximately the same length. The man's eyes were piercing, and he looked at Eisele with the cool dispassion of a bird of prey.

"My boss is dying," Eisele said, assuming the man was in charge of the frontier village. "We need to get him to a hospital."

"That's out of the question," the man said quickly.

"I haven't eaten anything since I've been here."

"You seem to be doing okay." Without turning toward her, he said, "Double-A, see if you can get him some food. There should be some leftovers in the mess hall."

"Sure," Double-A said. "Then it's time for his medication."

Eisele asked, "Do you think you could take the cardboard down from the windows? It's like a cave in here."

"I'll think about it, but no promises," the man said.

"Who are you?"

"I'm Axel."

"Thank you," Eisele said. "What was all that shooting about that I heard earlier?"

"Drills."

"Drills? For what?"

"You ask a lot of questions and make a lot of demands," Axel said flatly. "You're lucky we kept you alive. Frankly, there was a debate about it. My commanders voted and it was two to one in favor of keeping you alive. I was with the majority."

Eisele thought, *Commanders?*, but didn't say it.

Instead, Eisele said, "I thank you for that. But I'm really worried about my boss. I think he's spiraling."

Axel turned and beheld Spike Rankin in the next cot. As he did so, Rankin grunted weakly.

"I'm not sure we can do much for him at this point," Axel said. "We're limited in our field resources, and he looks too far gone."

"Please," Eisele said. "Just take him and drop him at an ER somewhere. They might be able to save him. He didn't do anything wrong. *We* didn't do anything wrong. We were just scouting for elk when we surprised Double-A and those other guys."

Eisele was surprised how pitiful and fawning he sounded, even to himself. And by the man's lack of reaction, he'd not made any headway.

"There might be people looking for me," Eisele said. "That can't be good for you."

"Is that what you think?" the man asked. "Why are you so special?"

Eisele hesitated for a few seconds. Would telling Axel that he was the governor's son-in-law help or hurt him? Would it cause Axel to release him or decide that he needed to take drastic action immediately? Either way, Eisele chose to keep that arrow in his quiver in case he needed it later.

"I'm not special," Eisele said. "But I have a family. Three little girls," he lied. He wanted more children. Megan wasn't as enthusiastic about the idea.

"Don't you think we all have families?" Axel said. "That doesn't make you unique."

Double-A returned with a tray of what looked like meat loaf and mashed potatoes. She placed it on Eisele's belly. Then she loosened his upper chest restraint and propped several cheap pillows under him so he could sit up and eat. Eisele stared at the plate of food. He wished he *was* hungry.

"Can you tell me what's going on up here?" Eisele asked the man. "I swear I won't say anything to anyone if that's what you want."

Axel smiled ruefully and shook his head. Obviously, Eisele's proposal wasn't even worth considering.

In his peripheral vision, Eisele could see that Double-A had bent over the next cot and fished out Rankin's wrist from beneath the covers to check his pulse. She held his wrist for a few moments, then glanced at her wristwatch. "I can hardly get a reading," she told Axel. "His heartbeat is weak and slow."

Axel turned to her as she lowered Rankin's wrist and tucked it back under the sheet. Then, making a sudden decision, Axel raised his own right arm and grasped that crutch with his left hand to hold it steady. He twisted the crutch pad a half turn.

Eisele felt a chill shoot through him as Axel unsheathed a ten-inch stiletto-like pointed blade from the crutch tube. The blade now protruded from Axel's grip, emerging from between his index and middle finger.

"What are you doing?" Eisele asked. Then, with his voice rising, "Axel? *What are you doing?*"

Axel ignored him while he plunged the blade into Rankin's

exposed ear and pushed it deep into his brain, nearly to the crutch pad itself. Eisele was stunned. Even Double-A stepped back and gasped as Rankin's body erupted with spasmic jerks, until it stopped moving.

Axel withdrew the blade and wiped it clean on Rankin's blanket, then slid it back into the crutch tube. He said to Double-A, "Get the guys to clear this cot. We might need it later."

Then, without another word, Axel glided out of the room through the open doorway. He didn't look back.

Stunned and horrified, Eisele glared at Double-A for confirmation of what he'd just witnessed. He couldn't speak.

"Time for your medication," she said while plunging a syringe needle into an open bottle of morphine.

CHAPTER TEN

THE NEIGHBORHOOD WAS known as "the Avenues" in Cheyenne, a historic district established in the 1920s and largely made up of single-family brick bungalow houses, as well as a few homes that had been turned into small one- or two-person office locations. Tall mature cottonwoods bordered the avenues on both sides of the streets and the gutters were choked with dried yellow leaves. When the wind blew, which was often in Cheyenne, the fall leaves fluttered down like a golden snowstorm.

Dead leaves swirled in the wind in such volume around Geronimo Jones's Suburban that they obscured his vision for a moment and he nearly drove by the address they were seeking.

"There it is," Nate said, jabbing his finger at a small wooden hand-painted sign in the yard of a bungalow that read:

> Cheryl Tuck-Smith
> Attorney-at-Law
> 314 N. Reed Ave.

Geronimo slowed down and parked against the curb in front of the law office. The streets were from another era and were so narrow that the big Suburban blocked nearly half of it.

"This thing seems a little out of place in the big city," Geronimo said to Nate as he patted the dashboard of his armored vehicle.

"It seems out of place everywhere," Nate said.

"So," Geronimo said. "How do you want to play it?"

"You're the talker," Nate replied.

"Weapons?"

"Always."

AS THEY ENTERED the front door, an old-fashioned bell tinkled. It startled a woman sitting behind a desk, who was absorbed in doing something on the screen of her phone. Her eyes got wide when she looked up and she involuntarily pushed back a few inches on her rolling chair. Nate assumed it was unusual for two large men—one Black with massive dreadlocks, the other white and rough-looking—to enter the law office unannounced at the same time. The lobby had obviously once been the parlor of a small home before being remodeled into a business office. An elaborate stone fireplace took up the entire right wall and the left wall had built-in bookcases filled with law books, primarily the statutes of the State of Wyoming. The receptionist's desk was just a few feet in front of them. A plastic plaque on the front of the desk identified her as Joann Delaney.

By her reaction, Delaney likely thought they were there to commence a home invasion, Nate thought. He slid in behind

Geronimo's wide shoulders, and they practically filled the small lobby.

She was a pert-looking woman in her midfifties with too much makeup. She had short reddish hair cut in a pixie style, and her long, curved, and painted nails likely clacked on the keyboard as she typed.

"I'm Geronimo Jones," Geronimo said in his gentlest baritone. "This is my associate, Nate Romanowski. We're here to see Cheryl Tuck-Smith. Is she in?"

"I don't want any trouble," Delaney said.

"And you won't get any from us," Geronimo assured her.

"Usually people call or email for an appointment," she said.

"And we apologize for not doing exactly that," Geronimo said. "But we've been on the road from Montana and we have an urgent matter to discuss with the attorney."

Delaney glared at Geronimo for a beat, then chinned toward a closed door over her shoulder and said, "She's on a call at the moment. I can ask her if she has a few minutes when it's done. But please be aware that the conference call may take a while and that she may have other business this afternoon."

Geronimo stepped closer to Delaney's desk and pointed at the single line on the three-line phone set that was illuminated. "I can see when she concludes the call," he said. "Until then, I guess we can wait. In the meantime, may I use your men's restroom? We've been driving all day."

"There is only one bathroom available to the public," she said.

"May I use it, please?" Geronimo asked.

After a beat, Delaney gestured toward a short hallway next to the closed door. She handed him a key on a rabbit's foot key chain from the top drawer of her desk. "It's the first door on the left," she said.

When Geronimo found the bathroom and went inside, Nate noticed that Delaney shot furtive looks at him standing next to the fireplace. Her hands were out of sight under the desktop and he realized she was furiously texting something on her phone without looking down.

"Stop doing that," he said. "Who are you texting?"

Caught, her face flushed. "Just my sister," she said.

"Your sister can wait. Our visit is unofficial. We'd like to keep it that way."

"I don't want any trouble," she said again. "The only reason I'm even here is to work off a legal bill."

"Then put your phone on your desk and leave it alone," he said.

"Okay, okay," she said, doing exactly that. She placed it screen-down and drew her hands away from it as if it were suddenly very hot.

"I'm not officially Ms. Tuck-Smith's receptionist," she said. "I just happen to be here at the moment. I don't know anything about her clients or her business."

Nate nodded once that he had heard her. She was scared of him, and probably more scared of Geronimo. Nate was fine with that.

"Really," she said, to emphasize her previous contention.

"Is that why you have your nameplate on the desk?" he asked.

Caught in a lie, she broke eye contact.

"You're pretty quick to distance yourself from your boss," he said. "I hope you never apply for a job at my company."

As Geronimo returned from the bathroom and placed the key

on her desk, the light on the phone set went dead. Geronimo gestured toward it and Delaney hit the intercom speaker button and said, "Cheryl, there are two gentlemen in the lobby who want to see you."

"Do they have an appointment?"

"No," she said while giving Geronimo a withering glance. "They're walk-ins."

Geronimo grinned and winked at Nate.

"And they're here concerning what?" the attorney asked. "I don't have time for donations today." She sounded annoyed and suspicious at the same time.

"Concerning what?" Delaney echoed to Geronimo.

"Start with C. W. Reese and Axel Soledad," Geronimo said. "We want to discuss your relationship with them."

Silence. Then, after a long pause, the attorney said, "What are your names?"

"Geronimo Jones and Nate Romanowski," Geronimo said. "We were hoping to get a few minutes of your time."

Another long pause. Then: "I have fifteen minutes."

EVEN SEATED BEHIND her very wide walnut desk, Cheryl Tuck-Smith looked out of proportion to her surroundings, Nate thought. She didn't rise when they entered her office, but she looked very tall even while seated. She had short blond hair, a long thin face, pearls over a cashmere turtleneck, broad shoulders, and very long fingers. Her nails were unpainted. Her demeanor was wary, and all business.

"Sit," she said to them.

Geronimo and Nate slid into hardback chairs across from her.
Nate studied the items on her walls: a law degree from the University of Wyoming, a hundred-year-old map of the state, and
photos of her in uniform with Army Rangers and a women's Big
Ten college basketball team, as well as photos with state and
national politicians, and people he vaguely recognized as fringe
personalities from the world of right-wing podcasting and
talk radio. Liv would have had a better idea who they were than
he did because she kept abreast of popular culture in general. In
all of the photos, Tuck-Smith was extremely easy to identify.
She towered above everyone else, except for one photo of her with
the starting lineup of the NBA champion Denver Nuggets from
2023.

There was also a mounted length of faded barn wood with
words burned into the surface: THIS IS THE GOVERNMENT OUR FOUNDERS
WARNED US ABOUT. Bullet holes marked the *O*'s.

Tuck-Smith's desk was empty except for a phone set identical
to the one on Delaney's desk, a coffee cup filled with pens and
markers, a banker's lamp with a green shade, and a stainless steel
.357 Magnum revolver within easy reach, with the muzzle pointed
away from her and toward them.

"That's probably not necessary," Geronimo said.

"I'll decide that," she responded.

"I'm Geronimo Jones and this is my associate—" Geronimo
started to introduce them again, but she cut him off.

"I heard," she said. Then: "You two look rough-and-tumble.
And you better get right to the reason you're here before my next
appointment. I make my living by billing for my time, and you

two are free riders who showed up without calling ahead or retaining my services. So get to it. I'll make a decision whether or not to charge you by the hour depending on what our discussion involves. And, gentlemen, my rate is not cheap."

Nate appreciated her no-nonsense manner, although it flustered Geronimo for a few seconds. He liked to ease into conversations, and he was a master at charming people and putting them at ease. Nate was the opposite of that.

"We're here because we understand that you're looking for Axel Soledad and contacting people he's been in contact with," Geronimo said. "We got your name from Mr. C. W. Reese of Gardiner, Montana."

Nate watched her closely for her reaction. There wasn't one, except for a barely perceptible twitch of her fingertips on her right hand on top of the desk. She seemed to recognize it as well and she went completely still. Nate attributed her stoicism to trained courtroom technique—to never let the jury, opposing counsel, or the judge know what she was thinking.

"About us," Geronimo said. "We're just a couple of master falconers who happen to be small businessmen as well. Axel is of interest to us because he's attacked our families in two different states. Mr. Reese led us to believe that you're tracking his movements and building some kind of case against Soledad. We hope you'll share some of that information with us."

Tuck-Smith frowned while she drummed her fingers on the desk. Better to keep them busy, Nate thought.

"Now, why would I do that?" she asked.

"Because we're the good guys," Geronimo said.

"We're going to kill him," Nate said.

Geronimo turned to Nate and winced at the statement. Tuck-Smith's reaction was notable. She didn't recoil. Instead, she displayed a cold smile. She turned to Nate and said, "You, I'm familiar with."

Nate raised his eyebrows in anticipation.

"Your name has been associated with some nasty business that occurred last winter at a cabin near Pinedale," she said. "After that, you seemed to have vanished off the face of the earth."

Nate didn't respond.

"I'm very sorry about what happened to your wife," she said to him. "It was such an unnecessary tragedy."

She said nothing more about the discovery of the three burned bodies found in the Sublette County rental cabin. Nate was grateful for that.

Instead, she turned to Geronimo. "I hope you have good homeowners insurance so you can get your house rebuilt. It's really a challenge to find good contractors in the winter these days. They're all building houses for newcomers."

"Ain't that the truth," Geronimo said.

"I also understand that the feds are after you both," she said. "I've been avoiding calls from a Special Agent Rick Orr for months now. I get the impression he's a bulldog, and he might be operating on his own."

Nate and Geronimo refrained from exchanging a confirming glance when they heard the name.

"You know a lot more about us than we know about you," Nate said.

"That's because she got access to the Bal-Chatri forums on our site," Geronimo said to Nate. "She's read all about us."

Tuck-Smith agreed with that and said, "That's why I'm good at my job. I do my homework. I was frankly a little surprised how chatty you falconers are with each other."

"Who gave you the password to get in?" Geronimo asked.

Instead of answering, Tuck-Smith reached up and mimed a *zipping my mouth closed* gesture.

"Should we trust you?" Nate asked.

"That's up to you. It's your call. But I would point out that you haven't retained me as your counsel, and as an attorney I'm an officer of the court. I'd also point out that you've come in here and admitted your involvement in a conspiracy to commit homicide, yet I haven't called 911 to report you. So take that for what it's worth."

With that, she looked at her wristwatch to conspicuously remind them that they had limited time.

"Look," she said. "I'm a pretty well-known person in certain circles that aren't looked kindly upon by our national media or the permanent entrenched bureaucracy in Washington. I fight them at every opportunity, and I usually win. They absolutely hate that; I know I'm in their crosshairs.

"I've been called a rogue lawyer and a conspiracy theorist. I really don't give a crap. My job is to serve my clients and to seek the truth no matter where that leads me."

To Nate, she said, "That's all you need to know about me. I believe you have some experience in being targeted by the feds yourself."

"That's correct," Nate said. "Is Axel Soledad your client?"

"Ah," she said. "Now we're getting down to brass tacks. No, Axel is not my client."

"Then who are you working for?" Geronimo asked. "Do you work for someone who is after Axel Soledad? Is that why you know about us? And why you visited with C. W. Reese?"

Tuck-Smith glared at Geronimo for a long beat, then said, "What I'm doing as far as Axel Soledad is pro bono. All of the time I've spent trying to locate him has been on my own dime.

"I'll tell you this," she said, her eyes flashing for the first time. "Axel Soledad is a danger to our country. He has to be stopped."

Geronimo was temporarily speechless.

"That's what we're going to do," Nate said. "But with us, it's personal."

"Which is fine by me," she said. "More power to you. I just hope you know what you're up against."

"Oh, we do," Nate responded.

"Do you know what he's up to?" Geronimo asked her. "You make it sound big."

"That's because it is," Tuck-Smith said. "He's been working toward this for years, and he's recruited enough like-minded followers to maybe make it happen. You've talked to C. W. Reese—you know how Axel operates. I've talked with a few more people like Reese who were approached by Soledad. People like you two: military background, lone wolves, men who feel betrayed by their government, disaffected . . ."

"I'm not sure that describes *us*," Geronimo said with a huff. "Speaking for myself, I mean."

Nate remained silent.

"Anyway," she said. "What I don't know is how many people have fallen for his bullshit and have joined up with him. Or what exactly he plans to do."

"Where will it happen?" Geronimo asked.

"Here," she said, jabbing her index finger into the desktop. "Either in Wyoming or northern Colorado. All of his movements in the past few months have been in the region. There are so many targets of national importance here when you think about it: oil fields, refineries, power plants, our nuclear arsenal—they're all here. All of his activities over the last few years have been designed to raise money and support for a big attack."

"If this is true," Geronimo said, "shouldn't you go to the authorities?"

Nate rolled his eyes as Tuck-Smith said, "I think if I told the FBI why I've been doing this, they'd just look at my history and call me a crackpot. They're too busy going after ranchers, so-called insurrectionists, antiabortion activists, parents who speak at school board meetings, and traditional Catholics these days. Plus, although I know there are good ones out there, I don't know which agents I can trust or how to find them."

"I understand," Nate said, to Geronimo's obvious annoyance.

"What about local law enforcement?" Geronimo asked her.

Tuck-Smith pursed her lips and said, "That's a mixed bag. Some are good, some are awful. A few would probably sign up with Axel. But since I don't know yet what jurisdiction Axel plans to operate in, how can I notify the locals?"

"What got you interested in Axel Soledad in the first place?" Geronimo asked her.

She looked at Nate and said, "You asked me if he was my client and I said he wasn't. But that doesn't mean he didn't want to be. Like I said, I'm pretty well known for fighting the feds and representing clients they consider marginal or even traitorous. I think Axel figured I'd fit right in. He thought I might be able to keep him out of jail until he could pull the trigger on his big plans. I played along for a couple of meetings, but the more I learned about Axel, the less I wanted to be his attorney—even if there were a few points he made that I agreed with.

"That's when I first heard your name," she said to Nate. "And that's the first time I heard of Geronimo Jones."

Nate leaned forward, intrigued.

"He considers you two his enemies," she said. "You are impediments to him and his plan. When he talked about you two—especially Mr. Romanowski—it was the one time I saw the crazy, irrational part of his personality on display. He wants you out of the way, and he'll do anything to make that happen. Axel hinted to me that friends of his keep track of your movements and your families and they're just waiting for the word to take action."

Nate and Geronimo exchanged a long look.

"Every man has a weakness," Tuck-Smith said. "Axel's is that he thinks he's smarter than everyone else. I found that if you flatter him, he can't help but brag about himself. It's classic hubris. He told me this when he was sure I'd be his counsel, so what I'm revealing to you is not privileged information."

"How did he take it when you told him you wouldn't take him on as a client?" Geronimo asked.

As a response, she patted the .357 Magnum and said, "That's the reason I got this. Axel has a way of getting rid of people who are a threat to him. I think he just hasn't gotten around to me yet. And it's why Joann gets so jumpy when people we don't know just show up."

"It's settled, then," Nate said. "Axel will be history soon. Though, that was pretty much the case before we showed up here."

Geronimo agreed.

"We're out of time," Tuck-Smith announced. "I've got a big board meeting on the docket. There's a new sagebrush rebellion brewing, and a real effort to take back our land from the federal agencies who run roughshod over us. I'm their legal counsel. I need to be present at this meeting because we're suing the feds and I'm writing the lawsuit."

"One more thing," Geronimo said. "How do we find Axel's location?"

"What's your cell phone number?" she asked. As she did, one of the buttons of her phone lit up and Joann Delaney announced over the intercom that the board meeting had been called to order and that they were waiting for her to join it.

Geronimo recited his number. It had a Colorado area code.

Tuck-Smith snatched up her phone and sent a contact record. Geronimo's phone pinged.

"Russ and Jolene Anthony are clients of mine on another matter," Tuck-Smith said. "When I met with them a few days ago, they were worried about their daughter, Allison. They talked about her like she'd been recruited into some kind of cult, and she's been gone for a few weeks now. Then they described the man she ran off with. They said he was ex-military, a master falconer like yourselves, and very charismatic. They also said that his legs are useless and he gets around on crutches."

"Soledad," Geronimo said.

"You're the one who shot him," Tuck-Smith said to him. "Why didn't you finish him off?"

"I thought we had," Geronimo said sourly.

"Don't screw it up this time," she said. Then: "I'll have Joann contact Russ and Jolene and tell them you're coming. If they don't want to see you, I'll let you know, now that I have your cell number."

Then Tuck-Smith stood and pulled a set of headphones on. Both Nate and Geronimo froze in their chairs as she did so. Nate had never been in the same room with a seven-foot woman before.

"Yes, I'm tall, get over it," she said to them. "Now, go."

She said it while she shooed them out of her office.

"*Thank you*," Nate mouthed to her.

"*No charge*," she mouthed back. Then: "This is Cheryl," she said into her headset while turning away. "I'm sorry I'm a minute late. Let the games begin . . ."

Nate looked over his shoulder to see if her last statement was also meant for them. Geronimo caught it as well.

When she winked at them, they knew it was.

ON THEIR WAY through the lobby toward the front door, the receptionist, Joann Delany, extended her arm and handed Geronimo a Post-it note that she'd hastily scribbled on. Geronimo took it and looked it over.

He read, "'Russ and Jolene Anthony, 103 Cherokee Creek Trail, Tie Siding, Wyoming.'" Then to Nate: "Where in the hell is Tie Siding?"

"South of Laramie," Nate said. "It's an hour or so west of here. Don't worry—I've been there. It's really off the beaten path."

"Of course it is. What isn't off the beaten path around here?" Geronimo said.

Nate nodded goodbye at the receptionist, who turned away and wouldn't meet his eye.

CHAPTER ELEVEN

"FROM WHAT I'VE been told," Susan Kany said to Joe as she drove slowly to Spike Rankin's elk camp along a narrow two-track road flanked by towering aspens on both sides, "the Centurions are a mix of defense industry CEOs, federal government officials, current and ex-military leaders, airline executives, and even a few astronauts. I've heard them described as the military-industrial complex in cowboy boots."

Joe chuckled at that.

"I went to the ranch last year when the Centurions were around," she said. "At the time I didn't know any better. All I knew was that there had been a big run on out-of-state fishing licenses sold at their tackle shop in a short period of time, so I thought it was a good opportunity to check fishermen. I'll tell you what—I wasn't exactly welcome there."

"How so?"

"They stopped me at the front gate of the ranch. They have a little guardhouse building, and there were like five people inside. Two older ladies apparently work there all the time for the

B-Lazy-U, but there were three buff guys in shades with handheld radios as well: security for some of the members, I think. They questioned why I was there and I had to show my badge and ID. They asked if I could come back later, but that made me suspicious and I said no.

"After ten minutes of the security guys talking to someone inside, they let me in. But as soon as I got within the ranch complex, a couple of other security types followed me to the river on an ATV. I checked a couple of fishermen on the river with their guides and they checked out—everything was kosher. But my minders never left me alone the whole time."

"Did you have any idea who the fishermen were?" Joe asked.

"You could tell by looking at them that they were muckety-mucks," she said. "They wore all-new Orvis gear straight out of the box, and they had two-thousand-dollar Sage rods. I looked up the names of the three guys I checked later. One of them was the CEO of a defense company that does radar and sensors for rockets and warplanes, one of them was the chairman of an airline, and the third guy was some kind of deputy undersecretary in the Defense Department."

"Interesting," Joe said.

"None of them could cast worth a hoot," she said.

"How many of them are out there?"

"They have two hundred and fifty members, and they've been around as a club for over sixty years."

"Have they always come here?" he asked. "From what you've told me, I'd expect them to go to some place more high-end and famous. You know, Jackson Hole or Aspen or something like that."

"I think that's what they're trying to avoid," she said. "This place has everything they want: a huge private airport, luxury ranches, outdoor things to do, no national press of any kind, and locals who keep their mouths shut."

"Do they invite members of the community to come to any of their activities?" he asked.

"Not really—none I know of," she said. "Of course, they have to hire people to work there during the week. Waitstaff, housekeeping, extra fishing guides and wranglers, and such. The Centurions bring staff and security folks, but they can't fly all of their people out here. Locals who go out there for the week have to sign an NDA."

"Who told you all of this inside stuff?" Joe asked with a sly smile.

"The night after I went out there to check licenses, I eavesdropped on a couple of the pilots who were having a few too many beers at the bar at the Hotel Wolf," she said. "The Centurions put their pilots up there for the week while they go out to the ranch and do whatever it is they do."

She looked over at him as she drove. "It's always amazing what people say around me when I'm not in uniform. One of them offered to buy me a drink."

"I understand," Joe said. He guessed that Kany looked pretty good in her street clothes, and then he felt immediately guilty for thinking it.

"Maybe you'll run into a couple of them," she said.

"Maybe," Joe said. "But I hope not to stay here more than a night or two."

"And get out of my hair? No offense."

"Yup," Joe said. "None taken."

———

THE MASSIVE ASPEN grove cleared and the road crossed a rocky alpine meadow before plunging into a heavy copse of pine trees. Joe glimpsed the signs of a camp between the trunks of the trees as they approached.

"Rankin's camp is straight ahead," Kany said. "It's tucked into those trees."

Joe liked the location for an elk camp. It was about four miles from the state highway and the road seemed to dead-end at the copse. The mountains rose sharply to the east, and the terrain eventually sloped on the west to the rugged North Platte River canyon wilderness area. From that camp, Rankin would have easy access to hundreds of thousands of acres of mountains, scrub, scree, foothills, and river bottom.

It was still but cool outside with scattered clouds that looked close to the summits of the nearby peaks. A mottled carpet of snow lay on the ground in the shadows of the trees.

Kany slowed even more as she entered the elk camp. Joe admired that. One of the worst traits of overeager new game wardens was to rush into a camp and panic the inhabitants, who were very likely armed and not expecting visitors. It was much better to enter an elk camp in the most transparent way possible, unless they were there to surprise people.

The camp was clean, simple, and well-planned, Joe thought. There was a natural opening in the heart of the copse and the camp was surrounded by trees. Two large taut wall tents had been erected on either side of the clearing, and a larger tent in the middle likely served as the communal eating and gathering place. The side tents were big enough for four and no doubt filled with cots and sleeping bags.

Most traditional elk camps were laid out by experienced outfitters, so their clients had their own sleeping quarters and privacy. The guide tents were far enough away not to interfere, but close enough to keep an eye on their people and to make sure no one wandered off in the dark.

There was an outhouse a hundred feet behind the tents, and stripped pine poles had been lashed high to the trunks of the tallest trees to hang game carcasses. To the side of the camp was a parking area that extended into the trees. A single vehicle was in it—an aged Ford Bronco with local plates.

A big firepit bordered by heavy, round river rocks occupied the space in front of the communal tent. A pile of folded camp chairs sat on a wooden pallet next to a neat row of firewood that looked freshly split. A teepee of kindling had been built in the firepit, ready for a match.

The camp looked ready for hunters to arrive, but they were not there yet.

Smoke wafted from a round tin chimney pipe that poked through the canvas roof. Joe could smell woodsmoke when he climbed out of Kany's pickup. He always loved the smell of smoke during fall in the high mountains.

"He's here," Kany said with triumph as she gestured toward the communal tent.

"Let's see what we've got here," Joe said, thinking, *Mark Eisele better be with him.*

He wasn't.

———

THE RIGHT CANVAS flap of the communal tent was thrown back as Joe and Kany approached it, and a fireplug-shaped woman wearing an apron, a red flannel shirt, and worn Carhartt bib overalls peered out at them.

"Hey there," Kany said with a smile.

"Good afternoon," said Joe.

The woman came out of the tent, but left the doorway open. Joe could see a Dutch oven filled with red chili simmering on the woodstove inside, as well as a pot of coffee. The cook peered at them and looked over the top of Kany's truck toward the road behind them. Her expression was pained.

"I could hear you coming down the road," she said. "I was hoping you was someone else."

Kany said, "Sorry to disappoint you. I'm game warden Susan Kany, and this is Joe Pickett. We're here to talk to Spike Rankin."

"Is he in trouble?" the cook asked.

"No. It's a friendly visit."

The woman put her hands on her hips and looked them over. She was in her late fifties or early sixties with shoulder-length white hair, thick round-framed glasses, and a ruddy expression. The cast-iron camp stove inside the tent crackled as it burned.

"I'd like to talk to Spike myself," she said. Then: "I'm Audrey Racines from Baggs." The town of Baggs was thirty miles away to the west. "I've been up here cooking for Spike for twenty-three years. This is the first time he hasn't shown up when he said he'd be here."

Joe and Kany exchanged a concerned look.

"When was he supposed to be here?" Kany asked Racines.

"Yesterday, damn it," Racines said. "It's been the same drill for-ever. Spike comes up here a week or two before the season opens to scout for elk and set up the camp. He sends me a list of how many clients he has and any food allergies, and how long they're going to be up here. Then I go shopping and I come up the day before to get everything set up and plan all the meals. Spike usu-ally goes down into Encampment or Warm Springs to pick up whatever we're low on or we forgot.

"But when I showed up yesterday, there was no Spike Rankin. He's been here to set things up, as you can see. But I haven't heard hide nor hair of him."

"And that's unusual?" Kany asked her.

"It's really unusual," Racines said. "I called and texted him, but he hasn't called back. Of course, cell service is rotten up here. But still, I should have heard from him by now. His hunters are due to show up anytime."

"Do you know what part of the mountains he was scouting?"

"Not a clue," Racines said. "When I'm up here at the elk camp, I stay right here. I never go out with them. My job is to keep the coffee on and the beer cooler full for when they get back."

"Does he usually have a radio or a sat phone with him?" Kany asked.

"He's got a sat phone in case a hunter gets injured or some-thing," Racines said. "If he needs to call in the EMTs. But he doesn't turn it on unless he needs to call out."

"What's the description of his vehicle?" Kany asked. "We can call it in and see if anyone has reported it parked somewhere. If not, we can put out an APB for southern Wyoming. Do you have any photos of Rankin I can send along?"

"Back at home, I have some elk camp photos from over the years," Racines said. "But I don't have none of 'em with me." Then, raising an index finger to her chin, she said: "Hold it."

With that, she ducked inside the communal tent and came out with a large three-ring album. "We've got hunting and camp photos in here going back ten years," she said. "Spike's in a ton of them. We keep this on the table so new clients can see there are plenty of elk up here."

"Perfect," Kany said.

Racines said Rankin drove a "tricked-up" gray 2018 Dodge Ram Power Wagon with local County Six plates, meaning Carbon County. The pickup had extra clearance and knobby tires, and a platform for an ATV on top of the bed in back.

She said, "It's hard to miss. It's quite a unit. My husband has dreams about owning one like it one of these days, to which I say, 'Fat chance, buddy. You need to make a lot more money than you do if you want to afford one of these.'"

While Kany called dispatch in Cheyenne to relay the vehicle details, Joe asked Racines, "Do you mind if I look around?"

"Feel free," she said. "I hope you find him. I'm at my wit's end. I don't want them hunters showing up with just me here. Some of them guys are hard to deal with as it is." Then: "And I'm getting worried about Spike. He shouldn't be gone this long, unless . . . something happened."

Joe tipped his hat to her and set about to circumnavigate the camp. As he passed Racines, she said, "You're pretty well known around this camp, Joe Pickett."

He paused and looked quizzically at her.

"Spike loves to tell his hunters about the time a brand-new game warden arrested the governor for fishing without a license up in Twelve Sleep County," she said with a laugh. "He does it so his clients know what kind of sticklers some of you guys are. It's a way of reminding them to always carry their licenses and conservation stamps with them and to stay on the up-and-up. 'Cuz you never know when one of those tight-assed game wardens might show up,' he says." Then: "That was you, right?"

"It was," Joe said. "That was a long time ago."

"Spike would probably like to meet you," Racines said. Then, with a long sigh: "I hope he shows up."

"Me too. Did he mention being up here this year with a new guy?" Joe asked.

"Yes, he did," Racines said. "His name is Mark-something. Spike said the guy was really wet behind the ears."

Joe didn't respond.

"He said it's getting harder and harder to find help these days. Nobody wants to work. They just want to sit around their houses all day and play video games and collect unemployment. That's a damned sight easier than packing a quarter of an elk out of the woods in knee-deep snow."

"True," Joe said.

"I worry about my country."

Joe let that one go.

THERE WERE TWO fit-looking sorrel quarter horses in a corral tucked into the pines not far from where the game-hanging poles were lashed up. Joe threw them some hay from a short stack of bales outside the corral and filled their water trough from a gravity feed bag hung from a branch. The animals were well-muscled and well-behaved, and since there were only two of them, Joe assumed Rankin used them not to hunt from but to pack out meat from areas too rugged to access with his Power Wagon or ATV. Like most experienced outfitters Joe knew, Rankin likely didn't want to put his clients on the back of a horse if they weren't extremely experienced mountain riders. Too many things could go wrong— and often did.

Joe confirmed his guess when he found two weathered pack-saddles under a tarp near the corral.

He untied the flaps to the tent on the left side of the clearing to find four roomy cots, a table with a full pitcher of water, and four bedrolls. That would be for the clients.

In the other sleeping tent were three cots. Two were on the right side of the tent, and a sheet separated them from a single cot on the left. That one had a rumpled sleeping bag on it, as well as a duffel bag underneath and a vanity and mirror at the back. Joe guessed that Audrey Racines had slept there the night before. The two other cots, for Spike Rankin and Mark Eisele, were un-touched.

It was impossible to know how long it had been since the camp had been set up but not used by Rankin and Eisele. Two nights? Three nights?

WHILE HE WAS inside the tent, Joe heard the rumbling of another vehicle approaching the elk camp. He left the staff sleeping tent and retied the flaps closed, hoping Rankin's "tricked-up" Power Wagon would nose through the aspen grove and he could go home to Marybeth.

Both Kany and Racines had also turned toward the road.

Instead of a Power Wagon, however, a new-model luxury Land Rover appeared. It had three people inside and North Carolina First in Flight license plates.

Rankin's hunters had arrived.

JOE MET THE Land Rover on foot and held up his palm to signal to the driver to park it. The vehicle stopped and Joe could see the driver angrily gesticulating to the passenger, who held up his hands in an *I don't know* response. A third man in the back seat had leaned forward to listen to their exchange. The back half of the big SUV was packed to the ceiling with gear and duffel bags, making it dark inside.

The driver's-side door exploded open and a slim, fit man in his sixties popped out. He had close-cropped, styled silver hair and his chin was thrust out. He wore tactical hunting pants and a tight beige chamois shirt with a red bandana around his neck. He was obviously angry.

In contrast, the passenger in the front seat eased his door open and slipped out of the SUV. The man in the back seat did the same.

"Who the hell are you?" the driver asked Joe.

"Not Spike Rankin."

"Well, that's obvious," the man said as he peered over Joe's head toward the camp. "Where is he? He was supposed to meet us here this afternoon. I paid a lot of money for this, and he won't answer his goddamned phone."

Before Joe could respond, the driver squinted at Joe and then at Susan Kany. "You're game wardens," he said. "Has Rankin done something wrong? Because if he has and we can't hunt, I'm going to sue his ass."

"Let's calm down," Joe said as friendly as he could. "I'm Joe Pickett and this is my colleague, Sue Kany. She's the local game warden. Audrey Racines back there is your camp cook. Let's relax and get this all sorted out."

"Jimbo," the passenger pleaded to the driver, "let's hear him out."

Jimbo shot a withering look at his friend, then turned to Joe and raised his eyebrows. "This better be good," he said.

Joe explained the situation without explaining the *whole* situation. He and Kany had come just an hour before to visit with Rankin, but no one was there except for Racines.

Jimbo was obviously enraged, but he listened patiently. As he did, his face got redder.

"So nobody fucking knows where he is?" Jimbo asked.

"That's about the size of it," Joe said. "But no need to panic. I'm sure he'll show up." Joe wanted to believe what he told Jimbo.

"What if he doesn't?" Jimbo asked. "I brought my clients all the way from Raleigh here to Bumfuck, Wyoming, for a ten-day trophy elk hunt. It cost a pretty penny, as you can imagine. Now I show up and the guy I sent tens of thousands of dollars to isn't even here to meet us. Instead, we find a couple of fish cops standing around twiddling their thumbs. That's called fraud where I come from in North Carolina. I don't know what you call it here in Bumfuck, Wyoming."

"*Jimbo* . . ." the passenger cautioned.

"*Raymond* . . ." Jimbo replied in a mocking tone.

His passenger, Raymond-something, was an overweight bald man with a round face, a tiny mustache, and reading glasses hanging from a chain around his neck. He, like Jimbo, was decked out in state-of-the-industry high-tech hunting clothes and boots. Raymond-something looked puzzled and embarrassed by the whole situation. Joe noticed he had glanced away as Jimbo complained, as if he were distancing himself from the scene.

The third hunter, whom Raymond-something referred to as Kent, was rail-thin and had an upside-down triangle of a face, a broad forehead tapering down into a tiny chin. He seemed to be amused by everything, and Joe observed that he was likely pretty drunk. His eyes were watery and his reactions to what was being said were slow on the uptake. Joe's impression was confirmed when he noticed an empty Coors can on the grass on the side of the Land Rover. Kent must have accidentally kicked it out when he swung outside.

"We're not fish cops," Kany said as she walked up and stood shoulder to shoulder with Joe. "We're game wardens from the Wyoming Game and Fish Department.

"We have full authority to enforce our state's laws. That includes arresting people who get out of line."

Joe nodded in agreement.

"If you're officers of the law," Jimbo said as he leaned forward and balled his fists at his side, "you should arrest Rankin for misleading us. That is, unless you're in cahoots with him."

"Jimbo, please," Raymond-something said. "Let's take a few seconds and talk this over."

Jimbo reluctantly agreed, and the two men turned and walked to the rear of the vehicle and stood behind it. Kent darted back inside the SUV for a fresh beer and then joined them. The three hunters engaged in an energetic back-and-forth in whispered tones so as not be overheard.

"That escalated quickly," Kany said out of the corner of her mouth.

"You just never know," Joe agreed.

He gauged the situation. "I don't think Jimbo is trouble," he said in a low tone only she could hear. "I think he's just embarrassed and out of his element. He probably talked up this hunt to his clients all the way out here, and now he doesn't want them to think it's his fault. He wanted to impress them."

"*That* impresses me," Kany said as she chinned toward the SUV. "That's a 2023 Land Rover Range Rover LWB. It starts at a hundred and seven thousand dollars. This one is probably worth more than that because it has all the bells and whistles on it."

Joe looked over in amazement at Susan Kany. "How do you know that?"

She shrugged. "I priced it online after I saw one at the airport the other day. One of the Centurions had one to take to the B-Lazy-U Ranch. I was just curious."

"Hmmm."

"What do you think they'll do now?" she asked about the hunters. "Go back home?"

"I doubt it," Joe said. "That would be too much of a debacle for Jimbo. He'll feel that he needs to take some kind of action."

The three hunters broke up and returned to the front of their vehicle. Jimbo took the lead and Raymond and Kent stood behind him.

Jimbo crossed his arms over his chest in a defiant stance. "I need the names of a couple of other local elk-hunting guides," he said, looking from Joe to Kany and back again. "And I need a list of lawyers who will sue Rankin's ass for fraud on my behalf—and maybe your department for perpetuating his fraudulent scheme."

"How about you just turn around and go home?" Audrey Racines suddenly said to Jimbo. She'd joined Joe and Kany. "We don't need jerks like you around here anyway."

Joe turned to Racines. "We really don't need your help right now," he whispered.

Racines's eyes flared, but she held her tongue.

"I'll tell you what," Kany said gently to the three hunters. "We'll get this figured out so everybody's happy and no one needs to sue anyone."

As she spoke, she approached the hunters and handed each one of them her business card. "I'll call down to town and get you reservations at either the Hot Springs Resort or the Riviera Motel. Whichever one has the three best rooms available. Both are very comfortable, and the three of you can soak in the local hot springs tonight and relax. I'll text you a list of local outfitters, and if need be, I can make recommendations. In the meanwhile, you can enjoy the town and have a few beers and a nice meal. I'd suggest you call ahead for a dinner reservation," she said. "You're sharing the town with a bunch of private pilots."

"I like the sound of that," Kent said, hoisting his can of beer.

"What about my deposit on the elk hunt?" Jimbo asked. His voice didn't contain the fury it'd had earlier.

"I'll text you the hotline for the Wyoming Outfitters and Guides Association," Kany said to him. "They police their own and they do a good job of it. But for the time being, let's get you boys settled in town and set up a fine hunting adventure. How does that sound?"

"Pretty good," Raymond-something said. "I'm getting hungry."

"I'll also send along a list of restaurants," Kany said.

"So you two aren't up here because Rankin broke the law?" Jimbo asked them.

"Nope," Joe said. "We were just checking in on him when you boys showed up."

"And you really don't know where he is?"

"No. But we plan to find him."

"Maybe he had an accident or something," Kany added.

Although it was obvious Jimbo wasn't completely satisfied with the answers, he turned with the others and got into the Land Rover. His three-point turn wasn't aggressive, and Joe and Kany watched as the vehicle rumbled away to go down the mountain.

"Well done," Joe said to her.

"I thought, 'What would Joe Pickett do?'" she said with a grin.

A FEW MINUTES later, Joe said to Kany, "You've got a two-horse district, right?"

Game warden districts were designated by HQ in Cheyenne as one-, two-, or three-horse districts depending on the size of the area and the difficulty of the terrain.

She confirmed it. Kany said she had a fine, well-trained mountain quarter horse and a stubborn mule.

"Let's trailer them up here and go look for Rankin first thing tomorrow if he still hasn't shown up," Joe said.

"That makes sense," she said. "Do we notify the search and rescue folks?"

"Not yet," Joe said. He didn't explain why, and he could tell she was puzzled by him again.

"When, then?" she asked.

"I think first we need to talk to the sheriff." Joe knew they needed some help.

They'd blown nearly an entire day without getting a solid lead on the missing outfitter and the governor's son-in-law. He recalled what Rulon had said about Sheriff Regan Haswell, but he chose to disregard it. Rulon may be enemies with the man, but Joe wasn't. And if Haswell was like most local sheriffs, he kept his ear close to the ground and might know more about Rankin's habits and his current whereabouts. He'd also likely know if Rankin had enemies or aggressive competitors who might have sabotaged him in some way.

"You get the stubborn mule," she said to Joe as she waved goodbye to Audrey Racines and climbed behind the wheel of her pickup. "His name is Henry."

"I'll take him," Joe said.

He wished he had brought Rojo with him. Marybeth kept the gelding tuned up and ready to go at a moment's notice.

"I'll drop you at the Wolf and get all the tack ready tonight," Kany said.

"Do you need some help?"

"No. I can handle it, *Dad*," she said with more than a little attitude.

He let it go. And he made a mental note to contact Ann Byrnes in the governor's office as soon as Kany let him out of the pickup in Warm Springs. He needed to keep her apprised of his progress.

Or, in this case, the lack of it.

PART FOUR

"The bird out of place is always the first to die."

—J. A. Baker, *The Peregrine*

CHAPTER TWELVE

T *HIS* IS TIE Siding?" Geronimo said with amazement at the two rambling structures on the west side of US 287 south of Laramie. The buildings were boarded up and appeared abandoned.

"Affirmative," Nate said from the passenger seat.

"It's not even a town."

"Think of it as a location."

One of the buildings was a large A-frame with the words **FLEA MARKET** painted on the side shingles, and the other, according to a hand-lettered sign in front, was a former post office and general store. Several junked cars and pickups sat on flattened tires between the structures.

"Who could live here?" Geronimo said as he slowed and took the exit.

The wind had picked up and the buffeting waves of it shook the Suburban on its springs.

"You'd be surprised," Nate said, gesturing toward tree-covered mountains looming on the western horizon.

They passed through an open ranch gate, under power lines, and over railroad tracks. In front of them was a long gravel straightaway bordered by yellowed grass and gray sagebrush that stretched as far as they could see through the windshield. The sky was huge and broken up by long parallel strands of cirrus clouds that looked scratched into the blue by cougar claws.

"We should have gotten something to eat in Laramie," Geronimo said. "There's no place to get food around here and I'm hungry."

"You're always hungry," Nate said.

RUSS AND JOLENE Anthony lived on a loop of road cleared in the trees on the top of a wooded mountain. There were a dozen other high-end homes within the enclave, all with views of the plains on the valley floor that stretched for thirty miles to the east. The homes were too far from the highway to be seen from below. It was a horsey mountain getaway location that had been carved out of a vast ranch holding, and it had obviously been designed for people who didn't want to be stumbled upon. Geronimo pulled into the circular driveway of 103 Cherokee Creek Trail and shut off the engine.

A towering flagpole boasted three flags snapping furiously in the wind: the U.S. flag on top, the State of Wyoming's in the middle, and a red U.S. Marine Corps flag on the bottom.

An attractive, outdoorsy woman in her fifties was watching for them, and she greeted them at her front door.

"You must be Jolene," Geronimo said.

"You must be Geronimo and Nate," she said with a nervous

smile. "We don't get a lot of visitors by design. Our attorney in Cheyenne let us know you were coming."

Jolene stepped aside and let them in. Nate acknowledged her as he went by.

"I have coffee, tea, and water," she said. "Russ no longer drinks alcohol, so we don't have any in the house."

"I'm fine, thank you," Nate said. He knew that Geronimo was probably hoping she'd offer them some food. To Geronimo's credit, he didn't make a fuss when she didn't.

The home was spectacular, with a massive elk-antler chandelier in the great room and furniture crafted from more antlers and steer hides. It was built so solidly that the sound of the howling wind outside was squelched into silence the second she closed the heavy door.

"Russ is in the study," she said. "We thought that would be the best place to talk." Then: "I hope you can help us rescue Allison."

As they followed her across the great room into a book-lined office with leather-covered padded chairs surrounding a desk, Nate and Geronimo shared a glance.

"*Rescue Allison?*" Geronimo mouthed. "*What?*"

Nate had no response.

AFTER INTRODUCTIONS AND extra-firm handshakes, Russ Anthony took his place behind the desk and motioned for Geronimo and Nate to sit. They did. Jolene perched on the arm of a chair next to the desk and leaned forward, as if she didn't want to miss a single word that was spoken.

"Let's get right down to business," Russ said as he settled in and leaned back in his chair. "I don't like to beat around the bush, especially where our daughter is concerned."

Russ was older than Jolene by at least a decade. He had dark brown eyes, a silver crew cut, and a square jaw. He wore a sweater over a button-down shirt, jeans, and cowboy boots. His manner said ex-military, Nate thought.

That presumption was confirmed when Nate studied the photos and plaques on the walls surrounding Russ Anthony. Half of them were of Anthony with groups of fellow soldiers in tropical, desert, and arctic conditions. The other half of the photos were of a dark-eyed younger female in a contemporary dress uniform as well as military fatigues. She smiled brightly in one surrounded by fellow Marines posing in front of a bunker built with sandbags. Her no-nonsense countenance in most of the shots must have come from her father, Nate thought.

"Let's talk about your daughter," Geronimo said. "And then we'll let you know why we're here and how we might be able to help each other."

Russ's eyes got large and he said, "Didn't Cheryl brief you before you left Cheyenne?"

"Not really," Geronimo said, "except to say that you might be able to help us locate a man named Axel Soledad."

Jolene physically recoiled at the mention of his name, Nate noted.

"If you find Allison," Russ said, "you'll likely find Soledad. As far as we know, she's with him."

"Where are they?" Nate asked the couple.

"We'll get to that," Russ said with a wave of his open hand.

"First let me tell you how Allison got in this situation and why it's important to us that you bring her back."

Nate winced, and he assumed Geronimo did so as well. "Bringing her back" was a complication neither man had anticipated when they arrived.

"Allison is our only daughter," Jolene added.

"That's her in those photos behind me," Russ said without turning his head. "She followed me into the U.S. Marine Corps. We couldn't be prouder of her, even though I have my issues with the Corps these days, and especially what our so-called 'leaders' are trying to do to it."

When Anthony said the word "leaders," he did air quotes around it.

"Not now, Russ," Jolene said, cautioning him. Then to Geronimo and Nate: "When Russ gets going on what he thinks is happening to his beloved Marines, he really gets wound up. I don't think we have the time right now."

Geronimo nodded his head in agreement.

"Anyway," Anthony said, "we're a family of Marines. Four generations of 'em. Not former Marines—there is no such thing. Once a Marine, always a Marine."

"Gotcha," Geronimo said. "We understand."

"Are you two special operators?" Anthony asked.

"Affirmative."

"I could tell by the way you come across," Anthony said. "Only special ops guys would be comfortable coming across as raggedy-assed as you two. Marines have a little more . . . decorum."

"Please get on with it," Jolene pleaded to her husband. She

could tell that Geronimo reacted negatively to his comments about decorum. Nate, on the other hand, didn't react at all.

"Allison was—is—a star," Anthony said. "She always has been. She was a three-letter athlete in high school and she aced basic training even before they dumbed down the physical requirements to add more women. She was assigned to a unique unit called Sniper Team Reaper 2. She grew up with firearms, and she's a deadly shot. She never gets flustered."

Anthony went on to describe Allison's deployment to Afghanistan in the waning months of the U.S. presence there, and that her job was to oversee units of Marines and to take out any threats to them.

"Her closest friend in the Corps was a female soldier named Brittany Newsome, who happened to be from Laramie, just down the road," Anthony said. "They entered basic together, and those two were like this," he said, crossing the first two fingers of his right hand. "Lance Corporal Brittany Newsome. She was a beauty both inside and out, just like our Allison. Both of them were in Kabul during the debacle of our sudden withdrawal from Afghanistan.

"Then we come to August 26, 2021," Anthony intoned. "Abbey Gate at the Kabul Airport."

The dramatic way he said it made Nate think the man had told the same story over and over.

Anthony said, "Allison was in a tower overlooking the chaos below as hundreds of Afghans were rushing the entrance gate, trying to get to the American aircraft landing at the airport to evacuate our people, as well as the few privileged Afghan nationals who had received permission from us to leave. It was a nightmare of bodies—entire families—pleading with Marines guarding the gate to let them through. You've seen the photos, I'm sure. Afghan mothers handing their babies to twenty-one-year-old Marines, people trampling old men and women underfoot—it was a clusterfuck, a total disaster."

"It made me sick," Geronimo said. "It made me ashamed."

"You're not the only one," Anthony said. "All of the Marines there that day felt the same way you did, believe me. They didn't enlist in the U.S. military to be tasked with the job of *preventing* innocent civilians from escaping certain death. A lot of those people trying to get out were our longtime friends, and they'd worked by our side for years. It was horrible the way we turned our backs on them.

"Anyway, Brittany was on the ground with her unit keeping those Afghans from accessing the airstrip. Those were her orders from Washington, from people who weren't even there. Allison was up above her, in agony, trying to keep an eye on her friend and her fellow Marines."

"That's the day when a suicide bomber got through and killed thirteen Marines," Geronimo said.

"It is," Anthony said. "Thirteen brave Americans. Including Brittany Newsome."

"Allison saw it happen," Jolene added.

Nate grunted and looked away.

"That's only the half of it," Anthony said. "Most people don't know the whole story of that day. Too many people, especially our so-called leaders, *never* want to hear it."

"Go on," Geronimo said.

"Two days before the terrorist attack, Allison's unit received intel that they should prepare for an ISIS suicide bomber to show up at Abbey Gate. The intel specifically said for them to be on the lookout for a bomber posing as a cameraman arriving by motorcycle," Anthony said, his voice rising. "Another intel report gave a detailed physical description of the suicide bomber. It even said the terrorist would be carrying a backpack with three yellow arrows embroidered on the material. I mean, this intel was *really* specific.

"And in the early evening of August 26, Allison spotted the terrorist approaching the crowd. She wasn't the only one. Two other Marine snipers saw the guy who matched the description getting closer and closer to the people and Marines below them. He stuck out like a sore thumb. He appeared nervous and jumpy, and he wore a backpack with three yellow arrows on it.

"The rules of engagement that came from Washington were ridiculous," Anthony said with disgust. "The rules of engagement didn't allow well-trained Marines to be Marines. They couldn't do anything without specific approval from the thumb-suckers inside the White House. Allison literally had this guy in her cross hairs as he entered the crowd. And when she asked for permission to take him out, you know what they said?"

"What?" Geronimo asked.

"They said, 'Do not engage.'"

He let that sit there for a moment. Then Anthony widened his eyes and repeated, "*Do not engage.*

"So she asked again," Anthony continued. "By now, she was starting to panic. The terrorist was walking straight toward the line of Marines at the gate, including Brittany. But Allison got no reply this time. Since the only thing she had been told was 'Do not engage,' there was nothing she could do. Then you know what happened next," Anthony said.

"We find out later that the bomber was well known to us. He was a prisoner at the Bagram Airfield that had been built and run by the U.S. military until the weenies in Washington ordered them to evacuate it and leave all of the weapons and equipment to the bad guys. The terrorist just walked out when the Taliban took it over. And within days, he strapped on that suicide vest and blew it up at Abbey Gate, killing thirteen of our finest Marines."

"It was not something Allison could shake off," Jolene said. "When she came home, she was a different person than she was when she deployed. Allison felt responsible for Brittany's death, as well as for the deaths of the other twelve Marines. She was bitter and despondent, as you can imagine. She railed against her superiors, the administration, and even the Corps itself."

"It broke my heart," Anthony said as his eyes suddenly filled with tears. He swiped them away with the back of his hand. "Allison was warned not to go public with what actually took place because the higher-ups were embarrassed. They'd let the future suicide bomber walk out of prison. And none of the officials who let it happen have been made accountable. Unlike Allison, they feel no shame or guilt. No one lost their jobs, much less ended up in prison, where they belong. And all of them are too cowardly to resign."

"That's where Axel Soledad comes in," Nate said. He'd been so quiet that his voice seemed to startle Jolene.

"That's where Soledad comes in," Anthony intoned. "They met in town at the Buckhorn Bar. Allison was spending too much time there, and Soledad apparently sought her out. He was a shoulder to cry on, and he hated the military elites for his own reasons. Allison got sucked into his orbit very quickly, and you must believe me when I tell you that wasn't typical of our girl. It was like Soledad cast a spell on her."

"It's like she joined a cult," Jolene said sadly. "She did whatever he said. And then she was gone. They were *both* gone."

"To where?" Geronimo asked.

They didn't know, and Allison had contacted them by cell phone only once in the last two months. When she did, she said she was fine. In fact, she sounded calm and purposeful, just like the old Allison, Jolene said.

"But she didn't mention where she was?" Geronimo asked.

"She said she'd tell us everything one of these days," Jolene said. "But that she couldn't tell us now."

Anthony said that because he had a buddy in the Albany County Sheriff's Office, they were able to make an official request to the phone companies to determine the location of Allison's call. It was illegal to do so, because Allison wasn't suspected of a crime and she'd left Tie Siding voluntarily, but that didn't bother his buddy, he said. Marines did favors for other Marines.

"And where was she calling from?" Geronimo asked.

"Warm Springs," Jolene said.

"That's over the top of the Snowy Range to the west," Anthony said, pointing vaguely in that direction.

"I know where it is," Nate said to Geronimo.

"Not that we could find her there," Jolene said. "We've been over there a dozen times in the last two months. We've asked people there about her, and we passed out her photo. No one knows her."

"We're guessing she called as she passed through Warm Springs on her way to someplace else," Anthony said. "And since that call, she turned her phone off for good. My buddy says she hasn't used it in over sixty days, so we can't track her."

"She's with Soledad," Jolene said as her eyes filled with tears. "I'm worried about her. There's something creepy about that man."

Both Geronimo and Nate nodded in agreement.

"Please find her," Jolene pleaded to them.

"We'll do what we can," Geronimo said. "But she's a grown woman. If she doesn't want to come back with us, we can't force her."

"Sure we can," Nate said.

ON THEIR WAY back to the state highway, Geronimo whistled and said, "Man, I feel for those people. I really do. And it pisses me off all over again to hear what we did over there."

"Agreed," Nate said.

"This has gotten very complicated."

"It has," Nate said. "But we don't need to let that distract us. Our target hasn't changed. Our mission hasn't changed."

"I feel like we're getting closer," Geronimo said, thumping the steering wheel with the heel of his hand for emphasis. "We've finally got a legitimate lead on Soledad."

After they'd cleared the trees, the gravel road rose sharply up a hill. As they neared the top, Nate shot his hand out and clamped hard on Geronimo's arm.

"Stop," Nate hissed.

"What?"

"Stop. Back up. *Now.*"

Geronimo did so.

Nate said, "I just got a glimpse of them, but there are two ve-hicles down below on the flat on either side of the road, pointing in our direction. Two SUVs that weren't there when we drove in. They look like they're waiting for us to come down the mountain."

"An ambush?" Geronimo asked. "How did they know we'd be here?" Then: "Did that lawyer screw us?"

"I don't think it was her," Nate said. "I didn't get that vibe from her at all."

"The Anthonys?"

"No way."

"So what are we going to do?" Geronimo asked. "I don't know how we can get to the highway without driving right by them."

Nate's mouth spread in a cruel grin. "As my friend Joe Pickett would say, things are about to get Western."

FIVE MINUTES LATER, Nate returned to the Suburban after crawl-ing to the top of the rise to scope out the situation a half mile below them to the east. As he walked back to the vehicle, he placed the pair of binoculars into their chest harness and zipped his fa-tigue jacket over it.

"They haven't moved," he said to Geronimo while he opened the passenger door. Then he instinctively checked to make sure all five cylinders of his .454 were loaded. "I'm pretty sure they didn't see us when we drove to the top and backed away. If they had, they would either have retreated to a better position or chased us. No, they're still waiting for us down there."

"How many subjects?" Geronimo asked. In Nate's absence, he had reloaded his combat shotgun with alternating rounds of buckshot and slugs. Buckshot for human targets, slugs for disabling vehicles.

"Two men in the vehicle on the right, one in the SUV on the left."

"Armed?"

"Too far away to confirm. But I think we should proceed as if they are."

"Gotcha," Geronimo said. "So what's the plan?"

Nate said, "We can't communicate, so we go old-school. Give me twenty-five minutes. That ought to give me enough time to get into position. If something goes wrong, like they see me coming, you'll hear shots. If that happens, drive down that hill like your hair is on fire."

"Copy that," Geronimo said. Then he extended his huge right fist. "*Yarak.*"

Nate fist-bumped Geronimo in silence.

"Say it," Geronimo insisted.

"*Yarak,*" Nate said.

NATE'S ROUTE TO the prairie floor was circuitous and tough going. He cut into the heavy pine forest to his right and waded through and over downed timber as he traversed the mountainside. It was tangled and dark in the trees, and the forest floor was littered with deer and elk scat. The smell of elk was pungent, and he kept an eye out for them. As he entered a shadowed alcove, a covey of pine grouse broke noisily from the cover and slashed through the low-hanging branches and he reached for his weapon in response. Following the grouse, he heard the heavy footfalls of a small herd of elk out ahead of him and saw brown and tan flashes of fur through the tightly spaced pine trunks. Then it was silent. After a few breaths, Nate continued.

He'd observed through his binoculars that a dry wash ran through the sagebrush from the side of the mountain they were on through the valley floor and beyond. The SUVs were parked on either side of the gravel road ahead of a culvert that accommodated the wash. Nate's plan was to slip down the side of the mountain, using the heavy trees as cover, then duck into the wash and continue down it to the vehicles. The wash appeared to be deep enough—a jagged slash cut into the alkaline terrain by decades of flash floods—that he could approach the vehicles without being seen.

Nate was puzzled why the two vehicles had parked out in the open. It wasn't the most optimal ambush location. In fact, the best place to get the drop on Geronimo and Nate would have been just on the other side of the rise in the road. That way, they could have parked in the trees without being seen until the Suburban cleared the top of the hill.

Which meant to Nate that the subjects were either amateurs—or professionals with a plan too clever for him to fathom at the moment.

Or, he thought with a grimace, the subjects on the road below them were civilians doing something that had nothing at all to do with Nate, Geronimo, or the Anthonys. Maybe a drug deal was going down. Or something completely innocent. If so, Nate could signal Geronimo to stand down as he approached.

He glanced at his wristwatch. He'd been away from Geronimo's Suburban for seventeen minutes. He had eight minutes to move up the ditch and take a position with a clear view of the targets and cover to hide behind. Nate picked up his pace.

NATE KEPT LOW in the wash, scuttling through it without raising his head. There was no need. He knew where the SUVs were, and if he stood up and looked, they'd see him coming.

His thighs began to burn and his back ached as he pushed down the draw in a crabwalk. He noted mountain lion tracks in the soft sand of the wash, as well as rabbit pellets. Nate felt more than saw how close he'd gotten to the vehicles, and he dropped to his knees and bent forward to stay low. He grasped the grip of his .454 in the shoulder holster with his right hand and eased it out. Then he waited for less than a minute before he heard Geronimo's Suburban approach.

He kept his head down.

Not until the roar of Geronimo's engine was less than thirty yards away did Nate rise into a shooting stance with his weapon out in front of him. As he raised the .454, he thumbed back the hammer at the same time.

It all happened quickly, and he let his killer instincts—his sense of *yarak*—take over.

The two men in the vehicle closest to him scrambled out of the SUV, holding semiautomatic rifles. One of them yelled to the driver of the other vehicle to get out and arm up.

Nate observed in a second that the three subjects looked to be unfamiliar with their weapons, and one of them had banged the barrel of his rifle against the doorframe as he leapt out. Their actions ranged from the sheer panic of the driver of the nearest SUV, to what appeared to be frozen terror taking over the driver of the other vehicle, who stood motionless in the middle of the road with his rifle at his side as Geronimo sped toward them. The three of them looked young and hip and out of place, which was a surprise to Nate. The passenger of the nearest SUV sported a man bun and unseasonable river sandals over bare feet. He nervously bounced up and down while reaching to chamber a round in his weapon. None of the three had glanced over to the side to see Nate twenty feet away with his weapon aimed at them.

To be sure, Nate waited until the second driver unfroze, racked the slide of his rifle, and fired two quick shots in the general direction of the oncoming Suburban. One of the bullets smacked the windshield, leaving a white star-shaped impact on the darkened glass.

As soon as the shots were fired, Nate proceeded, because he was now sure of their intent.

BOOM. The second driver did a sideways flip when the round hit him in the left side of his neck.

BOOM. The passenger of the first vehicle turned his head toward the sound of the shot and never saw the bullet coming. He dropped away like a wet sock.

BOOM. The driver of the first SUV thought he could scramble and take cover on the other side of his vehicle, not realizing that the .454 round aimed at him would penetrate both the driver's-side *and* the passenger door before blasting through his heart.

Two seconds later, Geronimo's Suburban shot through the space between the two vehicles, and the right tires thumped over the dead body of the sprawled-out passenger. The Suburban came to a skidding halt twenty-five feet farther out, near the culvert.

Geronimo leaned over inside the cab and pushed open the passenger door. Nate holstered his revolver as he climbed back in. "Let's go," he said.

"Who were those guys?" Geronimo asked with amazement.

"Amateurs," Nate said. "Two of 'em didn't know which end of the rifle to point at you."

"How does that make sense?"

"It doesn't," Nate said. "They looked more like unemployed graduate students than people Axel would recruit."

He turned and checked out the license plates of the two vehicles before he could no longer see them. "Colorado and New Mexico," Nate said. "Not locals."

"Well, how are we going to find out who they are?" Geronimo asked, then corrected himself to say, "*Were*."

"We can't," Nate said. "We left three bodies in the middle of a public road in broad daylight. We can't stick around to check IDs." Then: "How did our birds fare?"

"No injuries, thanks to the bulletproof glass. That includes me, by the way."

Geronimo gestured toward the west at the Snowy Range mountains that stretched across the horizon.

"On to Warm Springs?" he asked.

"Not yet," Nate said. "We've got to make another stop first."

B-Lazy-U Ranch Interlude

The Guests

THE NEW WAITRESS approached the server station at the side of the bar in the saloon and told the bartender, "Dirty gin martini, up, Hendrick's; a glass of chardonnay; a double Maker's Mark on the rocks with water on the side; and a vodka soda with a lime."

When the bartender raised his eyebrows she quickly added, "Tito's." With that, the bartender shot her a thumbs-up and slid down the bar to start the cocktails.

The din in the room was rising in volume as Centurions and their spouses arrived for the opening cocktail reception. Most of the men were in their sixties or seventies, she guessed, with a few young fit men with short haircuts and earnest faces among them, listening intently to what the older men said. The wives generally split from their spouses after ordering drinks, and they quickly found each other. Their conversations were largely about which activities they'd signed up for in the coming days and if the fall weather would hold up enough for them to ride horses, fly-fish, do goat yoga, or hike.

The new waitress wore her uniform, along with a red bandanna to keep her hair in place. The jeans she'd been assigned were so tight they felt painted on, which she assumed was the idea.

Most of the guests wore Western clothing as well, or at least their interpretation of it: jeans, belts with silver buckles, cowboy boots, and all manner of cowboy hats. The mood was energetic and a little raucous as Centurions greeted their colleagues and fellow members they hadn't seen since the last Centurions Week at the B-Lazy-U.

The new waitress marveled at the genuine enthusiasm the guests showed when they encountered Peaches Tyrell, who was also taking cocktail orders.

"Oh my God, it's Peaches!" one of the women cried out. "How are you doing, girl?"

Peaches, to her credit, greeted every guest by name and never stopped smiling. The new waitress was stunned by Peaches's effortless recall and hospitality.

THE NEW WAITRESS stepped to the side to let Peaches approach the bar and call out drink orders to the bartender.

"Everyone knows you," the new waitress said.

"This is my fortieth year serving the Centurions," Peaches said. "A few of 'em have been here every year, but there are always a couple of new faces and names to learn."

"Are all the Centurions men?"

"Almost all. They let a lady general in a few years ago and some defense industry biggie, but I think they felt they had to. But yes, the rest of them are men. I don't judge—that's not my job."

"You're kind of amazing."

Peaches shrugged. "Not really. This is much easier than it was when I started with this group. This is a walk in the park."

"Meaning . . ."

"It used to be different. Wilder. A lot of the guys didn't bring their wives then, and I was a lot younger and curvier. Some of those boys got a little handsy, and a few of them thought my job included cabin visits after the saloon closed down."

She spoke with a half smile that belied what she was saying.

"And it used to be that, on the weekends, the ranch organized a ladies' spa day in Warm Springs. They'd load up a bus and take the women to town. No sooner had the wives left, then a couple of vans from Steamboat and Rock Springs would show up filled with young women. I can't call them 'ladies,' unless I call 'em 'ladies of the night.' They'd clear them out before the wives got back in the evening."

The new waitress raised her eyebrows.

"That got shut down thirty years ago," Peaches said. "Now it's a lot more civilized."

"Interesting."

"You do know who these people are, don't you?" Peaches asked.

"The Centurions?"

"The people in this room," Peaches said. "Over there's the secretary of defense, surrounded by his lackeys. He won't go near the head of the Joint Chiefs over there in the corner, because I guess they really don't like each other. I can't keep a lot of their titles straight, to be honest. 'Undersecretary of this or that,' 'special assistant to the blah-blah-blah.' It'll drive you crazy. Plus, their titles change from year to year. One year, they'll be a senator, and the next year they'll be the CEO of a lobbying outfit on behalf of a defense contractor. Or the other way around. It's musical chairs out in D.C., and you'd need a scorecard to keep track of their official titles from year to year. What I've learned is that presidents and administrations change, but most of this group stays the same . . . Luckily for me. Otherwise, I'd never remember their names."

"Point out the secretary of defense to me again," the new waitress asked. Peaches chinned toward a large man with steel-gray hair and a hangdog expression. She did it without being obvious.

"And the head of the Joint Chiefs?"

Peaches pretended to be surveying the room for new arrivals. Her eyes lingered on a stout, fireplug-like man with coiffed hair and a booming voice. The new waitress followed Peaches's gaze and she recognized him.

"I've seen him standing next to the president on television," she said. "In fact, the last couple of presidents."

"Now that he's announced his retirement, I hear that he's headed to Boeing or Raytheon," Peaches said. "I heard a couple of the guys talking about that tonight."

"It really *is* musical chairs," the new waitress said.

"And we're bound to hear all kinds of national security secrets," Peaches said. "If you care about those kinds of things, which I don't. A lot of people would like to be a fly on the wall here during this week, but they can't get in.

"But, oh, how these guys love to come out here," she enthused. "Once a year, they can drop all their titles and take off their ties and hang out with their buddies. Not all of the wives get along, though. Some of those women are more competitive than their husbands."

THE DRINKS ARRIVED and both the new waitress and Peaches delivered them and took new orders. They reconvened at the bar a few minutes later. The new waitress blew a strand of hair from her face and tried to catch her breath.

"Wait until orientation night," Peaches said. "Then you'll really witness something you've never seen before, I can guarantee you that."

"Orientation night?"

"Every year, the Centurions vote in new folks to replace the members who died in the past year. These guys don't really retire, but if they're too feeble to fly out here, they're given some kind of special award and eased out. There are always exactly two hundred and fifty Centurions, and the list is pretty long to get in, I guess."

"So what happens on orientation night?" the new waitress asked.

"It's crazy," Peaches said, grinning and shaking her head with awe. "It all takes place out on the ranch grounds. We set up luminary candles all over the grass and turn all the electric lights off. All the Centurions and their significant others sit on lawn chairs or blankets in the dark. Then there's a big ceremony where the new Centurions march down the mountain holding torches until they arrive on a stage. The new members have to dress in Roman armor and such, and they have to kneel on the stage so the Imperial Legate and the Legion Legate can touch them on each shoulder with swords and swear them in as official Centurions for life."

"The *what?*"

Peaches arched her eyebrows and closed her eyes for a moment to recall the details of what she was about to say. "The *Legatus Augusti pro praetore* and the *Legatus Legionis* are the big cheeses of the Centurions. I learned those words quite a few years ago when I asked. All of the members come up through the ranks. There are broad-band tribunes, and camp prefects, and narrow-band tribunes, and other ranks I can't remember. They're structured like a real Roman army, I guess. It's all pretty wild."

"It sure is," the new waitress said. "I can't wait to see it. I can't believe this thing is a secret from the public and that nobody has ever heard of it."

"You signed an NDA, right?" Peaches asked.

"Yes."

"Then they'll let you on the grounds. Otherwise, they wouldn't let you even get close. But someone has to serve drinks, right? *We're* pretty important, too," Peaches said with a wink.

THE NEW WAITRESS laughed at that.

The bartender filled their trays with orders. Peaches had so many drinks to deliver that balancing her tray required a deft hoisting maneuver. As she turned to deliver her orders, she shot a quick glance over her shoulder to the new waitress.

"You forgot your name tag," Peaches said.

"Oh, damn," the new waitress said. She reached into the back pocket of her jeans and found the badge she'd been given that morning and pinned it above the right pocket of her Western shirt.

"Don't forget again, 'Allison from Wyoming,'" Peaches said with a warm smile. "These folks love to ask about where you're from. It breaks the ice."

Allison smiled to herself and thought, *That's not all that's going to be broken here.*

CHAPTER THIRTEEN

MARYBETH PICKETT WAS behind the desk in her office at the Twelve Sleep County Library when she looked up and saw the shadows of two broad-shouldered men through the upper pane of smoked glass in her door. She was in the midst of finalizing the annual budget for the facility after the county commissioners had once again slashed her request by fifteen percent.

The adjustment was not as painful as it'd once been, she reassured herself, because over the years she'd learned to pad the request by twenty to thirty percent so the inevitable cut wouldn't be debilitating. She hated that she had become such a bureaucrat since she'd been named director of the library, but the commissioners had all but forced her into it. Especially the hardcore retired feedstore owner, who asked her out loud, "Why in the hell do we fund a library when we have the internet?"

Kestrel was playing quietly with books and toys directly behind Marybeth in the corner of the office. She'd just gotten up from a nap, and it took the toddler a while to fully wake up. That in-between time was always a wonderful period to be with and around the child, and it was when Kestrel's innate sweetness showed through.

A man's voice said, "Knock-knock" as he rapped on the door and then opened it.

Sheriff Jackson Bishop stuck his head in and grinned at Mary-beth like a Hollywood leading man. He wore a crisp silver cowboy hat and his blue eyes twinkled.

"Can I bother you for a few minutes?" he asked.

Before she could answer, he fully opened the door and entered. There was another man behind him she didn't recognize. The man was older, in his sixties, and he had a kindly, scholarly air about him. He wore a trench coat, which was very unusual attire in Saddlestring.

"Come on in," she said. "I'm working on our budget."

"I figured you might be," Bishop said as he removed his hat and gracefully sat down in one of the hardback chairs facing Mary-beth. "They gave you a haircut the other night at the commission-ers' meeting."

What he didn't need to say was that the sheriff's department budget had sailed through the proceedings with no cuts at all. In fact, the retired feedstore owner had proposed a fifteen percent increase overall, citing potential threats to the community from illegal migrants, who had yet to arrive.

Sheriff Bishop placed his hat on his lap, and Marybeth noted that he didn't do it crown-down as Joe would have insisted on.

"This is Special Agent Rick Orr of the FBI," Bishop said, glanc-ing toward the man who loomed over his shoulder. "He came by the office today and asked a bunch of questions, only a few of which I could answer. But I told him you might be able to help him out."

"I guess that depends on what the questions are."

"The inquiry I'm working on involves Nate Romanowski and a man named Axel Soledad," Orr said, breaking in. Then he removed a card from his breast pocket and slid it across the desk toward her. His address was Langley, Virginia.

Marybeth was intrigued, and she waved to the empty chair next to the sheriff for Orr. He sat down.

"You're a long way from home," she said.

"I rarely travel out west," he replied. "It's . . . interesting."

She wasn't sure what that meant.

"It's no secret that Nate has been a friend of our family for years," she said while feeling her defenses go up. "I haven't seen Nate for nearly a year, though. I'm not sure I can help you."

Every word of it was true.

"My understanding is that your husband is away at the moment," Orr said. "I'd like to ask the same questions of him."

Marybeth was familiar with several of Joe's interactions with federal agents in the past and she knew not to say too much, and certainly not to lie when giving her answers. Some unscrupulous feds loved to go after civilians for violating a federal statute known as 18 U.S.C. 1001, which criminalized false statements or concealing anything from a federal investigator. The statute could also be twisted to include memory lapses or misstating dates or timelines. A number of FBI agents didn't record their conversations with subjects, so it would be their word against hers in court if it ever came to that.

She knew nothing about Special Agent Rick Orr, but his

demeanor suggested he wasn't out to entrap her. Still, she sat up straight and resolved to be careful with her responses.

"I can give you his cell phone number," she said, "but Joe will tell you the same thing. Nate has been off the grid for months. We're watching his child for him until he returns."

"That would be little Kestrel," Sheriff Bishop said, rising in his chair so he could get a good look at her.

Marybeth felt the hairs go up on the back of her neck. Something about the way Bishop looked at Kestrel set off alarm bells. The reaction was entirely instinctual, and unexpected.

"What about Axel Soledad?" Orr asked, oblivious to what was going on.

Marybeth turned to him. "I've heard the name, of course," she said. "My understanding is he was working with Dallas Cates to go after Joe and Nate, as well as our local judge and the ex–county prosecutor. But I never laid eyes on him, and I know very little about him. Why are you asking about Nate and Soledad?"

Orr's eyes twinkled as he said, "I'm sorry. I really can't comment on an ongoing investigation. I just want to assure you that neither you nor your husband are suspects at the moment."

"Well," she said icily, "that's nice to know. Especially since Joe is in law enforcement and he takes his job very seriously. And, as you can see, I'm the director of the county library."

"I'm well aware of both of those facts," Orr said.

"So she lives with you?" Bishop said, once again back to Kestrel. "And you bring her to work with you every day?"

Marybeth turned to the sheriff and studied him for a moment. She was unsure why Bishop's sole interest seemed to be aimed at

Kestrel. He was apparently uninterested in Orr's line of questioning, or her answers.

She said, "We changed our staffing policy during the pandemic to allow employees with children to bring them to work, as long as they didn't interfere with their jobs. The same applies to me."

"Don't trust day care, huh?" Bishop asked.

"If you weren't aware of it, Sheriff, our day care center in town has a waiting list."

"Interesting," Bishop said. "I didn't know that. I don't have kids myself."

"Obviously," Marybeth responded with ice in her tone.

"I'm sorry to interrupt your conversation about day care," Orr said, "but I just have a couple more questions for Mrs. Pickett."

Bishop looked over at him and waited for Orr to proceed. Marybeth was grateful, even though she had to be prepared for whatever was coming.

"Another name has come up in regard to my inquiry," Orr said. "His name is Geronimo Jones. We know he lived outside of Denver, but his residence burned down in a suspicious fire and he hasn't been on-site for weeks. Neither has his wife or child."

"What about him?" Marybeth asked.

"Have you spoken to him recently?"

"No, I haven't spoken to him." *Sheridan has*, Marybeth thought.

Orr studied her demeanor while she spoke, and Marybeth felt her cheeks flush slightly. The man was a professional and he knew she was withholding something. He stared at her in silence for a long thirty seconds.

"I believe he spoke with my daughter," Marybeth said. "He, like you, was looking for Nate."

Orr's expression softened. He believed her, and what could have become an issue between them was apparently resolved to his satisfaction. For now.

"Did he find him?" Orr asked.

"I honestly don't know," Marybeth said.

"Would Sheridan know?"

"I can't answer that," Marybeth said.

"Perhaps you can give me your oldest daughter's contact information as well," Orr said. "Again, none of you are suspects. I would just like to talk to her."

Marybeth looked away for a moment. She felt trapped, and she wasn't sure why. Then she leaned forward on the desktop toward Orr.

"I don't know what you hoped to accomplish here today, but I think we're done talking without my lawyer present," she said. "You're the FBI and you have access to the most intrusive databases in the free world. You have Joe's number, and you probably know exactly where he is at the moment. And you have Sheridan's contact details, even though you pretend you don't. I know this because I never said her name or mentioned that she was our oldest."

At that, Orr chuckled as if to say, *Touché*. Then: "I understand you might know a little about accessing law enforcement databases."

"I've assisted my husband with several cases over the years," she responded.

"You're probably planning to do a deep dive on the name

'Richard Orr, Special Agent' the minute we leave your office," Orr said with a twinkle in his eye.

"You read my mind," Marybeth said.

After a long, tense pause while Marybeth and Orr eyed each other, Bishop cleared his throat and said, "So, are we done here?"

"Yes, you are," she said.

"I believe we are for the time being anyway," Orr agreed. He pushed himself to his feet and held out his hand to Marybeth.

"It was a pleasure to meet you," he said. "Give my regards to your husband and Sheridan."

She shook his hand limply. It was cool to the touch.

"I guess I'll see you at the next commissioners' meeting," Bishop said to Marybeth as he fitted his hat back on his head.

"Probably so," Marybeth said, not looking forward to it.

"By the way, where is Joe right now? I haven't seen his truck around the last couple of days."

Marybeth said he was out of town, but she didn't say why.

"He's out of his district?" Bishop asked. "In the middle of hunting season?"

"The governor asked him to do something in southern Wyoming, near Warm Springs," she said. "He should be back soon."

"Take care of that little sweetheart," Bishop said as he nodded toward Kestrel.

Marybeth didn't reply.

TWO MINUTES AFTER Orr and Bishop had left and closed the door, Marybeth's breathing returned to normal. She knew she was probably more shaken than she should be, but she also trusted her instincts. Orr had been playing games with her, but he hadn't revealed what they were. And Bishop's unhealthy interest in Kestrel Romanowski's circumstances unnerved her.

Quickly, she called Sheridan on her cell phone.

"Yes, Mom," her daughter answered. Her tone was dutiful, but not overly enthusiastic.

"Sheriff Bishop and an FBI agent from headquarters named Rick Orr were just in my office. Orr asked questions about Nate, Geronimo, and your dad. Orr is aware that you talked to Geronimo."

"Well, I did," Sheridan said.

"I know that. But Orr is up to something and I don't know what. I'm pretty sure you'll hear from him soon. If you do, I want to give you some advice."

"Okay," she said warily.

"Tell him the truth, but no more. Don't speculate about Nate's whereabouts, or Geronimo's. Don't give him any reason to come back at you later, claiming you misled him or lied. Answer like you're on the witness stand: yes, no, or I don't know. Got that?"

"Got it."

"Good. Now I've got to let your dad know."

"You said Bishop was there as well?" Sheridan asked.

"Yes."

"What did *he* want?"

"I'm not really sure," Marybeth said. "I think he was here to make the introduction, but he seemed most interested in Kestrel. And where you were."

"Did you tell him?"

"Not really. He knows where you work."

"Why does he care?"

"I don't know, other than he thinks anything that goes on around here is his business," Marybeth said.

"I don't trust that man," Sheridan said. "He's creepy."

"Let's talk more about that. What are you doing tonight?"

"No plans at the moment."

"Come over for dinner."

Sheridan hesitated a moment. "I can do that." Then: "What's going on, Mom?"

"I'm not sure, and of course your dad is out of town. But please bring a change of clothes, just in case you decide to stay over. I could really use some company, and we can talk about Sheriff Bishop."

"I'll see you after work."

"Thank you," Marybeth said. "I'd appreciate that."

SHE PUNCHED OFF and speed-dialed Joe's number. He answered immediately, but his voice was hushed.

"I'm in a meeting," he said. "I'll call you right back." Then he disconnected.

Frustrated at her husband and still awash from the strange conversations with Bishop, Orr, and Sheridan, she gathered up Kestrel and plopped her on her lap. Kestrel loved to sit there and watch what happened on the computer monitor, hoping Marybeth would open up a video application that featured *Peppa Pig* and *Bluey*.

Instead, Marybeth reached around the child to her keyboard and called up the first of many search engines she planned to access in the next few minutes while waiting for Joe's return call.

She keyed in: RICHARD ORR SPECIAL AGENT FBI LANGLEY VIRGINIA.

CHAPTER FOURTEEN

JOE SAID, "I'LL call you right back," and slipped his cell phone into his uniform dress pocket.

"Sorry about that," he said to Sheriff Regan Haswell, who sat behind his desk with a bemused expression on his face. "That was my wife."

"Gotcha," Haswell said. "I used to have one of those."

Susan Kany bristled at the remark and squirmed a bit in her chair.

The Warm Springs branch of the Carbon County Sheriff's Department was located on East Springs Street with its back facing a public parking lot and the rear of the Hotel Wolf. Haswell apparently rotated between his county office in Rawlins and the branch in Warm Springs, according to the receptionist out front. It was fortuitous that they'd caught him at the right time.

Haswell was thin and dark and had a trim mustache and probing brown eyes. He wore jeans, boots, and a beige and brown uniform shirt with a bolo tie festooned with ivory elk teeth. He was younger than Joe had imagined him to be, maybe midforties.

These days, Joe thought, most people he dealt with were younger than he was. He still wasn't used to it.

The sheriff had nodded a greeting to Kany when the two of them entered his office, and Kany had acknowledged him back. Kany had told Joe on the way down from Rankin's camp that she didn't think the sheriff respected her authority yet, and he didn't seem to place a high priority on the cases she brought forward to his office. She attributed that to the fact that Haswell was tight with a group of similarly aged men, longtime locals who treated Game and Fish regulations as recommendations instead of statutes. They camped together while elk-hunting and drank together at the Rustic Bar and the Wet Fly Saloon at the outskirts of town.

"So, Joe Pickett," Haswell said, "what can I do you for?"

The man pointedly ignored Kany's presence in the room, which substantiated her theory, Joe thought.

"We're trying to locate an outfitter and his employee," Joe said. "The outfitter is named Spike Rankin."

"I know Rankin," Haswell said. "He's a hard case, but a good guy. He has a fine reputation around here. He seems pretty by the book to me, but you might know otherwise. What do you think he's done wrong?"

"Nothing that we know of," Joe said. "But he's missing from his camp, along with his apprentice."

Joe gave a quick briefing of their visit to Rankin's camp, as well as the arrival of the North Carolina hunters.

When he was through, Haswell cocked his head and eyed Joe suspiciously.

Haswell said, "It was good of you two to suggest that those

out-of-state hunters spend some time and money in our fair county. We appreciate that, and I appreciate the tax dollars."

"You can thank Susan," Joe said.

Haswell narrowed his eyes and leaned forward in his chair. "So are you telling me that two game wardens are spending their time looking for a licensed outfitter in my county who hasn't done anything wrong? Is he a witness in an investigation or something?"

"Not really," Joe said. He knew that his manner wasn't placating Haswell, an experienced local cop who had obviously sniffed out Joe's obfuscation.

Kany tried to save Joe by clearing her throat and saying, "We were wondering if your office has run across his vehicle anywhere. It's a local gray 2018 Ram Power Wagon. It has extra clearance and knobby tires, and a platform for an ATV on top of the bed in back. Here, I've got the plate number . . ." She fished a notebook out of her pocket.

"I know the vehicle," Haswell said. "And we know where it is. It was called in this morning."

Both Joe and Kany looked up expectantly.

But instead of answering, Haswell looked hard at Joe. "I'm compadres with your sheriff in Twelve Sleep County, Jackson Bishop. He's a good man. We went through the academy together, and we're on the same page when it comes to law enforcement."

Joe had no idea where this was going.

"Suppose I call my buddy Jackson," Haswell said, "and tell him what you told me? Do you think he might be a little more forthcoming with what is going on here? Like why the local game warden from the Bighorns comes all the way down here out of his district to Warm Springs to visit an elk-hunting guide? Because something about that just doesn't make sense to me."

Joe sat back, caught. He said, "Spike Rankin's employee happens to be Governor Rulon's son-in-law. They're both missing. Governor Rulon asked me to look into it because we go way back."

Joe felt Kany's eyes bore into the side of his head, and Haswell grinned.

"So now we know the rest of the story," Haswell said. "Our governor doesn't want folks to know that his son-in-law is a doofus who might be in trouble. Is that it?"

"Pretty much," Joe said.

"Were you aware of this?" Haswell asked Kany.

"Not at all," she said through gritted teeth.

"Well, *that's* interesting," Haswell said, chinning toward Joe. "The governor doesn't alert state troopers, or the local sheriff, or the local game warden. Instead he sends you like some kind of secret agent man. That kind of says to me that our highest elected official doesn't have much confidence in us here in Carbon County. That almost seems like an insult."

Joe didn't respond.

"Don't you think that sounds like an insult to us both, Susan?" Haswell said.

After a beat, Kany said, "Yes."

"And Joe here didn't tell you about all of this?"

"No, he didn't."

"My, my," Haswell said, shaking his head and making a *tsk-tsk* gesture.

Joe said, "About Rankin's pickup. Where was it located?"

"Somewhere up on North French Creek Road on the way to Battle Mountain," Haswell said. "It was parked on the shoulder and nobody was around. I'd need to contact dispatch to get the exact location for you."

"Thank you," Joe said. When he finally turned his head to look at Kany, he saw that she wouldn't meet his eyes. Instead, she stared straight ahead at the sheriff. She was angry.

"I'll get that info and we'll put out a county-wide BOLO on your Spike Rankin and the doofus son-in-law," Haswell said. "What did you say his name was?"

"I didn't," Joe said. "But it's Mark Eisele."

"Mark Eisele," Haswell repeated as he jotted down the name. "Within a couple of hours, every LEO in Carbon County will be alerted. And I suppose the press will find out pretty quickly as well. Then we'll have a full-blown kerfuffle on our hands, won't we?"

"I suppose," Joe conceded.

"And the governor isn't going to like that very much, I'd guess."

"That would be correct." Then: "Can I ask you to hold up for a few hours on the BOLO until we confirm that it's Rankin's pickup on French Creek Road? There's no good reason to panic until we know for sure either way."

Haswell started to argue the point, but he apparently thought better of it.

"You're right. I'll hold off until you let me know either way."

"Thank you."

"But if it's his truck up there, this is gonna be fun."

"Maybe for you," Joe said with a sigh.

In the parking lot, Kany wheeled on Joe. "You embarrassed me in there," she said. "You embarrassed me in front of a sheriff that doesn't think much of me in the first place. What else have you withheld from me?"

"That's about it," Joe said, looking down at the top of his boots. "I'm sorry. The governor asked me to keep this all on the down-low."

"Why? So the press wouldn't find out? That makes no sense."

"No, so the First Lady and his daughter wouldn't know," Joe said. "He's a lot more scared of them than he is of the press. It's complicated."

"Are there tire tracks on my clothes from where you threw me under the bus?"

"Again, I'm sorry," Joe said. "It wasn't my intention to bushwhack you."

She stepped into Joe with her nostrils flared. "I mean, I've got other things to do, you know. Do you prefer to be on your own from here on out?"

Joe said, "I usually am," he said. "I understand how you feel. I'd feel the same way. No hard feelings."

"All these things I've heard about Joe Pickett turn out to be full of crap. I looked up to you, Joe."

He briefly looked away.

Kany glared at him with her hands on her hips while he retrieved his gear bag from the back of her pickup and turned to walk across the lot to the hotel. He could feel her eyes boring holes into his back, and he couldn't help but think that Susan Kany was a stand-in for one or all of his daughters and how *they* would feel in the same circumstances.

It hurt.

Then Kany called after him. "I'll pick you up at the hotel in an hour with the horses."

He paused and turned. "Are you sure?"

"I'm sure. I might have come on a little strong there. You were doing what the governor asked you to do, after all. I don't know what I'd do if Rulon asked me to be his personal agent. Besides, I really don't want you running around blind in my district."

"This isn't the first time he's gotten me into trouble," Joe said.

With that, Kany climbed into her pickup and eased out of the lot toward her state-owned home and corrals. Her expression as she drove away was a mixture of anger and humiliation. He felt for her.

JOE PAUSED ON the wooden front porch of the Wolf and placed a call to the governor's office. He was transferred to Ann Byrnes.

"Joe Pickett here," he said.

"And . . . ?"

"We haven't found Rankin or Mark, but we've got a lead in the case. We just found out where they were last seen and we're headed up there tonight to try to track them down."

Byrnes said, "The governor will be very happy to hear that. I'll tell him as soon as he gets off the phone with the feds."

"There's something he won't be happy to hear," Joe said.

"Oh, and what is that?" Her tone was suddenly icy.

"The cat's out of the bag," Joe said. "I've bought us a few hours, but I thought you should be prepared for the fallout."

As Joe TRUDGED up the stairs of the Hotel Wolf with his over-night duffel slung over his shoulder, he speed-dialed Marybeth. The bartender–slash–hotel clerk had assigned him the same room he'd occupied before, number nine, because it was one of the few in their inventory covered by the notoriously low state employee lodging rate.

"Sorry it took me so long to call you back," he said as he fitted in the key and pushed the door open. The room was as he remembered it: small, quaint, and clean.

"It's okay," she said. "I was a little worked up earlier, but now I'm home and Sheridan just showed up."

"Tell her hello."

Joe listened as Marybeth covered the mouthpiece and turned her head away and conveyed the message to their oldest daughter. "Same here," he heard Sheridan say.

"Tell her I met someone who knows her," Joe said.

Marybeth said, "Hold on—I'll put us all on speakerphone so I don't need to be the middleman."

After Marybeth switched to speaker and lowered the phone to the countertop, Joe said: "You go first."

He listened with growing concern as Marybeth briefed him on the visit from Special Agent Rick Orr and Sheriff Jackson Bishop.

"Rick Orr?" Joe said. "I've never heard of him."

Joe's experience with various agents from the FBI varied widely over the years. He'd liked and worked well with Chuck Coon, who had supervised the Wyoming office out of Cheyenne. And he'd clashed, sometimes seriously, with others recently who'd been sent out from Washington, D.C., or who'd showed up on their own with their own personal agendas.

The three of them discussed Orr's visit and Bishop's interest in Kestrel's circumstances. Sheridan said that Bishop "creeped her out" and that her friends thought the sheriff had a God complex. She also said she had a good impression of Susan Kany from college.

As they spoke, Joe moved to the window and pulled the lace curtain back. The room afforded a bird's-eye view of First Street. As he did, Kany's pickup appeared below with a two-horse trailer attached. It idled in front of the hotel because there wasn't enough diagonal parking on the street to accommodate the length of it.

"In fact, she's here," Joe said. "I'll call you later tonight, Marybeth. I hope to have good news and tell you that I'll be home tomorrow."

"Are you going to Battle Mountain, then?" Marybeth asked.

"That's where we'll start. That's where Rankin's truck was called in. Sheridan, I'll give Susan your best regards."

"Good," said Sheridan. "And please try not to do or say anything to embarrass me."

Joe sighed: "You're too late for that."

CHAPTER FIFTEEN

I N THE BED in the dark room, Mark Eisele painfully turned over to his right side. The restraints made it difficult, but he was able to press his weight into the old mattress firmly enough to get some slack in the nylon straps. The wound in his left butt cheek throbbed from lying on it, and it was a true relief when he was able to complete the half turn. The problem was, when he did so, the wound on his right shoulder screamed at him until he was able to adjust his upper body slightly.

It was good to know that there was a little more slack in the straps then there had been at first. Apparently, they'd stretched out a little. He doubted he could wriggle out of them like a butterfly emerging from its chrysalis, but the idea gave him a shot of hope.

The band of light under the boarded-up window was pale orange, meaning dusk was approaching. It also meant that he'd been in his medically induced coma since very early that morning, when Double-A had delivered the shot.

As Eisele slowed his breathing and relaxed his muscles to further ease the pain, he recalled what he had witnessed in a fog that morning. Two men in combat fatigues had entered the room with headlamps on and unfurled a thick plastic body bag on the floor next to his bed. One of them had asked the other, "Where we gonna take him, anyway?"

"Axel said the old meat cellar."

"Ah."

Through hooded eyes, Eisele had watched the two men lift Spike Rankin's body from his bed and lower it into the open body bag. They'd done so with ease, and Eisele had gotten a glimpse of Rankin's thin white arm hanging under him like the tail of a comma. Then one of them bent over the body bag and zipped it up.

Eisele recognized the two men from his first encounter with them on the rim of Battle Mountain. They'd been with Double-A.

ALTHOUGH HE HAD every reason to doubt the veracity of his memories at the moment, he thought he recalled overhearing several conversations through the door from the room next to his. Through his narcotic stupor, at different times during the day, he'd been slightly awakened as people gathered in groups for chit-chat and discussions. The subject matter had varied depending on who was out there.

One group of both men and women had complained about the exercises they'd been doing outside. A woman said that if she heard "Fire, move, fire, move" or "Aim like it's a pumpkin on a post" one more time, she'd lose her mind. They discussed the weaponry they'd been using, and a man had quietly explained how to switch his weapon from semi- to full-auto. Then the voices had faded, or Eisele had slipped back into unconsciousness.

Another, smaller group talked about the building they were in as once being called the Summit Hotel. Apparently, Eisele was in a room off the old lobby area. He'd heard someone start to ascend some stairs and another call out to be careful because some of the steps were rotten.

There was talk among a few men about how they had eyes on and inside the ranch. That the operation was getting close. Eisele heard the words "tomorrow night."

None of it made a lot of sense to him, but he discerned that the number of people coming into and out of the Summit Hotel lobby numbered around twelve to fifteen. There could be more outside, or in other structures, of course. Either way, it seemed like a lot of people for this operation, whatever it was. He also guessed that the people he'd heard talking belonged to distinct groups. The mixed-sex group sounded younger, and they were very talkative. The woman who'd complained about the repetitive commands up-talked in a way that made every statement sound like a question. Were they college-age?

The others were men only, and in groups of three or four at most. They spoke in low tones and came off as businesslike and serious.

Although Eisele came to no firm conclusions, he thought that the information he'd overheard could be important if he got out of there. If he could escape this chrysalis, the first thing he'd do is warn the governor.

And then ream him up one side and down the other for getting him into this situation in the first place.

WHEN A KEY turned in the door, Eisele feigned sleep. Someone entered, and he recognized the footfalls and breathing as belonging to Double-A.

He stayed still as she gently pushed him to his back again, and he felt a tightening of his upper restraint as she pulled it tight. No more rolling over for him, he thought.

He felt her warm fingers as she pulled back his shirt to examine the shoulder dressing, then tugging gently at the waist of his loose scrubs to look at the other wound. She did both moves carefully, and he felt a wave of unexpected affection. He had no idea, until that moment, how much the touch of a woman could mean to him. She probably didn't care anything about him, but it meant everything to him at the moment.

Did she know what he was feeling? he wondered. Did she know he was faking sleep?

He wanted to show her he was awake and lucid, and ask her questions, but before he opened his eyes, the room filled with another, more malevolent presence. Axel Soledad was back.

Eisele didn't move. He didn't want to speak or do anything that might provoke Soledad. Spike Rankin's display of weakness was likely what had led to his ruthless murder. Eisele didn't want to do the same. In fact, he didn't want Soledad to even notice him.

"What's going on?" Soledad asked. His tone was sharp. "What are you doing here?"

Eisele felt the beam of the headlamp move from his face as Double-A turned to greet Soledad.

"I'm on a break," she said. "It's time to give him morphine, and then I have to get back."

That seemed to placate Soledad, and his tone softened. "Is everything on track?"

"Yes. Everything is on track."

"Is anyone suspicious?"

"Not that I can tell," she said. "I got bumped up to senior server already, thanks to a woman named Peaches. I've been in the room and seen them all."

"Those bastards," Soledad said.

"It was so strange to see him in person," Double-A said. "He was not more than two feet away. I took his order and served him a couple of drinks. He's a scotch-and-soda guy. Shorter and older than he looks on television standing next to the president. Also cruder. He tried to flirt with me, even though he's here with his wife."

"I figured he was an asshole," Soledad said. "No one could be that pious in real life."

"I can confirm they're all here, just like you said."

"Of course they're all here. These criminals wouldn't miss this gathering for the world. Did the shipment arrive on time?"

"Yes. It's secure."

"So that's what they make you wear?" Soledad chuckled. "They make you dress like a sexy little cowgirl?"

Eisele couldn't help himself. He opened his eyes slightly, because he wanted to see her outfit. He'd only seen her in baggy fatigues before, but now she wore a skintight Western shirt tucked into tight blue jeans. It was worth the risk to look, he thought.

"Don't waste too much of your time on him," Soledad said

dismissively while throwing a side-eye toward Eisele. "We might need those medical supplies later."

"I don't need to change his dressings at the moment," she said. "He's healing up nicely."

"Great. We need him to be healthy and recovered when we put him in the meat locker next to his buddy."

"I can't just let him suffer," Double-A said. Eisele suddenly loved her with all of his heart.

Soledad snorted a laugh. "I don't care about that, as you know. Our mission here isn't to nurse anyone back to health."

"I know that, Axel." This time, her tone was sharp. "I'm not an idiot."

"I know you're not. I'm sorry. I have a lot on my mind right now."

Eisele kept his eyes closed and his face passive when the light from her headlamp fell back on him. He got the feeling she was looking away from Soledad more than checking on his condition.

Soledad said, "I got the word that we might have a problem."

"Oh?" she asked.

"A guy called Nate Romanowski is looking for me again," Soledad said. "He's with a big Black dude named Geronimo Jones. They're both ex-operators and falconers. Romanowski could really be a problem."

"I've heard you mention his name," she said. She was still not fully reengaged with Soledad, Eisele thought. There was a rift between them he'd been unaware of until that moment. It was obvious Double-A didn't like being addressed in the derisive manner Soledad had used at first.

"Yeah," Soledad said. "If it wasn't for the network of patriots out there I wouldn't have the intel. It seems those two paid a visit on a weak man named Reese in Montana, who told them I tried to recruit him. I'll deal with him as soon as this operation is over.

"And just today, they met with a lawyer I've had dealings with. They must have spooked her enough that she talked out of school. I'll deal with her, too."

"Are they getting close to us?" Double-A asked. There was alarm in her voice.

"I'd say they're getting warmer," Soledad said. "I sent a couple of our dipshit anarchists to take care of them this afternoon, outside of Laramie. I'd sent them there for supplies and redeployed them to intercept Romanowski and Jones."

He paused. "It didn't work out. Our dipshits got jumped. I don't know if they did any damage before they were taken out, but as you know, those idiots are pure amateurs. It's one thing to stage a student protest in the office of the dean, and another thing to intercept a couple of armed ex-operators. But they were all I had available. I wish you or a couple of your team had been there instead."

"So where are Romanowski and Jones now?" she asked.

"I don't know. Thank God we're hard to find here in Soledad City."

"Axel," Double-A said, "we can't have them screwing this up. There are too many moving parts as it is."

"I'm well aware of that. I planned this all in the first place, if you'll recall."

She went silent. Even without looking, Eisele could tell she was seething.

"But you don't have to worry," Soledad said, moving close to her and lowering his voice. Eisele imagined him putting a hand on her shoulder. "I've got a plan B. I've *always* got a contingency plan."

"Let's hope it works," Double-A said.

"Oh, it'll work. If I need to, I'll pull the trigger on it and Nate Romanowski will suddenly have much bigger things to worry about than me or us. I know how to rock his world to the core. I've done it before."

"Does it involve innocent people?"

"Don't you worry about that," Soledad assured her. "That's my concern."

Eisele heard Double-A breathe out a long sigh. Whatever Soledad's contingency plan was, she didn't want to know. Eisele did, though. He wanted to know as much as he could about these people and what was going on, in order to increase his odds to escape with his life.

What was the "operation" they were engaged in? Who were the anarchists and who was on Double-A's team? Why was it so important that they'd kill Spike Rankin and stuff his body into a meat cellar? Or keep Eisele literally in the dark in a smoky old room in an abandoned hotel?

"I think I need to get back," Double-A said to Soledad. "I don't want anyone down there to miss me."

"Give them my regards," Soledad said. "And please don't fret. Everything is falling into place just like we talked about. And you, my dear, are the key to it all."

"Thank you," she said. "But just so you know, I'm doing this for me. Not for you and your cause."

"It's all the same," he said.

He felt the sheet being pulled up and tucked under his chin as Axel Soledad left the room. Then he felt her warmth as she leaned in over him and whispered into his ear.

"You'd *better* be sleeping," she hissed. Then he heard the now-familiar sounds of her preparing the next dosage of morphine.

Within two minutes of her leaving the room, Eisele drifted back into darkness as Double-A started up her ATV outside the hotel.

CHAPTER SIXTEEN

A T THE SAME time, back in the city of Cheyenne, Geronimo Jones sat behind the wheel of his idling SUV in an alley off Randall Avenue, waiting for Nate to return. Geronimo was alert and anxious, and he kept an eye out for vehicles or movement both in front of him and via the rearview mirrors. The houses on the street were single-family homes that were older and constructed with red brick. The block was tree-lined with old cottonwoods and Austrian pines that had held up over the years despite the notorious blizzards and summer windstorms in Cheyenne. He'd seen activity in at least two of the houses as people moved past windows. One older white woman in an apron appeared to be constructing a multitiered cake.

No one entered the alley while he sat and waited, but he knew it would be only a matter of time. Time they didn't have.

They'd looked up the address for Joann Delaney on Geronimo's phone, and had parked in the alley behind her house. The posted office hours for the Tuck-Smith Law Office went from nine a.m. to four p.m., so they'd hoped she'd come straight home, alone.

They hadn't had to wait long for the receptionist to return home. She drove a blue compact Ford sedan, and both men had slunk down in their seats and watched her pull into her driveway, emerge with a white plastic sack of groceries, and go inside. Soon after, a pair of drapes were closed on a side bedroom window, followed by a light switching on in the kitchen at the back of the house. Nate had given her five minutes to put away her items and get settled inside before saying, "Keep it running. This shouldn't take long."

Which is what Geronimo was doing. He also spent the time mulling a plausible cover story just in case the Cheyenne PD descended on him because one of the residents on the block reported seeing a Black man in a military-looking type of vehicle with bullet strikes in the windshield loitering in their alley. He had yet to come up with one, especially one that explained the three hooded falcons perched behind him and the semiautomatic combat shotgun in the front seat.

To pass the time, Geronimo clicked on the dashboard radio and let it scan through local stations. There weren't many. His anxiety increased when he heard a news broadcaster for a local AM radio station announcing that authorities had been called to the scene of what was described as an "alleged gun battle at a rural location west of Tie Siding, where three fatalities have been reported."

That made him sit up and squirm in his seat. The broadcaster added that the Wyoming Highway Patrol could not yet confirm if the shootout was "gang- or drug-related" at this time.

"Stay tuned to KGAB for further updates," the announcer said, before moving on with the news about a new grizzly bear sighting in the Bighorn Mountains.

"I'll stay tuned, all right," Geronimo said aloud. If law enforcement at the scene was looking for a specific vehicle or suspects seen leaving the area, it hadn't been mentioned.

That was a relief. He and Nate hadn't seen any other vehicles in or around Tie Siding as they exited the area, and the report seemed to indicate that. Still, it was possible that every trooper in the state of Wyoming was on the lookout for a matte-black Suburban with Colorado plates.

"Come on, Nate," he whispered, looking at the back of Delaney's house. "Move it along. What are you doing in there?"

THE QUESTION WAS answered two minutes later, when Nate pushed through the back screen door of Delaney's home. He made his way across the backyard toward the alley. His shoulder holster was exposed beneath his open jacket, and he carried something small in his right hand, held down low at his side. Geronimo leaned over and opened the passenger door as Nate closed the gate behind him and slid inside the vehicle. He held something oblong and translucent in his bloody right hand, and he flipped it on top of the dashboard, where it stuck.

"Holy mother of God," Geronimo gasped. It was a human ear with a tiny diamond earring pierced through the lobe. Geronimo recalled last seeing it on Joann Delaney at her desk.

"It was Delaney who gave us up," Nate said. "She's a disciple of Axel Soledad."

"You took her ear."

"Just the one," Nate said. Then: "Let's get out of here, and don't drive like your hair's on fire. We don't want to raise any alarm bells. The interstate is just a few blocks away, so take it easy. You'll see the entrance to I-80 West right in front of us."

"Her *ear* is in my car," Geronimo cried.

"Just the one," Nate repeated.

THEY WERE ON I-80 near Lone Tree when Nate said, "She claimed she didn't know that Axel would send gunmen after us, but I'm not sure I believe her."

"Did she tell you this before or after you twisted her ear off?" Geronimo asked.

Moaning with annoyance, Nate leaned forward and grasped Joann Delaney's ear by the lobe and flipped it out the open passenger window like a discarded cigarette butt.

"Happy now?" he asked.

"Yes."

"After," Nate said. "She wasn't very cooperative before that. She could have made it a lot easier on herself, but she's a true believer— the worst kind. I didn't enjoy one second of it, but we needed the intel and she could have gotten us both killed."

"What else did she tell you when you threatened to tear off other parts of her?"

"Axel's been doing what Axel does," Nate said. "Just like we thought—he's been collecting people with grievances and molding them. Like he tried to recruit Reese in Montana and Cheryl

Tuck-Smith. Axel's got some kind of plan in place, but Delaney didn't know what it was exactly and I believe her on that."

"Who has he recruited? Did she tell you that?"

Nate indicated that she had. "He went back to the well and gathered up some of the antifa 'activist' types he used to fund and rub shoulders with, apparently. The ones who want to burn everything down—the real lunatic fringe. It seems Axel's been training them in weapons and tactics."

"That sounds like the three we ran into," Geronimo said. "But they had the weapons without the tactics."

"I think you're right. They were unfamiliar with combat of any kind, and they set themselves up to be taken down. I'm not real worried about the rest of them. But Delaney said Axel has also brought in some military vets—folks who are trained and very bitter. People like him, who want nothing more than to get revenge on the elites who sent them overseas and betrayed them."

"Like Allison Anthony," Geronimo said.

"Delaney didn't say her name outright, but she's the first person I thought of, too."

"Man, that's too bad."

"It is."

"Did Delaney know what Axel is up to? Or where he is?"

"No and yes," Nate said. "She absolutely didn't know Axel's plan, other than in broad strokes: to strike a blow against the D.C. military-industrial establishment. Delaney is in favor of that as well. She lost a son in Iraq."

"Oh," Geronimo said. "I'm sorry to hear that."

"Me too."

"But you still twisted her ear off to get intel."

"Yes," Nate said, "I did. And I'd do it again to get the info we got."

"Will she try and warn him?"

Nate took a beat before answering. "No," he said. "She doesn't want me to come back."

As they shot by the Abraham Lincoln visage that marked the highest point in the nation on I-80 (which was once known as the "Lincoln Highway") and plunged down the mountain canyon toward Laramie, Geronimo said, "On to Warm Springs?"

Nate nodded. Then: "Specifically a location called Battle Mountain. Delaney thought Axel has established a compound there to stage whatever it is he's going to do. She heard him mention it once."

"Battle Mountain," Geronimo repeated. "That sounds familiar to me."

"It does?" Nate asked.

Geronimo suddenly turned to Nate with his eyes wide as he drove.

"What?" Nate said.

"October, Warm Springs, Battle Mountain," Geronimo said. "Did she mention the name of a specific dude ranch there?"

"No. Why? Keep your eyes on the road."

Geronimo corrected his drift over to the shoulder of the road and said, "Have you ever heard of the Centurions?"

"No."

Geronimo spoke as if everything were falling into place for him.

"I had a buddy once in special ops who was assigned to them," he said. "The dude was flown to the Warm Springs airport in October to work security for a visiting four-star general at this big secret gathering of defense industry CEOs, Pentagon brass, and politicians. They call themselves the Centurions.

"My buddy said he's never seen so many private jets in one place as he saw at that little airport," Geronimo continued. "When the four-star arrived, they shipped him out to some old dude ranch in the mountains, where the Centurions have their annual gig. Dude said *everyone* was there: his boss's boss's boss. These Centurions play cowboy and have meetings to discuss who knows what. Then they all fly out together after the gig is done and come back the next year to plan the next stage in the future of the world."

"You're not kidding, are you?" Nate asked.

"I shit you not," Geronimo said. "My buddy said it kind of blew his mind."

"I'm surprised he told you anything," Nate said.

"Yeah, well, you know how it is. We're in some shithole pressure cooker overseas, and when we get sent back home for a little mission, we tend to loosen up and blow off steam. That was my buddy. He told me all this one night when we were clubbing in Tampa and he got into some potent weed he couldn't handle. Basically, what he told me that night was that if someone were to drop a bomb on the Centurions, it would wipe out most of our military-industrial complex in one big bang. The next morning, he found me and told me to never repeat what he'd said."

Nate sat back in the passenger seat and stared out the windshield with a blank expression on his face.

With a cold half grin that Geronimo couldn't decide was serious or playful, Nate said, "It might not be such a bad idea, actually."

"Nate, really," Geronimo admonished him. He thumped the steering wheel a few times with the heel of his hand and said, "I mean, *come on*."

"Think about it, though," Nate said. "You've got all these patriotic kids from good families who volunteer to serve their country. They're generally not the born-with-a-silver-spoon-in-their-mouths East Coast Ivy League types, they're the kids from here, or the South, or from some farm or ranch.

"They go through all kinds of hell in basic, but they stay with it because they believe in America and what it supposedly stands for. Then people like the Centurions ship them off to Third World countries, where they see their buddies get maimed or killed—and for what? It's not like we fight our wars to win anymore, because we don't. Instead, we quit early and bugger out, leaving a lot of dead people and betrayed allies. Then it's on to the next conflict somewhere, where we do it all over again. I can see where the anger and bitterness come from. I can see where Allison Anthony comes from."

Geronimo said, "That's the longest speech I've ever heard you make. I wish I could argue with you about it."

"We were there," Nate said. "We know what it's like to risk our lives for nothing, for a country that forgets why we were ever there in the first place. We know what it's like to accept losing, when every damned time we could have and should have won."

"Stop," Geronimo said. "You've made your point."

BATTLE MOUNTAIN

———

As THEY ENTERED the city limits of Laramie on I-80, Geronimo said, "We need to be cool around this town. I heard a report on the radio about a shootout near Tie Siding earlier today. The cops think it might be drug- or gang-related."

"What's this world coming to?" Nate asked. Then, gesturing toward an exit sign off the interstate to Wyoming State Highway 230, he said, "Take that one. There's a gun store up ahead. We need to stock up on ammo before we get to Battle Mountain."

"There's my man," Geronimo said with some relief. "We're back in the hunt."

CHAPTER SEVENTEEN

JOE AND SUSAN Kany had found Spike Rankin's pickup off an unmaintained Forest Service road in a pocket of aspen about a quarter of the way up the east side of Battle Mountain. The location had been provided by Sheriff Haswell's office, and they'd pinpointed it using the onX Hunt GPS app on Kany's phone. Kany parked short of the vehicle in a flat, grassy meadow that would allow her to turn her truck and the horse trailer around and head back without having to back up.

Joe glanced at his watch as they approached the gray Power Wagon on foot.

"We've got maybe an hour and a half of light left," he said. Kany nodded and walked shoulder to shoulder with Joe. She'd left Ginger back at her state-owned home.

Kany glanced at her phone as they walked and said, "No cell signal."

"Story of my life," Joe replied.

The early evening was cool, and shadows from the standing aspen were growing long across the meadow and making the grass look like it was overlaid with jail bars. A slight breeze rattled the dry leaves on the stand and a few fluttered down onto a carpet of yellow.

The truck was just far enough off the main Forest Service road that it couldn't be seen from it. A muddy Polaris RZR was strapped down on a platform that covered most of the bed.

"They must be on foot," Joe said. He approached the driver's side from the back of the pickup and Kany split off to look into the cab from the passenger side.

"It's unlocked," she said with surprise as she pulled the door open. Joe did the same on the driver's side and he leaned into the cab. The interior was cluttered with maps, insulated coffee mugs in their holders, blaze-orange caps and neck gaiters wadded up on the top of the dashboard, and an empty binocular case tucked in between the two front seats. The back section of the cab was piled high with clothing, boots, ropes, saddlebags, and canvas panniers. He thought it looked a lot like *his* pickup: a working office on wheels.

Joe moved out of the doorway and leaned down next to the rear tire. The key fob for the truck had been placed on top of it, just behind the bumper. It wasn't a surprise to find it, since most fishing guides and outfitters Joe knew always left the key with the vehicle to avoid the possibility of losing it or getting it damaged out in the field or in a river. That Rankin had left the truck un-locked and the key with it said to Joe that the outfitter was confi-dent no one would come by the vehicle while it sat there.

Kany ducked out of the cab and found a small soft-sided Yeti cooler in the bed of the Power Wagon. She brought it to Joe and they opened it up. It was filled with bottled water, several cans of beer, and white-bread sandwiches sealed up in a quart-sized Ziploc bag. There was a bed of partially melted ice in the bottom of the cooler.

"They didn't take their lunch," she said. "That tells me they planned to come right back to the truck."

"I agree."

"It also means they're probably within eight to ten miles from here at most, since they didn't take their horses or the ATV."

Joe nodded his agreement with that as well, then backed away from the truck to get a good view of the mountain terrain. It was vast. Battle Mountain loomed to the southwest and filled up the entire horizon. It was densely wooded, except for a few granite knuckle-like promontories that poked out of the sea of dark green. The top of the mountain was bald and already dusted with snow.

"That's a lot of country," he said. "Are there any roads on this side?"

"Not really," Kany said. "There are a few old logging roads to the south, but they're all but impossible to use. Dead trees have fallen over the tracks and the Forest Service doesn't maintain them anymore.

"I tried to go up there last spring just to get more familiar with this area," she said. "There's an old mining town up there called Summit I wanted to check out. But I gave up after a few miles because I was tired of getting out of the truck to move dead trees."

"What about the other side?" Joe asked, gesturing toward the summit.

"That's where the B-Lazy-U Ranch is located, in a valley on the other side of Battle Mountain. That's the ranch I was telling you about earlier. But as far as I know, none of the ranch roads come over the top to this side."

"It looks like good elk country," Joe said.

"It is," Kany responded. "But there's so much black timber that it's hard work to get up in there. That's why it isn't hunted all that much, even though most of it is public. I remember one guy telling me the only way to get an elk down from the top of Battle Mountain is to quarter it and pack it out on foot or horseback. Either that, or stay up there a few weeks and eat it one meal at a time."

"No wonder Rankin hunts here," Joe said. "He knows he doesn't have to share it with a bunch of local road hunters."

"True," she said. Then: "We had better saddle up before we lose our light."

KANY RODE A red roan gelding named Badger and Joe followed her on Henry, a wide-backed mule. Henry was laconic but sure-footed, and he was lazy enough that Joe constantly clicked his tongue and prompted the animal to keep going. He'd tied his field gear bag to the back of his saddle and his shotgun filled the saddle scabbard.

In the bag were items he'd assembled and collected over the years to be of use in practically any situation: extra layers of clothes, dry socks, a compact one-man tent, a compressed down sleeping bag, a first-aid kit, matches and a fire starter, a tin plate and utensils, toilet paper, insect spray, shells for his shotgun and .40 rounds for his Glock, parachute cord, a headlamp, a water purifier within a Nalgene bottle, and several MREs that he hoped he'd never have to try and eat.

They took a well-trodden game trail through the trees that meandered up the mountain. The elk and deer that used the trail chose a route that avoided overhanging branches for the most part, but Kany and Joe had to bend forward several times and dismount once to keep going.

As they rode, the forest got darker. Unseen squirrels high in the trees announced their presence by chattering relay-style up the mountain. Badger spooked a small flock of pine grouse where it got wide on the trail and the horse crow-hopped and backed up into Henry—but he didn't bolt. Henry took the flight of grouse and Badger's reaction to it in stride and later turned his head to look back at Joe as if to say, *Flighty damned horses, right?*

THERE WAS NO sign of Spike Rankin or Mark Eisele. The game trail was too hard-packed to reveal boot prints, and neither man had shed clothing to be retrieved later or dropped any objects that would confirm that they'd been there. Joe knew he was flying blind, hoping against hope that they'd locate the men. But Rankin and Eisele had been missing for three days now. Although it was conceivable that they'd pitched an overnight camp while scouting in the remote wilderness terrain, there had been no evidence at the elk camp or at Rankin's vehicle that they'd packed enough gear to carry on their backs to survive.

And that uneaten lunch indicated that they had planned to return on the day they left.

Multiple scenarios ran through Joe's mind as they rode, and

almost all of them had bad endings. Rankin and Eisele had been attacked and killed by a grizzly bear, or fallen off a precipice, or been brained by a falling tree, or they had surprised someone—a poacher or a lunatic survivalist, perhaps—who kidnapped or murdered them.

"This doesn't bode well," Joe said aloud to Kany.

"No, it doesn't," she agreed as she pulled Badger to a stop and turned him toward Joe. "And if we keep going, it'll get too dark to go back down."

THEY SAT SIDE by side, facing opposite directions, and discussed the situation.

"What do you mean you'll stay up here?" Kany asked Joe with alarm. "That's nuts."

"Who knows?" Joe said. "I might spot a campfire somewhere on the side of the mountain, or I might hear something that'll give us a jump on them in the morning."

They agreed that Kany would return to Warm Springs that night and start the process of informing Haswell, coordinating the local search and rescue team, and requesting spotter aircraft from Game and Fish headquarters in Cheyenne, as well as the Civil Air Patrol. Kany said she'd return with the search team as soon as she could the next day, unless she heard differently from Joe.

She dug into her saddlebags and handed Joe a handheld radio, as well as a black plastic case containing a satellite phone.

"The batteries are charged up a hundred percent," she said. "I took them off the charger this afternoon."

"Good for you," Joe said. "I usually forget."

"Keep the phone on tonight," she said. "And make sure you turn the radio on in the morning. I'll get in touch when I arrive with the cavalry."

"Will do." Then: "Rulon is going to be upset when he hears we're mounting an all-out search for his son-in-law, but it can't be helped. We've done all we can do on our own, and we can't spend another day out here fumbling around. This mountain is too big and isolated."

"Agreed. It's something we should have started two days ago, if I'd known."

Joe winced. He knew she was right.

"Can you do me a favor when you get home?" he asked. "Please call Marybeth and let her know what's going on. I try to call her every night, and I will if I can get a satellite signal, but just in case . . ."

"Sure. Text me her number."

"Our cell phones don't work, remember?"

"Oh, that's right." She seemed flummoxed for a moment.

He scribbled out Marybeth's number on a sheet in his pocket notebook and tore it out and handed it to her. "We used to call this 'writing' back in the day," he said.

"Thanks, Dad," she said with sarcasm.

Joe thought she sounded, once again, just like one of his daughters.

He watched her ride Badger through the openings of the dark tree trunks back down the mountain, until he could see her no longer. Then he turned Henry back onto the trail and goosed him to make him resume the climb solo.

SEVERAL HOURS LATER, under a moonless sky awash with endless clouds of stars, Joe winced as he finished eating a package of "Chicken, Noodles, and Vegetables in Sauce" and several "Peppermint Candy Rings" that had been among the MREs in his gear bag. They'd both been in there for a while. Both were "Warfighter Recommended, Warfighter Tested, Warfighter Approved," according to the packaging. Both had also expired the previous year, which is something he wished he had checked at some point.

He took several sips from a half-pint of bourbon and screwed on the cap. The liquor warmed his mouth and belly.

Henry was picketed in a small meadow on the left side of his one-man tent, and Joe could hear the mule munching grass and occasionally letting loose with bouts of loud, percussive flatulence.

Joe let his small campfire burn down to coals before getting to his feet. He could feel his thigh muscles burn from the ride up, and his back was stiff. He stretched and moaned and he pulled on a thick wool Filson vest against the evening cold. He fitted the headlamp over the crown of his hat and twisted it on a quarter turn, which provided a soft yellow glow. It was enough light that he could gather up his shotgun, binoculars, and the satellite phone.

Then he tossed several gnarled lengths of pitchwood on the fire to build it up again so he could locate his camp when he returned.

AFTER A FIFTEEN-MINUTE hike farther up the mountain, Joe found the granite promontory he'd seen earlier that towered above the tops of the trees. It had a graduated slope on its left side all the way to the top. He left the shotgun at the base and climbed it hand over hand, careful not to grasp or step on loose rocks that might result in a tumble back down.

He was breathing hard when he ascended to a lichen-covered table-like flat on the summit. Then he turned off the headlamp and sat cross-legged on the cool rock, letting his eyes gradually adjust to the near-total darkness. A gentle cold breeze wafted through the treetops below him from the east. It smelled sharply of pine.

When his breathing calmed, the starlight slowly revealed the terrain around him. Joe surveyed the undulations and folds in the mountainside on either side of him through the binoculars. He was looking for signs of a camp, if not a campfire. He saw neither. And he heard nothing, not even squirrels.

It took a while to notice, but he became aware of a slight glow over the mountains to the southwest. The glow, he surmised, was likely from the lights of the dude ranch Kany had told him about. It was so faint that even if there were a sliver of a moon in the sky it would have likely drowned it out. What was the name of that place? he asked himself.

The B-Lazy-U.

Then he had a thought. What if Rankin and Eisele had stumbled across the ranch boundary while scouting for elk? Given the high security and secrecy of the Centurion gathering, was it possible the two men were being detained there?

Joe's speculation seemed implausible to him. If Rankin and Eisele had been caught on the ranch, wouldn't they have the ability—and the facts—to talk themselves out of it? Especially when Eisele revealed his connection to the governor of Wyoming?

Still, stranger things had happened. Gung ho security personnel could overdo their assignment. Perhaps Joe could ask the sheriff or members of the search and rescue team to ask some questions of the ranch management the next day. Who knows, he thought, maybe someone had seen the two elk-hunting guides.

THE SATELLITE PHONE grabbed a strong signal very quickly, probably owing to the fact that there were no obstructions above him and a perfectly clear sky. He called Ann Byrnes on her cell phone and gave her the bad news.

"Oh, the governor isn't going to like this," she said softly. "Telling the sheriff was one thing, but this . . ."

"I realize that," Joe said. "But it is what it is. This whole county will be mobilized tomorrow to help search for them. Word *will* get out."

"I'll let him know tonight so he can prepare for it."

"You mean so he can let the First Lady and his daughter know," Joe said.

"Yes. I wish you had better news."

"So do I."

"Where are you now? Warm Springs?"

He smiled to himself. "I'm in the dark on the side of a mountain with a flatulent mule."

"What on earth?"

"I was hoping I could see a sign of Mark and Spike—maybe a tent or a campfire. But no such luck."

"When the governor hears this, he might order you to stay there for the rest of your life," she said.

He looked out over the dark timber sea and up at the brilliant, piercing stars. "I've been in worse places," he said.

THEN HE CALLED Marybeth. Before he could outline his location, she said, "Susan Kany just told me." She didn't sound pleased at all.

"Joe, I thought we talked about this. You assured me you wouldn't do crazy things like this anymore—that you were older and wiser than you used to be."

"I am, I think," Joe said. "But this is an emergency, and I'm completely prepared. I was hoping I'd see or hear something that would help me find them. It was a shot in the dark."

Joe heard Marybeth assure Sheridan that her father was okay after all, even though he was alone in the dark in unfamiliar mountains.

"He's on a little camping adventure," Marybeth said with more than a little disdain in her voice. He could hear Sheridan chuckle, which was good.

Joe was pleased Sheridan was still there at the house with Marybeth, especially given the curveball the FBI agent and Sheriff Bishop had thrown at her that day. Sheridan could help ease Marybeth's anxiety from being alone at home with only Kestrel.

He asked, "Did you find anything out about—"

"Special Agent Rick Orr," Marybeth said, completing his question. "Yes, I did, and it only compounds the mystery as to why he visited my office."

She said she had to use several proprietary databases and a dark web channel to learn anything about him. "He's simply not searchable on the internet," she said. "That can only happen by design. He's got zero social media presence, and Sheridan confirms it. Simply put, Orr doesn't want to be looked up."

"Interesting," Joe said.

"Yeah. I had to get into the records at their headquarters in D.C. to find him listed. He's nowhere in their public information. What I found is that Orr is the head of a task force called Special Investigations, Counter-Intelligence Unit. There's no description of what exactly that is, and I couldn't find any other names assigned to that group. It's like he's a one-man band."

"I wonder why he's asking about Nate, then?" Joe said.

"I don't know, and I'm not sure I can even guess. But I can tell you something that intrigues me. I found it using an AI engine I've never used before. It turns out that FBI Agent Rick Orr has been on the scene of a lot of historic events dating back quite a while. Here, I wrote out the list."

Joe listened as Marybeth said, "Ruby Ridge, 1992. Waco, 1993. He was at the Bundy standoff in Nevada in 2014, and the Malheur National Wildlife Refuge siege in 2016. And he was on-site for the January 6 riots or insurrection at the Capitol. Whenever there have been significant domestic extremist incidents, Rick Orr has been there."

Joe didn't respond. He wasn't sure how.

"I don't know what it means," Marybeth said. "I'll keep digging. So will Sheridan, she says. But it isn't too much of a stretch to think that Orr is here because he thinks something big will happen. Either that, or he's involved somehow. But I just don't know."

"Wow," Joe said. "I don't want to think that Nate has been

using his time planning some kind of attack. I just don't want to think that."

"Me either," she said solemnly.

Then, after a long pause, she said, "You love it right now, don't you?" she asked. "You're enjoying yourself."

As usual, she could read his mind.

"I kind of do," he confessed.

"Do I even need to tell you to be careful? To stay safe and to not do unwise things?"

"You don't need to tell me that."

"Well," she said with a sigh, "please check in, in the morning. And keep your phone on tonight, like Susan advised you."

"I'll do both," he said.

"Joe, promise me you'll stay put until Susan and the search and rescue team reach you tomorrow. We don't want *three* missing people in those mountains."

"Not to worry," he said. Then: "Good night. I love you."

"I love you, too, you idiot."

JOE SOMEHOW GOT turned around as he descended the promontory, and found himself searching for handholds and footholds that he hadn't used on the way up. Finally, with his muscles trembling, he stepped down and felt soft earth beneath his boots.

"Made it," he said to himself. Then: "Where is my shotgun?"

He circled around the base of the rock until he located it about fifty yards from where he'd come down. It was too easy to get confused about directions in the dark in a sea of trees, he admitted to himself.

Although he attempted to use the same trail to get back to the fire and his camp that he'd taken on the way up, he wasn't sure at first that he was on it. Game trails looked the same under the light of his headlamp.

In fact, he realized ten minutes later, he'd taken the wrong trail. This one veered off and cut across the mountain, rather than descending to lead him back. He knew he'd need to backtrack to the promontory and start over.

And he'd need to remain calm.

That's when he noticed an old logging road coursing through a meadow to his south. The starlight made the depressions of the two-track stand out as twin ribbons in the grass.

A road? he thought. Kany had said there weren't any.

Before trudging back to the promontory, Joe walked out into the meadow for a closer look. After twisting the lens of his headlamp to bring it to full illumination, he was surprised to see that the grass in the tracks had been crushed down flat into the soil. There were recent tire tracks going in both directions based on the tread marks.

It was puzzling, he thought. They hadn't seen a single other vehicle that afternoon, and the elk season in the area had yet to open. Yet the road had been recently traveled by multiple vehicles.

He was also surprised to see that someone had used a chain saw to clear downed trees where the road entered the forest on the other side of the meadow. There were yellow piles of sawdust on the grass where the trees had been cut, as well as fresh cuts on the remaining logs still resting in the timber.

Was this the road Kany had mentioned? he wondered. The road that went to Summit, the old mining town? The road that was impassable due to the fallen trees that blocked it?

He walked up the two-track into the trees for a hundred yards, seeing by the light of his headlamp. Not only had fallen trees been cleared along the surface, but green branches had been cut back on the sides of the road to allow vehicles to pass. Since it wasn't an official Forest Service road, who had taken the time to open it up?

Joe stopped and stared ahead into the dark past the reach of his beam. Where did the road lead, and who had been using it?

"Hmmmmm," he said aloud.

CHAPTER EIGHTEEN

A<small>T MIDNIGHT, N</small>ATE drove the Suburban on WYO 230 through the Snowy Range, while Geronimo hunched over his iPhone in the passenger seat. The glow from the screen turned Geronimo's dark skin multihued as he swiped and enlarged topographical images on several navigation and GPS mapping apps to better familiarize himself with the terrain in and around Battle Mountain.

They'd stopped only twice since leaving Cheyenne. Once to buy ammo and junk food at the West Laramie Fly Store, and again to gather road-killed rabbits from the pavement of the highway to feed their falcons.

The only time Geronimo looked up was when Nate slowed suddenly to let a herd of elk run across the road in the beam of his headlamps. Later, they passed a dark collection of cabins and a log-built structure to their right that was marked with a **WYCOLO LODGE** sign constructed of short lengths of wood to spell the words.

"Where are we?" Geronimo asked.

"We're crossing briefly into Colorado," Nate said. "It's a place where they'll welcome the goofy green license plates on this thing."

"Well, that's good, I guess."

"Then we'll veer north again back into Wyoming to Battle Mountain."

"Gotcha," Geronimo said. "I could get a better idea where we are and where we're headed if I could keep a cell signal for more than five minutes."

Nate shrugged. "I have a general knowledge of the area, and I learned it without maps on a cell phone. I've hunted sage grouse with my birds around Warm Springs, and I was here once in the winter helping out Joe."

Geronimo looked out the passenger window at the heavy timber that opened up to reveal a deep drop-off that went nearly straight down to a small mountain stream.

"This is some harsh-looking country. I don't think I'd like to be here in the winter," Geronimo said. "I suppose that's why they call it the Snowy Range."

"That's right," Nate said, leaning forward and looking around. "I once brained a guy with a frozen fish not too far from here."

"You did *what*?"

"I'll have to tell you about that sometime," Nate said. Then: "Do you miss your daughter?"

"Of course. Where did that come from?"

Nate shrugged again. "I find myself missing my daughter. Sometimes I think I see her out of the corner of my eye, but when I turn my head, she's not there. Sometimes she appears in my dreams."

They went through a narrow canyon and emerged at a junction

known as "Three-Way." The highway to the left went to Walden, Colorado, and WYO 230 continued to the right and climbed back into the mountains and led to Warm Springs, according to the sign.

Nate barely slowed down when he turned to the right.

"Now these Colorado plates will annoy people again," he said.

"Sometimes it's hard to keep up with where your head is at," Geronimo complained.

THEY PULLED OVER on the Wyoming side of the border, where the highway crossed the North Platte River, which was a wide inky ribbon that rippled with reflected starlight.

Nate gestured to the east. "There's no moon to see it, but over there is Battle Mountain."

The mountain loomed, a black inverted U that stretched as far as they could see north and south. The only way to delineate the dark mountain from the sky was by the fine line on top that blocked out the wash of stars and a derby-shaped hat of snow that topped the summit.

"Do you know why it's named Battle Mountain?" Geronimo asked.

"No. Do you?"

"As a matter of fact, I do. I looked it up on my phone."

"Okay, why?"

Geronimo said, "In 1841, a mountain-man dude named Jim Baker and another trapper were butchering a couple of buffalo cows they had shot, when hundreds of Cheyenne and Arapaho took exception and attacked them. The two of them ran like rabbits to a little fort on the Little Snake River, where there were a dozen other trappers. But the Natives kept coming.

"Baker and the other dudes killed their horses and used them as breastworks when the Indians charged time and time again. It was like a mountain-man version of the Thermopylae–Three Hundred–type fight. The only way the mountain-man dudes survived was when they realized that the attackers would always stop to pick up their dead. So, the trappers picked their targets carefully and took them out one at a time. They had one-shot rifles back then, so the trappers made sure they always kept half of their weapons loaded and ready to go at any one time. Finally, the Indians just decided it wasn't worth it and they went home. Jim Baker couldn't believe they'd held them off. After that, the settlers to the area referred to that mountain as Battle."

"That's a good story, if it's true," Nate said. "What did you say the name of the ranch was where they do the Centurions thing?"

"I'm not sure. Lazy-something, I think."

"Ah," Nate said. "Now I remember. The B-Lazy-U. It's been around for decades. It's isolated, but from what I understand it's a pretty cool place. Old-school."

"That sounds about right," Geronimo said. "So how do we get there?"

"The entrance is straight ahead on the right."

Nate eased the Suburban into gear and drove north.

EIGHT MILES LATER, Nate slowed on the shoulder of the highway and pulled over. The only light they could see in any direction was from a small building to their right a hundred yards from US 230.

Nate turned off the headlights and raised a pair of binoculars, leaning his elbows onto the steering wheel to steady his view.

"It's a kind of guard shack under the archway that leads to the ranch," he said. "I suppose they use it to check in guests. But now what I see are a couple of guys inside and an SUV parked next to it."

"Security?" Geronimo asked.

"Probably."

"Are we going to try to get through?"

"Affirmative."

"What's our story?"

Nate shrugged. "I'll think of something. But in the meanwhile, I think we need to get all of our weapons out of view. We don't want them to think we're here to storm the place."

They got out and opened the long, hidden compartment under the floorboard in the back seat and filled it with guns and boxes of ammunition.

"The gangsters I got this unit from thought of everything," Geronimo said.

THE GUARDS AT the gate didn't wait patiently for the Suburban to arrive. As Nate turned off the highway onto the gravel road that led to the facility, a pair of headlights came on and the occupants drove a shiny black Ford Expedition up the road to meet them. The SUV used the middle of the road and filled it, and it stopped so Nate couldn't go around it. The driver didn't kill the bright headlights, even when he and another man got out.

"Stay cool," Geronimo said. But his voice was tense.

Nate raised his arm to shade his eyes from the high beams. He could make out the forms of the two men as they approached. They wore jackets and cargo pants, and holsters with the handgun grips jutting out. The men split up near the grille of the Suburban, one going to Geronimo's side and the other to Nate's.

There was a tap on Nate's window, and Nate lowered it.

The man was in his twenties with tight military-style white sidewalls and a three-day growth of beard. He had a squared-off face and a thick neck, and he spoke in an East Texas twang.

"Are you boys lost?"

"No, sir," Nate said. "This is the B-Lazy-U, isn't it?"

"That's what the sign says," the man said. "The other sign right next to it says **Private Property**."

"I can't see either one right now," Nate responded. "Your head-lights are in my eyes."

East Texas didn't apologize, and he didn't head back to his vehicle to turn off the lights, either.

Nate glanced across the seat as Geronimo whirred down his passenger window. A similar-sized man, maybe a few years older, leaned forward and eyed Geronimo. He was dark-eyed, with a lightning bolt–shaped scar on his right cheek and a neatly trimmed handlebar mustache. When he raised his hand he had a flashlight in it.

The beam flashed on and moved from Geronimo's face to Nate's, and then to the console between them. Looking for weapons.

"Keep your hands where we can see them," East Texas said.

Nate placed his hands on the top of the steering wheel and Geronimo complied by reaching out and resting his on the dash-board.

"We aren't looking for trouble," Geronimo said.

"Then what are y'all doing out here so late?" East Texas asked.

Before Nate could respond, Handlebar moved the beam from the front seat to the back and said, "Well, look at this."

Without turning his head, Nate knew Handlebar had found the hooded falcons perched in the back.

"We're in the bird abatement business," Nate said to East Texas. "The B-Lazy-U hired my company to get rid of problem starlings in their barns by flying our birds around. We're both master falconers. That's what we do."

"I've never heard of the bird abatement business," East Texas said. "Do you have any ID?"

Nate said, "I'm now taking my hand off the wheel to get something out of my pocket. Okay?"

East Texas stepped back from the window and turned slightly so Nate could see that he was gripping the gun on his hip. "Sure. Do it slowly."

Nate did, then handed a business card out the window. East Texas used the light from his vehicle to read it.

"Nate Romanowski, CEO," he read. "Yarak, Inc." He mispronounced it "Yar-ACK," not "Yar-ock." Then:

"'We Make Your Problems Go Away.' That's quite the jingle."

"Actually," Nate said, "it's our motto and it *should* read 'We Make Your Problem *Birds* Go Away.' I plan to add the word 'birds' when we reprint the cards."

East Texas narrowed his eyes and squinted at Geronimo. "What's your name?"

"Steve Richards," Geronimo said.

"Again, I ask, what are y'all doing here this time of night?" East Texas said, pocketing the card.

"We got lost," Geronimo offered. "This place is hard to find."

"That's the point," Handlebar said.

"You boys will need to do us a solid and turn this car around," East Texas said. "You aren't going anywhere tonight."

"Really?" Nate asked.

East Texas turned to Handlebar. "Are their names on the visitor or vendor list?"

Handlebar drew out his cell phone and called up a document. "Nope. No Nate Romanowski, no Yar-ACK."

"There must be some kind of mistake," Nate said. "We've come a long way."

"You'll have to sort that out with the management of the ranch," East Texas said. "And you're not going to get that done tonight, or tomorrow for that matter. This place doesn't open back up to the public for two more days. There's a private function going on, and you boys aren't on the list for it, so kindly turn around and go."

"Go where?" Nate asked. "We're in the middle of nowhere."

"That's the point," Handlebar repeated.

"And don't come back tomorrow and try to talk your way in," East Texas said. "Even if we're not here, it's eight miles to the ranch, and there are two more checkpoints before it. So just forget about showing up for a while. Take your hawks and go to Warm Springs. I hear they have a hot spring in town."

"That doesn't sound so bad," Geronimo said reasonably.

"This is going to cost me money," Nate complained. "I can't afford downtime."

"Not our problem," East Texas said, stepping back and motioning for Nate to turn around.

———

As THEY DROVE back toward the highway, Geronimo said, "That was just outlandish enough that it sounded authentic. I think they bought it, even if they didn't let us through."

Nate grunted. "They were obviously military guys, just like your friend. They're probably kicking back and enjoying a few days in the mountains off the base where they don't have to shave. I didn't want to have to take them out."

"Me either," Geronimo said. "They reminded me of me back in the day."

Nate said, "So there's only one road in and out of the ranch and it's through a pretty deep canyon. There's no way to get there except on that road, and they've got three checkpoints set up."

"Meaning what?"

"If Axel plans to hit them, I don't think he'd try a frontal assault. Too much security that would stop them, or at least seriously slow them down. He's got to have another plan if the Centurions are the target."

Geronimo agreed.

Nate watched closely in his rearview mirror as they left. He clearly saw Handlebar approach East Texas and ask to see the card Nate had given him. Interesting, Nate thought.

WHEN THEY WERE back on the highway heading north, Nate said, "*Steve Richards?* You don't look like a *Steve Richards.*"

"I had to be fast on my feet," Geronimo said with a grin. "And don't be racist."

"Okay, *Steve*." Then: "We have to find that compound Joann Delaney told us about. That's where Axel will strike from."

"How are we gonna do that?" Geronimo asked.

"I don't know yet."

Geronimo stuck his pointer finger in the air as if to preview a profound thought. "How about we come back tomorrow and tell the Centurions what we think is going on?"

"Do you think they'd actually let us in?" Nate scoffed. "And you think they'd believe us if they did? We have no evidence of an imminent attack. We just hate Axel."

"Well . . ."

"Plus, who do we tell? I'm not sure we can trust all the security guys, and we'd need to get through them. For sure, Axel will have someone on the inside and maybe more. That's how he operates. I saw that guy with the mustache get my card from the Texas guy. I wonder who he might call to let them know we were here."

"Man, you can be paranoid."

"It's served me well," Nate said.

Geronimo sat in silence as they drove through dark ranch country. The only lights to be seen were distant pole lamps near ranch houses, and the piercing stars overhead.

"Based on what that security guy said, these guys are about ready to clear out of here," Geronimo said. "Which means . . ."

"It'll be tomorrow," Nate said, finishing the thought. "Axel will crawl out from under his rock tomorrow."

PART FIVE

"The hunter must become the thing he hunts."

—J. A. Baker, *The Peregrine*

CHAPTER NINETEEN

A T FOUR-THIRTY IN the morning, Axel Soledad nodded a greeting to each member of his team as they entered the lobby of
the old hotel. Most of them were disheveled, bleary-eyed, and
grumbling about the very early hour. They shuffled across the
wooden floor to where an urn of coffee had been set up. Some
made tea.

His attack team was made up of two distinct contingents:
civilian activists and military veterans. After filling their cups, the
individuals sat down in chairs at old tables or leaned against the
far wall. As usual, the vets separated themselves from the activists,
and they stood in a knot in the far corner of the room.

"Someone forgot the almond milk," one of the activists complained.

"Fuck your almond milk," one of the vets responded.

In all, the vets in the room numbered four. Two others were
elsewhere. There were nine activists in the room, and they were
soon joined by a tenth, who'd been in the kitchen because he also

served as the camp cook. When he came into the room he brought a carton of almond milk.

"Hey," one of the activists asked Soledad, "we're missing Caleb, Tosh, and Andy. Are they still sleeping?"

"They're not available," Soledad said. "They're on a side mission in Laramie."

"Will they be joining us?" another asked.

"Negative," Soledad said. "They've got another purpose."

What he didn't tell them, and what he *wouldn't* tell them, was that Caleb, Tosh, and Andy had all been killed by Nate Romanowski the previous day. That they'd set up a flawed ambush outside of Tie Siding that had failed miserably.

Soledad cleared his throat and addressed the entire room. "The mission is about to begin," he said. "Let's go over our plan and strategy one more time."

One of the activists moaned, and said, "We've been over this a thousand times already."

"This will be a thousand and one," Soledad said.

"What about the land acknowledgment before we begin?" asked a purple-haired activist.

"Fuck your acknowledgment," one of the vets grumbled.

"Maybe later," Soledad said to placate her. He had no intention of revisiting the topic. For weeks, when speaking to the activists, he had led them in a kind of invocation they'd insisted upon:

> *The land on which we sit is the traditional unceded territory of the Cheyenne Nation. We acknowledge the painful history of genocide and forced occupation of their territory, and we honor and respect the many diverse Indigenous*

people connected from time immemorial to this land on which we now gather.

AS HE PROJECTED an aerial drone photograph on the wall behind him, Soledad tried not to reveal how rattled he'd been two hours before. That's when he'd received a call from a burner phone carried by Marshall Bissett, one of the vets, who was doing a security stint at the front entrance of the B-Lazy-U Ranch. Bissett was one of his best men, and a true believer. He'd infiltrated the security team by simply showing up at the property and announcing that he'd been ordered by his superior officer at the "Dam Neck Annex of Naval Air Station Oceana near Virginia Beach" to help provide security for the secretary of defense. Since the security team had been assigned by different authorities and they'd never worked together as a unit before, they hadn't been briefed on the entire makeup of the contingent. But they all knew about the location of SEAL Team Six, and no more questions were asked of Marshall Bissett.

"Nate Romanowski showed up at the front gate a half hour ago," Bissett had reported. "He was with a big Black guy who said his name was Steve Richards, but he matched the description of Geronimo Jones."

"Where are they now?" Soledad asked.

"We sent them on their way. But I have no doubt that they plan to come back."

"This answers several questions I had," Soledad said.

"What questions?"

"I was tipped off that Romanowski and Jones were at the Anthony house near Tie Siding yesterday. I'd sent three activists into

263

Laramie for supplies, so I diverted them and told them to set up an ambush. Of course, they fucked it up. Now we know what happened."

"Romanowski got the jump on them," Bissett said. "Just like those other three up at that safe house near Pinedale."

"Exactly right. And now, after a long absence, he's on our doorstep the night before we launch."

"That's a problem," Bissett said.

"I'll handle it," Soledad said. "I need to make a call."

Which he did, two minutes later, to Twelve Sleep County sheriff Jackson Bishop. As he'd promised months before, Bishop answered his burner phone right away.

"What?" Bishop said. "I'm kind of busy at the moment. I met this new barmaid at the Stockman's Bar and she came home with me . . ."

"Everything is on track for Battle Mountain," Soledad said bluntly. "But we've got a Romanowski problem. I need you to do what we talked about."

"Now?" Jackson asked, obviously distressed about it. "Tonight?"

"No. You can't break into their house. Do it tomorrow, when she's the most vulnerable."

"What am I going to do with a two-year-old girl?" Jackson said.

"Just hold her and wait to hear from me."

"Jesus, Axel. This is bad."

"It's necessary."

"I'm going to lose my job over this."

"We all make sacrifices," Soledad said, and punched off.

———

THE ANARCHISTS CONSISTED of six men and four women, and they'd come from all over the country. All had been students at various elite universities, and they'd participated in demonstrations, walkouts, protests, marches, campus encampments, and acts of disobedience or violence that led to their expulsion (or, in a couple of cases in Ivy League schools, their graduation with honors).

Axel had recruited them by arriving at their campus encampments and providing funds for tents and food. He also gave fiery speeches, telling them that he was one of them and he was just as against the oppressors as they were. He railed against the patriarchy and the military-industrial complex, and he led them in mantras where they chanted scripts sent to them on their iPhones. He told them he'd been radicalized and now believed in their commitment to resistance and their wish to overthrow capitalism and the American government. And that he was there to help them do it.

Basically, Soledad told them whatever they wanted to hear. He kept a list of most-fervent true believers, and he kept in touch with them via secure texts and messages. He promised he would lead them on an act of resistance that would strike a blow to the oppressors that they would never forget.

When he'd built his list up to sixteen hardcore believers, he summoned them to the old mining ghost town and started their training in weapons and tactics. Although none of them were natural warriors and a few recoiled at the sight of guns, they eventually came around. They believed in their cause enough to take up arms and use them. He never told them about the three people

265

he'd sent to occupy his safe house near Pinedale, where they'd run up against Nate Romanowski. No great loss there, except for Bethany. Bethany he'd liked.

But in his heart, Soledad despised them all. They were entitled, bitter, dirty, and profoundly ignorant of history. He didn't even like looking at them sitting there with their nose rings, multi-colored hair, bored expressions, COVID masks, and Palestinian kaffiyehs.

Easily replaceable cannon fodder, as far as he was concerned. But they could still be useful if they did what they were told.

And there was the added benefit that he wouldn't feel any re-morse later when he either cut them loose, set them up, or aban-doned them.

It was a trait he shared with the Centurions gathered at the ranch in the nearby valley.

THE VETS ON his team were different. He admired them. Like him, they'd all fought overseas in different conflicts: Iraq, Af-ghanistan, Syria, Sudan, the Congo, or Somalia. These vets had signed up to protect their country and had instead been sent to places to fight that they'd barely heard of, all so the Centurions could fly their private jets to Wyoming and play cowboy for a weekend.

Allison, code-named Double-A, who had infiltrated the ranch staff and was fully on the inside, had been at Abbey Gate. She was the de facto commander of the group of veterans, all of whom were male, and they respected and obeyed her.

Bissett, the second-in-command, had received extensive injuries and a prominent facial scar when the MRAP he was riding in was blown up by an IED in Iraq. Two of his buddies had died on the scene, and two others were severely injured. After returning to the States, Bissett had spent years fighting with the Veterans Administration over medical treatment and facial reconstruction surgery, and the fight had turned him from a patriotic ex-soldier into a man passionately antiwar.

Both had been forbidden to talk about their experiences in the military. Both would be getting their revenge very soon in a very personal way on the people who had ruined their lives.

Although he admired the vets on his team, Soledad was wary of them. Unlike the others, who knew nothing, the vets were competent, skilled, and independent thinkers. He was careful around them. He never spoke of his own history except the betrayal by his superiors, which they could understand. Not once did he talk about the things he'd done or the people he'd killed in the intervening years.

Soledad could conceive of a scenario where the vets turned on him.

But if he could hold them together for one more day, he had no doubt they'd complete their assignments.

USING THE TIP of his crutch on the projected image to illustrate their strategy, Soledad said, "This is a Google Map image of Battle Mountain and the ranch. We're on this side of the mountain, and the ranch is over the top in the valley. You can see it here."

He moved the crutch slowly from the tiny scattered buildings of Soledad City over the summit of the mountain to a ragged white line that ran vertically on the mountainside to the west.

"Here's the granite ridge that overlooks the ranch. It has enough cover that no one from below can see you. To get there, it's seven miles of rough country. It'll take most of the day on foot, and we'll send along the support ATVs with water, food, and ammo. But you've got to move slowly and quietly and stay in the trees. We don't know about any overhead surveillance, but we don't want to risk your movement if there is. As you know, the government likes nothing better than spying on its citizens."

That resulted in a low rumble of support from the activists, Soledad noted. Two of the vets nodded their heads.

"Stay behind the ridge and don't look over it at the ranch. Keep out of sight. We can't afford to have some dude ranch cowboy look up and see your head skylined against the sky. Stay hunkered down there until you get the word from me over the radio. Got that? Next image."

A closer aerial view of the B-Lazy-U appeared.

"Here is the ranch yard layout. Here is the lodge, the cabins, and the lawn. Right here, even though it's not in this image, is where they put up a stage to welcome the new Centurions into the order. The guests will all be sitting on the lawn watching them and sipping cocktails. There will be loud music, and from what I understand, some fireworks. Do *not* react to either.

"We'll know when the ceremony is over from our people inside," he said. "That's when all of the guests will leave the lawn and regroup in the lodge for cocktails and such. Security will be very light—all of their security guards will still be at the checkpoints out on the road. No one will be looking for an attack from the mountain."

Soledad gestured to the vets. "You'll lead the attack, as we discussed. Everybody else will follow them down through the trees. Don't break up or get ahead of them."

He moved his crutch around the exterior of the lodge building. "There are five doors into and out of the building. Here are the main doors above the front porch. There are also two exits on each side of the lodge and two in back. This is the loading dock, and there's a door next to that.

"You all know which entrance you've been assigned. Make sure you're with your team and find cover and get a clear view of your door. Once you hear shooting inside, you know to aim at the door and spray anyone coming out. Keep an eye on the windows on the ground floor, second floor, and third floor. It's possible they might try to open the windows and escape. Don't let them."

He turned to the vets. "You'll be the first in. Two through the front, one through each side door. Our people inside will come from the kitchen in back, so the Centurions will be surrounded on all sides. Go for high-value targets first. I've provided you with their photos so you know who they are. Be careful not to get caught in a cross fire, and keep an eye out for guests who might be armed.

"There will be collateral damage, like we discussed," Soledad said. "Staff, wives, and caterers will be in that crowd. Try to spare them if you can, but don't worry if a few of them go down. It might not be possible to avoid that."

"They knew what they were getting into when they took the job," one of the anarchists added bitterly.

"That's right," Soledad said.

To the vets, he said, "Walk the room when it's over. Make sure you got all the right ones. Double-tap the high-value targets, just to be sure."

To the activists, Soledad said, "When the shooting stops, you'll know all is clear. I'll let you know over the radio as well. That's when our inside shooters will need to exit the lodge. Don't get too excited and make a mistake and shoot them when they come out. Our guys will be wearing full body armor, helmets, and balaclavas. Do *not* take a shot at one of them."

"Or we'll kill you all," one of the vets grumbled.

"Go back to your dorms and get ready," Soledad said. "Be ready to move at dawn."

The vets left immediately, anxious to gear up.

Then, as the full room gathered themselves up to leave the old hotel, Soledad said to the anarchists, "All your lives you listened to your professors telling you about the good old days when they marched in the streets and fought against the pigs. But they *never* did something as important as this. You're about to be heroes of the resistance, true children of the revolution, and people will know your names."

When they were gone, he smiled to himself and took smug pride in choosing the people he'd gathered together in Soledad City. They'd swallow anything.

In the next room, Mark Eisele struggled against his constraints. He had heard it all, and until Soledad's briefing, he would never have believed what they were about to do.

He recalled seeing the B-Lazy-U Ranch from the top of the ridge when he and Rankin had been shot up by Double-A and her team. Now he knew why they were up there: to scout out the target.

He had to alert his father-in-law, the governor. He had to alert anyone who would listen.

Tears came to his eyes as he strained against the nylon straps that held him down, but he managed to stretch them enough that at least the top one had an inch of slack in it.

He reached up and slipped his right hand under the strap with his palm against his chest. The shoulder wound screamed at him and his buttocks wound throbbed.

Eisele soon felt his fingertips under his chin, but he couldn't advance his hand any farther. His arm was stuck at the elbow by the strap.

Then, with a grunt, he was able to get his arm free. The skin of his forearm burned from chafing it against the underside of the strap.

When the door opened and Soledad looked inside to check on him, Eisele quickly lowered his free arm down along his body and lay still. Would Soledad notice that his arm was on top of the constraint?

Eisele went cold with fear.

Should he continue to feign sleep or try to talk his way out of the situation? His heart whumped in his chest.

He listened over the sound of whooshing blood in his ears for the *zzzzzt* sound of Soledad unsheathing his long blade from his crutch.

Then, outside the room, there was a disturbance in the hotel lobby. Someone came back in and slammed the door.

"Axel?" a male voice called out.

"In here, Sergeant."

A figure approached Soledad from behind and said, "We've got a problem."

"What now?"

"Two of the anarchists say they won't budge until you lead them in the land acknowledgment. That purple-haired girl is one of 'em, and her boyfriend, the pencil-neck geek."

"You're kidding me," Axel spat.

"I wish I was. Those people you brought in here are children, and children throw tantrums, because nobody ever told them to knock it off. I think you should pistol-whip those two and show 'em we're not screwing around here."

There was a pause as Soledad considered his options. Eisele remained still.

"That might make a few more of them revolt," Soledad said. "We need them all, at least for now."

"So what are you going to do?" the sergeant asked.

"I'll go lead them in the fucking land acknowledgment," Soledad said. Then his voice got icy. "We can deal with those idiots after all of this is over."

"If that's what you think."

Eisele listened as Soledad left the room. His gait was unmistakable on the hardwood floor of the lobby: a footstep followed by the *thunk* of his crutch pad. But he continued to fake sleep, and he'd managed to slip his free arm under the sheet to conceal it. The sergeant hadn't noticed.

———

WHEN THE SERGEANT was gone, Eisele slipped his free arm out from beneath the sheet and reached down on the side of his bed until he felt the cold metal of the ratchet tie-down mechanism. He could reach it, but he couldn't turn his head to view it. He used his fingers to trace the ratchet, trying to locate the release, aware that he had trouble with the procedure even with two hands. Rankin had chided him about it.

Could he trip the release and loosen the strap?

He decided to give it an hour or two before trying. Eisele wanted to make sure that Soledad's people had left the area.

CHAPTER TWENTY

IN THE MORNING, Joe groaned aloud as he shinnied out of the one-man tent onto the frost-covered grass. Although he'd been physically exhausted from the day before, it had been a tough night and he'd slept soundly only in stretches. His sleeping pad was too thin and he felt the impressions in his back of every small rock and pine cone beneath the floor of the tent.

He grumbled, "Getting too old for this" as he rose to his feet and stretched painfully.

The mule eyed him coolly while munching a mouthful of meadow grass.

"Good morning, Henry," he said. "Looks like you had a better night than I did."

Using torn pages from his notebook, he started a fire and fed sticks into it, then foot-long lengths of dry, broken branches. He squatted and held his palms out to the fire to warm his hands. Then he placed a small soot-blackened pot of water on the grate to boil. That always took so long at elevation.

Susan Kany had not called during the night and he was concerned to see that there was only a twenty percent charge left on the sat phone. Nevertheless, he punched in her number.

"Good morning," she answered. "You're up early."

He glanced at his watch. It was six-fifteen. "So are you," he said.

"That's because someone called me. Did you make any progress finding those guys after I left?"

"Nope." Then: "Maybe. I found something interesting last night."

He described the two-track he'd stumbled upon and the location of it.

"Somebody cleared it with chain saws recently," he said. "And there are a bunch of tire tracks on it. I want to see it in the daylight, and I hope I can tell you more."

"It's *open*?" she said, clearly surprised. "That doesn't make sense to me. The Forest Service isn't exactly known for clearing old roads in the mountains."

"What if it wasn't the Forest Service who cleared it?" Joe asked.

"Then who would it be?"

"That's what I'm asking myself. Who would open an old road to a ghost town in the mountains?"

"Hunters, maybe?" she said.

"Maybe. Maybe it was *our* missing hunters."

"Then where are they?" she asked rhetorically.

"How's it going on your end?" he asked.

"Joe, it's barely six in the morning. Last night, I called the dispatcher and asked her to have Sheriff Haswell call me back, and I left a message on his cell phone. I haven't heard back from him yet."

"Ah."

"If I haven't talked to him in a couple of hours, I'll drive down to the Warm Springs resort and look for him there. He always has breakfast there. Every morning, like clockwork."

"Good. Let's get this thing moving."

She said, "Haswell needs to call up the search and rescue team, and they'll need to gear up. They're all volunteers, so they'll have to get off work and so on. I wouldn't count on us getting up there until the afternoon at the earliest."

"That's what I figured," Joe said.

"I left a message for the Civil Air Patrol for when their office opens at eight, and I did the same at headquarters to see if we can get a search plane into the air today."

"Let me know when you know something," Joe said.

Then: "I briefed the governor's chief of staff last night where we're at. I'm guessing I'm not the most popular guy at the governor's residence this morning."

She laughed at that.

"In the meantime," Joe said, "I'm going to make some breakfast and then saddle up Henry. My plan is to ride him up that road until I get to Summit. How long do you think that'll take me?"

"It's fifteen or so miles from where you're camped, I'd guess," she said. "It'll take most of the day. Henry isn't exactly a sprinter."

"As I've learned," Joe said. "So that's my plan. If nothing else, I'll find that old mining town and scratch it off the list."

"Keep your phone on," Kany said. "I'll let you know how things are going down here."

"I will," Joe said, "although I don't know if you'll be able to call me on this phone. It's losing its charge really fast. I don't know how much longer it'll last."

"Crap. There must be something wrong with it. Maybe the battery is shot. In any case, if it goes completely dead, I'll communicate with you by radio when we get close."

"I wish I could plug it into a tree or something," Joe mused. Then: "I'll try and keep you posted if I can find anything of interest in Summit or along the road. If nothing pans out, I'll head back and meet you wherever. By the way, thanks for talking to Marybeth."

"She didn't sound very happy," Kany said.

"It wasn't aimed at you; it was aimed at me. But we talked it out."

Kany chuckled and punched off.

A HALF HOUR later, outside Saddlestring at the state-owned home and game warden station on the banks of the Twelve Sleep River, Sheridan escorted Kestrel out into the garage and buckled the little girl in her car seat in Marybeth's blue Ford Bronco.

"You have a good day, sweetie," Sheridan said.

"Bye-bye," Kestrel said while blowing Sheridan an exaggerated lip-smacking kiss. Sheridan returned the gesture.

As Marybeth entered the garage, Sheridan said, "You look nice today."

Marybeth wore a dark suit with a white blouse and her string of pearls.

"I've got an all-staff meeting this morning," Marybeth said. "I've got to get them prepared for budget cuts from the county commissioners, and that's never fun."

Sheridan told her mother that she was also headed to town right behind her to run errands and that she'd try to meet her for lunch. "I've got to get a roll of chicken wire at the feedstore so I can repair our Yarak pigeon coop. A fox tried to break in a couple of nights ago to get at the birds.

"I've also got a meeting with our CPA. It took me a while to get up to speed on Yarak's recordkeeping after Liv—"

Marybeth quickly placed her index finger up to her lips as a signal to Sheridan, who caught herself and didn't finish her sentence in front of Kestrel.

"Let me know if you hear from you-know-who," Sheridan said after a beat.

"I'd *better* hear from him," Marybeth said with a concerned look on her face.

ROAD DUST FROM Marybeth's Bronco still hung in the air on the gravel road when Sheridan departed for Saddlestring in her SUV. She had a full day ahead of her: chicken wire, post office, grocery store, the meeting with the CPA, then out to Nate's compound, where the office for Yarak, Inc. was located. She had bills, paperwork, and emails to catch up on, along with the repair of the pigeon coop. There was also a colony of gophers encroaching toward the mews from the sagebrush pasture, making holes in the ground a horse or cow could step into and snap their legs. That's why Nate's ancient 12-gauge pump shotgun was leaned muzzle-down on the passenger floorboard.

She was wary about the meeting with the CPA because Sheridan had questions she *hoped* he would have answers for. Should she scale back the bird abatement business since Nate was still gone, or ramp it up and hire additional falconers? Demand hadn't decreased in the past year with Nate away, and she'd been turning down some lucrative jobs because she couldn't handle them all herself.

If she did hire additional falconers, should they be given a salary or be paid by the job? What would the tax ramifications be for scaling up or down? What regulations would kick in for doing either?

Sheridan wished she'd taken more business classes in college and that she had paid more attention to Liv's side of the business before Liv was killed. Running a small business was much more challenging than she realized. There were days where she felt that she was flying blind and the business part of Yarak was overwhelming her time and knowledge. Sheridan wished she could return to the days where she was simply a master falconer sent on assignments.

As she turned onto the state highway from the access road, Sheridan saw her mother's Bronco a half mile ahead on the straightaway. There were no other cars in either lane.

And then, there was. Up ahead, behind her mother's vehicle, a sheriff's department pickup nosed out of the trees on the left and turned to follow the Bronco.

Since when, Sheridan asked herself, did the sheriff set up a speed trap on the state highway? And had her mother been speeding? Since the road was clear and there was no traffic at all on it, Sheridan thought it likely she had been.

Her guess appeared to be confirmed when the lights flashed on and rotated on the top of the sheriff's unit, followed by the *whoop* of a siren.

Sheridan punched the Bluetooth button on her steering wheel and called Marybeth.

"What's going on up there?" she asked.

"I'm being pulled over by the sheriff."

"Why?"

"I'm not sure."

MARYBETH CRINGED WHEN she saw the flashing lights in her rear-view mirror, then quickly looked down at her speedometer. She was going seventy-three in a seventy zone. Without disconnecting the call from Sheridan, she lowered her cell phone into her lap. She didn't want the sheriff to see her using it while driving.

The siren continued to wail behind her.

"Oh, come on," Marybeth said out loud. "Is that necessary? I'm pulling over."

From her car seat, Kestrel said, "Who is it, Grandma?"

"Oh, just an annoying sheriff," Marybeth responded. Her anger was muted by the fact that Kestrel had started calling her "Grandma" instead of her given name. It warmed her heart.

As she pulled over, several thoughts came into Marybeth's head. If she was being pulled over for speeding, it better be a warning and not a citation. Three miles per hour over the limit was *nothing*, especially in Wyoming. Was it something else? A burned-out taillamp?

Maybe the sheriff just wanted to talk to her about something and chose to pull her over instead of call? Or, she thought with sudden horror, had something happened to Joe?

She stopped on the side of the road and the pickup pulled in twenty yards behind her. The wigwag lights doused, and she looked into her side mirror to see Sheriff Jackson Bishop climbing down from his cab. She could read nothing on his face as he approached her on the driver's side.

Marybeth powered the window down. "What is it, Sheriff? I don't want to be late for work."

Bishop looked at her coldly. He was unsmiling and appeared nervous. She'd never seen him like that before.

"I need you to get out of the car."

"Why?"

She found it strange that he didn't ask for her license or registration. Then she saw him glance into the back of her Bronco toward Kestrel's car seat.

"Let's not make this difficult, Marybeth," he said as he placed his right hand on the grip of his holstered Glock.

"Make what difficult?" she asked.

"There's something I need to do here. I don't like it, either. But I'm the sheriff and you need to comply."

Marybeth felt a red-hot rush of blood to her face. "I do *not* need to comply," she said. "I don't believe in that nonsense. I'm also married to a law enforcement officer and I know you need to state a probable cause for why you pulled me over and asked me to get out of my car."

"He's not a LEO," Bishop said with contempt. "He's a game warden."

Then it hit her. He wanted Kestrel.

Marybeth gritted her teeth and said, *"You want her, but you can't have her."*

Before she could floor the accelerator and leave him standing there, Sheridan's SUV pulled up and stopped on the highway next to her Bronco. Bishop wheeled around, surprised by it.

Sheridan's passenger window was down and the muzzle of a shotgun extended out of it. Marybeth heard her daughter say, "Drop the weapon and get on the ground or I'll blow your head off." To her mother, Sheridan called out, "I heard everything."

Bishop looked over his shoulder at Marybeth. He was obviously frightened.

"I never wanted to do this," he said bitterly as he tossed his weapon to the pavement. "Can we just forget this ever happened?"

"Down on the ground," Sheridan warned. "*Comply!*" Bishop slowly shook his head from side to side as he lowered himself to his knees.

"Take off, Mom," Sheridan said. "I've got this."

"Are you sure?"

"Go," Sheridan commanded.

IN A SMALL dark motel room on First Street in Warm Springs, Nate and Geronimo assembled their weapons and gear on top of Nate's rumpled bed. It was at Geronimo's initiative.

"Our squad used to do this prior to any mission in Iraq and Somalia," Geronimo said. "It was kind of a ritual, but a useful one. We wanted every guy on the team to have a complete understanding of our overall firepower and capabilities. That way, we could position each operator on the strike team in the best possible location, and adjust them depending on the mission."

Nate said, "But there are just two of us."

"Which makes this even more important, if you think about it."

On the bed were firearms, boxes of ammunition, a pair of armored vests, and combat knives in sheaths. Piled on Geronimo's bed were optics, and field equipment including a first-aid kit, camouflage paint, and handheld radios.

Geronimo gestured to Nate's holstered .454 Casull and his accompanying Ruger Ranch Rifle chambered for 6.8mm SPC rounds. Three full fifteen-round magazines lay next to the rifle.

"Obviously, you've got long-range capability with your flat-shooting rifle. That weapon, even with open sights, is lethal up to three hundred yards. We already know what you can do with your hand cannon," Geronimo said. "You'll be our distance wing warrior."

"Gotcha."

Geronimo pointed at his weapons on the bed. "My Benelli is loaded with buckshot rounds. It's devastating up to forty yards, and I can hit my targets at one shot per second. It holds eight rounds.

"I'll have both of these on me," he said, picking up two identical 1911 Colt .45 semiautomatic handguns from the bed. "One under each arm. As you know, these old babies are bruisers close-in. I'll be our close-combat ninja.

"So," Geronimo said to Nate, "how do you propose we do this? We can't just blast our way in, and I *insist* that we spare the guards manning the checkpoints."

"I'm with you on that," Nate said. "We want Axel, not service members."

"How do we isolate him and take him out?"

"The hunter must become the thing he hunts," Nate said.

When Geronimo looked at him quizzically, Nate said, "It's

from *The Peregrine* by J. A. Baker. Baker wrote that after studying falcons in England. We need to get inside of Axel's head and imagine what he'd do, given the target and the terrain. Then we use that knowledge to go after him."

Using the scarred top of a small desk in the motel room, Nate used his fingertip in a thin layer of dust to plot out their approach. "The road into the ranch is heavily guarded, as we know. Even if we took on the guards or blasted our way in, the guys at the other checkpoints would know we're coming. The road goes along the North Platte River, so conceivably we could drop down to the water and hike upriver, where we couldn't be seen by the guards up on the road. But that's too risky. All it would take is for one of those guys to wander over from the checkpoint on the road to take a piss and see us.

"So what would Axel do?" Nate asked while moving his finger to the other side of the desk. "Axel would avoid the checkpoints, too. He's a special operator like us, so he'd study the situation and search for soft entry points into the ranch and exploit them. He'd move in from behind the ranch, where there aren't any roads and where heavy timber on the mountainside would conceal his approach. He'd come straight down Battle Mountain on the east side."

Geronimo nodded his head in agreement.

"This is all really rough country," Nate said. "It's filled with deep gorges and black timber. But if he comes directly down the mountain and not from the side or along the river upstream, it's easier terrain, even though it's a longer march. So what we need to do is intercept him before he gets to the ranch."

"How do we do that?"

Nate moved his finger to the center of the table. "There's a steep trail over here called Purgatory Gulch. I've gone down it and it's a bitch, but it takes you down to a river canyon, where it flattens out along the banks. We could go down there and cut across the side of the mountain to the south. We'll have to use the terrain and cover to our advantage, and it'll be tough going. But Axel won't expect to be flanked by anyone."

"I like it, except for the hike," Geronimo said. "How many bad guys do you suppose we'll be up against?"

"It's hard to say for sure from what little we know," Nate said. "I'm guessing his force is fifteen to twenty. It might be a few less because we've taken out a half dozen, but he might have picked up some new recruits along the way we don't know about. I'm not really worried about the hippies. I'm worried about the number of vets he has in his group."

Geronimo looked up at the ceiling. "The last thing I want to do is kill brother soldiers."

"Let's do our best to avoid that," Nate said. "I don't know how, but we can try. It shouldn't be that tough telling the vets from the hippies when we pull the trigger." Then: "If we take out Axel, we're done. We need to cut off the head of the snake and we can go home. I don't care about the hippies or the Centurions, to be honest. I just want Axel."

Geronimo lowered his eyes and took in the sketched map on the desktop, then he leaned forward and cleaned it of the dust and erased it so no one could ever see it.

"Then let's get going," Geronimo said. As he said it, his cell phone burred in his pocket. He took it out and held the screen up to Nate. It read: SHERIDAN PICKETT.

Geronimo punched her up on speaker. "Hello, Sheridan."

"Geronimo, are you with Nate?" Her voice sounded tinny and there was static on the line.

"He's right in front of me," Geronimo said.

"Good. I thought that might be the case. Please let me talk to him."

Instead of handing over the phone, Geronimo held the device out between them.

"I'm here," Nate said.

"Listen, I just cuffed Sheriff Bishop with his own handcuffs and he's rolling around in the back of my car. He tried to kidnap Kestrel from my mom."

"He did *what*?" Nate hissed.

"He pulled over my mom on her way to work and he was going to take Kestrel from us. I stopped him."

"How did you do that?" Nate asked, astounded.

"I stuck a shotgun in his face. It felt like something you would do."

"Is Kestrel okay? Is your mom okay?"

"They're fine. Bishop is really remorseful, and he keeps begging me to let him loose. Honestly, I'm not sure what I'm going to do with him."

Over the speaker, they could hear Bishop's muffled pleas.

"I had to gag him," Sheridan explained. "He was driving me insane. But I needed to let you know what he told me, which is that Axel Soledad ordered him to take Kestrel."

"He wanted to take us off the board," Nate said to Geronimo. "He knows we're close to him, and he wanted us to hightail it to Saddlestring."

"This guy is always a step ahead of us," Geronimo said. "I'm really starting to hate that."

He jabbed a finger at Nate and said, "See what happens when good people spend too much time around you? They *kidnap their local sheriff.*"

"Sheridan, you're amazing," Nate said, ignoring him. "Thank you."

"I wasn't going to hurt her!" Bishop yelled from the back seat. Apparently, he'd worked free of the gag.

"Smack him," Nate said to Sheridan. "And if he doesn't pipe down, twist his ear off."

"No," Sheridan said. "I'm not doing that."

Nate asked, "Where is Joe in all of this?"

"He's been out of town the last couple of days. The governor sent him on an assignment to try and locate a couple of missing elk-hunting guides."

"Where?" Nate asked.

"Down south, almost to Colorado. He's somewhere around Battle Mountain."

Nate and Geronimo looked at each other without speaking. Nate shook his head and said, "Sheridan, can you or your mom get in touch with him?"

"Mom can," she said. "I don't know his satellite phone number."

"Then please ask her to call him. We're in the same vicinity. Have Joe call Geronimo's cell phone so we can coordinate."

"I can do that. Is he in any danger?"

Nate hesitated a moment, then said, "He might be, but we won't know until we know where he is."

"Don't let him get hurt, Nate," Sheridan pleaded.

"I'll do my best, but now we have to go. Good work today. I owe you everything for what you did."

"Just come back soon with my dad," Sheridan said. "I'm serious."

"I hope to," Nate said. "But there's something we need to do first."

GERONIMO DISCONNECTED THE call and both quickly geared up. Geronimo carried his combat shotgun and Nate slung the rifle over his shoulder. Geronimo shouldered the motel room door open and Nate followed. They weren't worried about being seen because it wasn't unusual for people to openly display firearms on the streets of Warm Springs, especially on the cusp of elk-hunting season.

Leaning against Geronimo's Suburban was an older, silver-headed man wearing rimless glasses and a beige trench coat. To Nate, he looked like a college professor.

"I'm Special Agent Rick Orr of the FBI," the man said. "And you two must be Nate Romanowski and Geronimo Jones."

Both men froze.

"I've been looking for you for a long time," Orr said.

CHAPTER TWENTY-ONE

IT WAS ALMOST noon on the two-track trail through the timber when Joe heard the sat phone burr in his saddlebag. The day had turned out to be still and sunny, although the coolness of the encroaching fall seemed to emanate from low on the ground. He was riding Henry through a dense, ancient copse of lodgepole pine and he peered straight up to see if there was an opening to the sky in order to get the best reception possible.

Seeing there wasn't, he nudged Henry to pick up his pace into an opening to the side where there was a small mountain meadow. Henry wasn't one for picking up the pace, especially on the slow uphill grade, and he ambled off the trail in what seemed like slow motion.

When he was in the center of the meadow, Joe drew the phone out and activated it. As he raised the device to his mouth, he noted the dull blinking red light on its face, which indicated that the phone needed to be placed on a charger right away.

It was Marybeth.

"Joe, where are you?"

"Still on the mountain."

Her words came tumbling out. "Sheriff Bishop pulled me over this morning and he wanted to abduct Kestrel. Sheridan saved the day, but there was no doubt what it was he wanted to do."

Joe was stunned for a moment, and he reined Henry to a complete stop so he could concentrate. That was fine with Henry, who immediately dipped his head and munched meadow grass.

"Say that again."

She did, and Joe asked, "Is Kestrel okay now? Are you?"

"She's better than I am, that's for sure. I'm not sure she was even aware of what was going on."

"Where are you now?"

"In my office at the library," she said. "It seemed safer than going home. There are too many people here for someone to try to take Kestrel again."

"Smart move. Tell me about Sheridan."

After she was through, Joe said, "Bishop is in the back of her car? Where is she taking him?"

"I don't know. She doesn't know. I just talked with her."

"I'm not sure what to say. Did Bishop say why he was trying to take Kestrel?"

"It's about Axel Soledad, Joe. Axel ordered him to do it."

"*What?* Why?"

"According to Sheridan, Axel wanted to distract Nate with this and make him come here to try to rescue his daughter. I don't know why, and neither does Sheridan."

"This is *crazy*," Joe said. "I'm glad you're okay and Kestrel is okay, though. I need to talk with Sheridan—"

And with that, the satellite phone went dead.

Joe held it away from his face and shook it, hoping somehow that it would work again. But it didn't.

Although he knew it was probably pointless, he pulled out his cell phone and powered it on. Maybe, he hoped, he was high enough in the mountains or at a lucky spot with reception. There was no signal.

Then he turned on the handheld radio Kany had given him.

"Can anyone out there read me?" he said as he keyed the mic. He repeated the message several times and waited, to no avail.

It was obvious to him that Marybeth was leading up to something when she'd called. He couldn't even guess what it might be, other than "Come home as soon as you can."

He sat on Henry and weighed his options. Given what had happened that morning, he knew he had to get back to Saddlestring as soon as possible. Marybeth needed him, and he needed her. Bishop had obviously gone off the rails, which confirmed the worst of the rumors they'd heard about him. And Sheridan was in a very precarious situation at the moment. She needed his help as well, and maybe a good criminal lawyer.

What else had Soledad put into motion that might affect his family and Kestrel? Were there others in Saddlestring who were allied with Bishop and who might try to finish the job? Did Nate have any clue what had just happened, or why?

Joe looked back over his shoulder at the two-track through the trees. By his estimation, he was about halfway to Summit. Maybe more. If he returned to the road and retreated down the mountain without clearing Summit, had he done his duty to the governor? What about Susan Kany's efforts to mount a large-scale search and rescue operation?

If he could get to a place with cell phone reception, he could call Marybeth and brief Kany. Joe wished he was more familiar with the terrain. The kind of isolation he often craved—and sought out—was anathema to him now. In his own district, Joe knew of dozens of remote locations where, often inexplicably, he could catch a cell phone signal.

The ghost town of Summit, he recalled, was at nearly nine thousand feet in elevation. There might be an outcropping or promontory nearby where he could get a signal if he kept going. He knew for sure there wasn't anything like that behind him.

So he pulled Henry's head out of the grass and reined it over back to the road. Reluctantly, Henry began to move again.

Joe looked at his watch. He'd give it a few more hours of travel and, he hoped, he'd reach Summit.

"Let's move it along, Henry," he urged the mule.

EARLIER, NATE AND Geronimo sat across from Orr in a booth at a small diner on the bank of the North Platte River. All three had ordered coffee as well as biscuits and gravy with hash browns.

After the waitress left with their order, Orr said, "You boys came out of that motel room with a lot of hardware. What is it you're planning to do?"

"Are we under arrest?" Nate asked in response.

"I wouldn't say that," Orr said, turning to Nate. "But I would say you have some things to answer for, starting with the discovery of three bodies at a burned-out cabin in Sublette County a while back. What do you know about that?"

"Who were they?" Nate asked.

Orr's eyes narrowed. "They were identified as anti-government political activists. Two were from Denver, one from Portland. They were associated with a man named Axel Soledad."

"Just three of them?" Nate asked. "It sounds like a good start to me."

Nate could feel Geronimo cringe next to him as he said it.

"I know how this works," Nate said to Orr. "You ask me provocative questions and later you submit a report saying I lied to you or misled you on material facts. Then they come and get me and prosecute me for lying to an FBI agent in a show trial. Agent Orr, I'm not going to participate in this unless you arrest me or charge me with something. I'd already be gone, except I'm looking forward to my biscuits and gravy. I hear they make the best in the valley here."

Orr reacted in a way that surprised Nate. He smiled.

"That's not why I'm here," he said. "I'm not here to hassle you, although I've been following your exploits from afar for years."

"From D.C. headquarters?" Nate asked.

Orr nodded. "I've been involved in a domestic counterterrorism unit for a million years. I've been on the scene of dozens of cases, all the way back to Randy Weaver in Idaho and Waco and the Malheur National Wildlife Refuge siege in Oregon. And to make a long story short, I've seen a lot of deception and malfeasance from our side on the ground. It sickened me, to be honest.

"If I wasn't a year from retirement now, I'm pretty sure they'd figure out a way to kick me to the curb for the questions I kept asking my superiors and the commanders in charge of those operations. Instead, they've dismantled my unit, and they just ignore me entirely. So, they just sort of let me do my own thing now."

"You've gone rogue?" Geronimo asked.

"That's probably how they'd describe it," Orr said.

"Anyway, Axel Soledad came on my radar four years ago. His name kept coming up associated with urban and campus encampments and riots all over the country. Although we couldn't get enough evidence to bring him in, it appeared to me that he was fomenting and financing domestic violence and acts of terrorism. But he knew how to do it at arm's length so he could never be directly implicated. I took my suspicions to my betters, but they blew me off."

"Imagine that," Nate said. He sat back and studied Orr's face. The man seemed to be sincere. Either that, or he was baiting them into saying something that could land them in federal prison. For Nate, it wouldn't be the first time.

"So why *are* you here?" Geronimo asked.

Orr looked down at his mug of coffee for a moment, then back up at the two of them.

"I want to stop Axel Soledad before he does something momentous. I think you two want to do the same thing."

"With us, it's personal," Nate said.

"I get that." To Nate, he said, "I know what happened to your wife." To Geronimo, he said, "I know what happened to your home."

"Then why didn't you try to stop it?" Geronimo asked. "Isn't that what the FBI is supposed to do?"

"Back in the day, yes," Orr said. "But now it seems we have different priorities."

"What makes you different?" Geronimo asked.

Nate noticed that Orr's neck was flushed. He looked at a spot over their heads. "I guess I want to enforce the law and protect our country from bad guys, no matter what they represent."

Their food arrived. Orr picked at his breakfast, while both Nate and Geronimo wolfed theirs down. When they were done, Nate said to Orr, "So are we free to go?"

Orr was silent. Nate thought he read disappointment in Orr's reaction.

Finally, the man said, "I can't hold you. I guess I was just hoping you'd cooperate with me, since we share a common goal."

Nate could feel Geronimo's eyes on the side of his head. His friend was pleading with him to be reasonable.

"Can you at least tell me what you think Soledad is planning?" Orr asked. "If it's solid information, I might still have the juice back at headquarters to get a full-fledged investigation going. But it has to be airtight, and I have to bring receipts."

Nate looked up at him. "We suspect that Axel might be plotting to wipe out the heads of the U.S. military-industrial complex in one fell swoop. And we think he might be planning to do it today or tonight."

Orr's mouth dropped open and his eyes widened. He was speechless for a moment. Then he whispered, "When? Where?"

"Come with us," Nate said. "If we can confirm our suspicions, you can be a big hero. But not before we take out Axel Soledad first."

When the waitress returned with the check, Nate slid it across the table to Orr. "You get breakfast," Nate said. "It's time we actually got some return on our taxes from the government. That is, when I used to pay taxes, anyway."

On the way out to the Suburban while Orr paid inside, Geronimo said, "What do you think? Can we trust him?"

"Not sure," Nate replied. "But we can keep him close."

"Uh-oh," Geronimo said.

"You can't just hold me here," Sheriff Jackson Bishop said to Sheridan. "In case you've forgotten, I'm the duly elected sheriff of Twelve Sleep County."

Bishop was seated in the dirt in the corner of the Yarak, Inc. pigeon coop on Nate's property. His hands were cuffed behind his back. The ground was flecked with splashes of white pigeon excrement and errant feathers, and the two dozen birds housed in the coop had all moved en masse to elevated perches on the other side of the structure to distance themselves from him.

Sheridan was seated outside the coop within the open hatchback of her SUV, her feet dangling above the ground. She leaned forward and placed her chin in her hands and studied him through the chicken wire, pondering what to do.

"You're going to find yourself in Lusk for this," Bishop said, referring to the location of the Wyoming Women's Center prison.

"I hope not," Sheridan said.

"An attractive young woman such as yourself would have a very hard time there," Bishop said.

Sheridan ignored him and asked, "Was this really all about the sovereign movement? Is that why you were going to take Kestrel?"

Bishop groaned loudly and looked up through the wire roof of the coop. "It's complicated," he said. "I wasn't going to hurt her. I would never hurt a child."

"So you were going to do what, exactly?" Sheridan asked.

"I was going to deliver her to social services and tell them her father had abandoned her, which is the truth, as you know. While they sorted things out, she would have been fed and looked after. She would never have been in any danger."

"Kestrel was with my mom," Sheridan said. "She couldn't be in better hands, and you know it. This whole thing was done to try to smoke Nate out from wherever he is, right?"

"In a manner of speaking," Bishop said. "I was just doing what I was asked to do. Romanowski was getting too close to a big operation in another part of the state. I don't know the details, but I was told it would be a game changer. The guy in charge of the operation wanted to create a distraction and take Nate off the board. That's all."

Bishop was flailing, Sheridan thought. As she thought it, he came up with a new angle to try. "I would have probably saved Nate's life by doing this. Now it might be too late for him. If something happens to him now, it's on you."

"Nice try," Sheridan said. "So you take orders from someone other than the voters of your county?"

"It's not like that, really." Bishop paused, as if to collect his thoughts. Then he said, "Sometimes a patriot has to stand up and do things for the greater good. I think someday you'll look back on this and regret it when you realize I was on the right side in this fight and you're just a dupe for people who don't care about you. But let's put that aside for now and call it even. You let me go and I won't arrest you for kidnapping and assault."

"If I do that, do we pretend nothing ever happened?" Sheridan asked.

"Exactly."

"And you go back to your office and continue to be our sheriff?"

"Yes."

"I've got to really think about that," she said.

"You can't continue to hold me here," Bishop said, his voice rising. "Every minute that goes by makes it worse for you. I mean, what are you going to do with me?"

"I'm not sure yet," Sheridan said. "I didn't exactly plan this out. My morning was going to be running errands, until you screwed it all up."

AN HOUR LATER, Henry's ears perked up and rotated slightly toward something in front of them that Joe couldn't yet see. He trusted Henry's intuition and was instantly alert. The two-track curved ahead of them through the trees to the right and Joe couldn't see beyond the turn. He listened for the sound of a vehicle coming, but there was no bass rumble or vibration through the ground.

Joe pulled Henry to a halt and leaned forward in the saddle. He saw a flash of dull white through a space between the tree trunks. Then another.

Something was moving down the two-track toward him.

He reached to his side and untied the leather thongs that held his shotgun firmly in the saddle scabbard. That's when he heard labored breathing, and a pained grunt.

A figure staggered around the corner into full view. It was a young man wearing ragged oversized hospital scrubs. He had a gaunt face with haunted eyes and a half-open mouth.

Joe called, "Mark Eisele?"

The man stopped so abruptly that he nearly toppled over. He'd obviously not noticed Joe mounted on Henry in the middle of the shadowed road until Joe spoke to him.

"That's me," Eisele said. Then he took a step backward in obvious alarm.

"I'm not going to hurt you," Joe said. "I'm game warden Joe Pickett. I was sent here to find you."

PART SIX

"This was the peregrines' true hunting time; an hour and a half to sunset, with the western light declining and the early dusk just rising above the eastern skyline."

—J. A. Baker, *The Peregrine*

CHAPTER TWENTY-TWO

IT WAS ALMOST three-thirty in the afternoon when Joe and Mark Eisele reached the edge of Summit. Eisele was mounted on Henry with Joe leading the mule on foot. Joe wasn't sure Eisele could have continued to walk back based on his condition.

The ghost town consisted of fewer than a dozen intact structures: aging log cabin homes, the remains of a livery stable and large ramshackle barn, a blacksmith's shop, a storefront adorned with a faint GEN'L MERCH sign above the portico, and a large sprawling two-story hotel that looked like it was about to fall in on itself. Among the buildings were eight dented modern travel trailers that had been parked and mounted on cinder blocks to keep them steady.

The mining town appeared to be completely abandoned at first sight, but Joe was wary. He guided Henry off the two-track into a thick stand of twelve-foot-high mountain juniper brush, where they couldn't be seen from Summit. He helped Eisele dismount.

"I really don't want to come back here," Eisele said. "In fact, I never want to see this place again for the rest of my life."

Over the past two hours, Eisele had told Joe everything he'd seen, heard, and experienced from when he and Spike Rankin stumbled upon the armed team on the ridge while scouting for elk. Eisele said he thought they'd find Rankin's body in a meat cellar.

"I didn't go looking for him when I got loose of those restraints," Eisele said. "I just got out of that old hotel and didn't stop walking until I ran into you."

Eisele had pleaded not to go back, but Joe had explained the situation they were in with no way to liaise with the outside world and a dead satellite phone. And he told Eisele that it would take them much longer to go back down the mountain to the trailhead than it would to continue to Summit.

"They have to be able to communicate from there," Joe said. "Do you know how they do it?"

Eisele said he didn't, but he thought he'd heard what sounded like one-sided cell phone conversations on the other side of the door in the hotel lobby. Which meant there was either a cell signal available or they were using satellite phones.

"We've got to let your father-in-law know you're alive as soon as we can," Joe said. "And I've got to contact the game warden from this district so she can call off the search and rescue operation.

"So tell me about the layout of Summit and where I might find radios or sat phones."

"I don't have a clue," Eisele said. "All I know about that place is a dark little room off the lobby and what I could hear from outside. I know they have a kitchen somewhere, but that's about it."

Joe didn't press him further. Instead, he reached up and parted two juniper branches so he could get a better view of the ghost town. He saw no one about, and no signs of life.

"Do you think they're all gone now?" he whispered.

"I think they all left this morning after that meeting I told you about," Eisele said. "Whether or not they left anyone behind in Soledad City—I don't know. But I doubt it."

Joe turned and grimaced at Eisele in surprise. "Did you just say 'Soledad City'?"

"That's what they called it."

"As in *Axel Soledad*?"

Eisele was emphatic. "Yes. I met him, so to speak, and I heard the name 'Axel' time and time again. I heard Double-A call him that. She was the only one who was kind to me. I think if Double-A wasn't there that Axel would have done to me what he did to Rankin."

Joe felt his stomach clench and his heart race.

"Tell me about the people who were here," he said to Eisele.

FIFTEEN MILES AWAY, on the southern slope of Battle Mountain, Nate and Geronimo filled day packs with ammunition, water bottles, and other gear. They'd found a trailhead off the Forest Service road and parked the Suburban. Rick Orr had followed them from Warm Springs in his rental SUV and now stood with his back to them at the edge of the clearing, talking on his cell phone. As he spoke, he waved his free hand wildly and with emphasis.

"Who's he talking to?" Geronimo asked Nate.

"Probably D.C.," Nate said. "He's probably calling in an air strike on us."

"Very funny," Geronimo said.

"Let's release the birds."

Geronimo's expression turned suddenly serious. He no doubt knew what Nate was thinking. If the two of them didn't make it back, they didn't want the falcons to slowly starve to death inside the Suburban. It was better to release them and hope, if all went well, that they'd return to their falconers. Or just fly away forever.

Nate donned a heavy leather glove and lifted the peregrine and prairie falcon out of the vehicle and removed their hoods. Geronimo did the same with the gyrfalcon. All three birds were magnificently still, but Nate could feel the peregrine grip his hand with coiled-up anticipation. Then Nate held up each bird and released the leather jesses attached to their ankles.

The peregrine launched and dropped a foot until its wings caught air. Then it shot across the meadow, gaining elevation until it topped the pine trees and didn't look back. The prairie falcon did the same. The gyrfalcon needed more runway because it was larger, but it also climbed until it did a banked turn before a wall of trees, and it soared to the west.

"I kind of wish I could go with them," Geronimo said.

"I *always* do," Nate responded.

Orr watched the falcons fly away as he walked back to the vehicles, but he didn't comment on them. He looked very agitated, Nate thought.

"Cell service really sucks out here," he groused. "I could barely get one bar."

"Consider yourself lucky," Geronimo said. Then: "Did you call in the Marines?"

Orr stopped in front of them, briefly closed his eyes, and sighed. "Not even close," he said. "It's a typical bureaucratic clusterfuck. I told HQ what you told me, and I got put up the chain all the way to the assistant director. He said he couldn't take action without the approval of the big guy, who just *happens* to be out of town today and can't be reached."

"That's fine," Nate said. "We'll do this without them, like we planned to do in the first place."

"It isn't just that," Orr said, his eyes widening. "Do you want to know where the director is right now?"

"Where is he?" Geronimo asked.

Orr lifted his arm and pointed south. Nate noticed that his hand and pointer finger were trembling.

"He's at the B-Lazy-U?" Nate said.

Orr said, "Apparently, he arrived in Warm Springs on his jet a couple of days ago."

Nate grinned wryly. "The director of the FBI has his own private jet? And he's hanging out with the Centurions? Well, my, my."

Orr then told Nate and Geronimo that he wouldn't be accompanying them any farther. He pointed at his lace-up dress shoes and said, "I'm not equipped for where you're going, and I'd only hold you back. I'll stay here and get back in touch with the assistant director. I'll do everything I can to help you guys take down Soledad, even if that includes reaching out to other agencies who might have people on the ground near here to respond." Then: "How confident are you that they'll try to hit the ranch tonight?"

Nate shrugged. "We're flying blind at this point. All we know is Soledad is in the area, and the Centurions plan to break up and go home tomorrow or the next day after their big shindig. So if Soledad is going to hit them, it would need to be now."

Orr's face blanched once again. He said, "Why does this all have to happen in the middle of nowhere? Why can't it happen someplace where we have agents, local law enforcement, and fire-power available?"

"You just answered your own question," Nate said while turning on his heel toward the forest wall to the north of the clearing.

A few minutes later, Geronimo looked up while they walked and said, "*Damn.*"

"What?"

"Your peregrine is tracking us. It came back."

Nate continued trudging down the game trail without looking up.

"You knew it would stay with us, didn't you?" Geronimo asked with astonishment.

Nate grunted, "Yes."

"How did you know that?"

Nate took a deep breath as he trudged forward. After a long moment of silence, he said, "There are things that were revealed to me during my months in the Hole in the Wall Canyon living with my falcons twenty-four seven."

"Are you going to tell me what they are?" Geronimo asked with exasperation.

"Not now," Nate said.

EISELE STAYED BACK in the brush with Henry while Joe worked his way to Summit along the side of the road. He advanced from tree to tree, and he was terrified the entire time that someone would emerge from one of the buildings and spot him coming. Judging by what Eisele had told him, the people who had occupied "Soledad City" were heavily armed. If they saw a game warden in a red uniform shirt approaching the location on foot, they would likely shoot first and ask questions later.

Joe began to breathe easier as he cleared each building and structure. He worked around the edges first, leaving the old hotel for last.

He found a log lean-to where they had obviously parked ATVs, evidenced by the wide knobby tire tracks in the dirt and the spots of oil and gasoline within the shelter. Joe opened the doors of the camper trailers one by one with his shotgun ready. Most were cluttered and unkempt, filled with sleeping bags, clothing, wrappers, half-filled mugs of coffee, and a few books. In one, he reached in and came out with a long scarf-like item he recognized as a Palestinian kaffiyeh. He tossed it back in.

It was obvious to him that the trailers had been used very recently and that whoever had used them planned to return.

Joe approached the old hotel from the back while watching for any movement from behind the windows. Thirty yards from the building, he ducked behind a three-foot-high elevated mound of dirt that would shield him if someone inside took a shot at him. But there was no movement from the hotel.

As he moved around the dirt mound and looked back, Joe

realized the feature was the top half of an underground bunker of some sort. Several steps down a stairwell, thick yellow electrical cords came out along the ground from under the closed door. Joe followed the cords with his eyes and saw that they snaked through the grass and led to the hotel.

He descended the partially rotted set of stairs to the bunker and opened the door, which revealed a surprisingly large diesel electrical generator, which was turned off. Joe assumed that Soledad had put the generator in the bunker—which Joe now realized was an ancient meat cellar—to keep the sound of it muted when it was running. He placed his palm on the side of the unit. It was warmer than the air outside, meaning it had been recently used.

Joe backed out of the cellar and neared the hotel, walking as silently as he could. Then he entered it through an unlocked back door. There was a dark hallway that led to a larger room, presumably the hotel lobby. He stopped and simply listened for a moment.

Hearing no sounds inside, Joe proceeded with his shotgun at the ready. The lobby was filled with empty chairs and tables, as well as a laptop computer and a projector on a tall stool. The projector was aimed toward a bedsheet that had been tacked on the wall to serve as a screen.

The stairs going to the second floor were damaged, with several treads missing. The handrail was also snapped off in several places. He assumed they had not used the rooms on the second floor.

Joe walked behind the front counter and opened a door directly behind it. Inside were two cots that could barely be seen because the window was boarded up from the outside with a sheet of plywood. The cot on the right had rumpled bedding, and loose nylon straps were coiled on the floor on the side of it. The bed on the left had been stripped clean. It was exactly as Eisele had described where he'd been held. Next to the door, on a shelf at shoulder height, was a medicine bottle of clear liquid and a syringe. Joe assumed it was the morphine Eisele had been sedated with.

As he backed out of the room, Joe heard heavy footfalls on the wooden porch outside. Someone was coming. He quickly sidestepped so he was behind a pillar, and he shouldered his shotgun and aimed at the front door.

Joe saw the doorknob turn and he eased the safety off his weapon. Then Eisele pushed his way through and stood stock-still for a moment, blinking into the gloom of the room.

Joe lowered his shotgun and stepped out from behind the pillar. "You were right," he said. "They're all gone."

"I'm glad you didn't shoot me," Eisele said with a grimace. "That would have been a hell of an ending."

"We've got to search this whole compound before anyone comes back," Joe said. "There has to be a comms room around here. Do you have any idea where it might be?"

"I don't," Eisele said. "My familiarity with this town consists of that room behind you."

"I found a generator in the back," Joe said. "I'll go see if I can get it going. It would be helpful if we had light to see. Plus, I'm curious what's on that computer."

"I'll go take a look around myself," Eisele offered.

Joe approached the man and handed him his service .40 Glock. "Take this," Joe said. "I assume you know how it works."

"No safety, right?" Eisele said. "Just point and shoot."

"That's right. Maybe you can hit something with it, because I sure can't."

"I hope I don't need to find out," Eisele said as he slipped it into the back pocket of his scrubs.

Joe used the flashlight feature on his phone to illuminate the generator in the cellar. As he reached down for a silver toggle switch on the side of the unit, he caught a glimpse of a large bundle of some kind on the floor in the back of the cellar. He shinnied around the machine and got closer to it.

He recognized the bundle as a military-grade body bag. Joe didn't have to guess what he'd find inside, but he squatted down and reluctantly unzipped the top. Inside was Spike Rankin's pale white face and half-open eyes. There was a perfectly round puncture wound in his ear.

Shaken, Joe closed the body bag and returned to the generator. He quickly flipped the switch, and it rumbled to life, filling the cellar with sickeningly sweet diesel fumes. Then he got out of there as fast as he could and returned to the lobby.

Bare bulbs in fixtures suspended from the ceiling had blazed on. He hadn't even noticed where the lights were when he was first there.

Joe opened the laptop and the screen instantly illuminated. He was both surprised and pleased that it wasn't password protected. The desktop display was a photo of three ragged-looking soldiers in a tropical setting. Joe had seen Axel Soledad when he, Nate, and Geronimo had confronted him in Portland years before. In the photo on the laptop, Soledad was younger, slimmer, and obviously on active duty.

Then he studied the graphics on the screen. It was an Apple

MacBook Air, so he was somewhat familiar with it. Marybeth had the same model.

He located a folder on the desktop that read OPERATION OCTO-BER SURPRISE. Inside the folder were Word files. He clicked on one called ROSTER.

It was a list of twenty-two names divided into two columns. The column on the left was headed "Fodder" and the column on the right was headed "Vets."

Of the sixteen names under "Fodder," six had been crossed out. Joe read through the column twice. There were names like Bree, Hadid, Emi, Stephen, Gumoor, Tashia—people with decidedly younger names. None of the individuals were familiar to him, and he wondered why they were labeled as "Fodder."

The six names under "Vets" were intact, and they consisted of what Joe assumed were nicknames, such as Sergeant, Marshall, Gunny, Double-A, RPG, and MRAP.

Then he clicked on a PowerPoint folder and turned on the projector. The white sheet was suddenly filled with an aerial photo of mountain terrain. Joe studied it for a moment before recognizing it as Battle Mountain. Summit was located on the top right corner. On the bottom left was a property that looked like an oasis created within the sea of timber: manicured grass lawns, a uniform series of small structures, and a larger facility squarely in the middle.

Joe advanced to the second slide. It was the same aerial photo, but this one had graphics overlaid on it. Two arrows, one red and one blue, stretched from Summit through the forest and over the top of the mountain. Halfway down the other side, the blue arrow stopped at what looked like a long north-to-south granite ridge that poked up through the trees. The red arrow continued through a break in the ridge and was aimed directly at the property, which was now labeled B-LAZY-U.

"Oh no," Joe said aloud. "This is their battle plan."

As he said it, Eisele came back into the lobby from outside. He said, "Thank you for turning on the lights."

"Look at what they're planning," Joe said, pointing toward the sheet screen. "They're going after the Centurions."

Eisele studied the image. "It makes more sense to me now. This is what Soledad was talking about this morning. See that ridge where the blue arrow goes? That's where Rankin and I got jumped by the bad guys, including Double-A."

"Speaking of Rankin," Joe said, "I found his body outside in the cellar. I'm really sorry to tell you that."

"I can't say I'm surprised," Eisele said, looking down at the tops of his boots. "It really makes me sad, though. He was a really good guy."

Joe nodded in agreement.

Then Eisele looked up and grinned.

"What?" Joe asked.

"You were right. They have a communications room. I found it inside the old cabin right next to this place. And look what I found." Eisele handed a fully charged satellite phone to Joe.

"They took all the rest of their radios or whatever," Eisele said. "All they left was a bunch of empty charging stations. But they did leave this."

EIGHT MILES AWAY and over the summit of Battle Mountain, Axel Soledad navigated his three-wheeled ATV through tightly packed trees. He'd deliberately stayed in the rear of his strike force since they'd left Soledad City.

The vets led, followed by the activists. Soledad stayed behind all of them for several reasons.

The first reason was because he didn't like the optics of him riding the ATV while the others were on foot. He wanted *them* to lead, knowing that because of his injured legs he had no choice but to use the vehicle.

The second reason was that he was worried that some of the activists might decide to bolt before they were in place on the ridge. He wasn't worried about the vets in front. They were on a mission.

But already several of the activists had complained to him about the long march and the blisters that were growing on their feet from their boots. Plus, they didn't like having to pack their heavy rifles and day packs. If one or two of them decided to turn back, others might join them. But since he'd be directly in their path on the way back, he was confident he could dissuade them. And if that didn't work, he'd threaten them with their lives.

Soledad had ridden abreast of his team several times since they'd left that morning, and he'd offered bottles of water from the cooler strapped to his ATV. He'd also given encouraging words to them. "This will turn out to be the most important thing you do in your lifetime," and "This will be such a blow to the patriarchy that they may never recover from it," and "What you're doing this afternoon will be remembered forever," and whatever else he thought would bolster their morale.

The third and very unstated reason he hung back was that if the operation went pear-shaped on the ranch grounds, he could get the hell out of there in a hurry and save himself to fight another day.

An hour later, as the sun slipped behind the mountains to their left and muted the pale orange light that had fused through the forest, Nate and Geronimo scrambled their way through a tangled timber blowdown. They found themselves crawling over, under, and through a broken maelstrom of trunks, branches, and exposed pine tree root pans that looked like the outstretched palms of hands ordering, "Stop!" It was the isolated apex of a mountain microburst.

It was hard going, literally cutting southerly across the grain of the mountain terrain that sloped west to east. And they did so as quickly as they could, because they knew that once darkness enveloped the mountain in less than an hour they'd be blind.

After they'd traversed the blowdown and entered the standing forest on the other side, they entered a small mountain meadow that afforded a panoramic view of the mountainside ahead of them and the valley floor below. Nate paused for the first time since they'd left Orr back at the trailhead, and he stood there breathing hard to regain his calm. Geronimo very willingly took a break as well, and when he did, he leaned forward at the waist and placed his hands on his knees. His wide shoulders heaved with exertion.

From that vantage point, Nate could see the distant B-Lazy-U Ranch spread over an opening on the valley floor far below. Geronimo saw it, too, and nodded.

When he was once again breathing normally, Nate sat down and leaned his back against a thick tree trunk. He placed his hands in his lap and let the back of his head rest against the trunk. Then he closed his eyes.

Five long minutes passed. Geronimo spent the time glaring at Nate, then pacing near him. Finally, Geronimo said, "Nate, you need to wake the fuck up. We're burning our daylight. Are you okay?"

Nate didn't respond. His face was calm and his eyes remained shut.

Only when Geronimo squatted down and lightly cuffed Nate's jaw did Nate open his eyes. For a few seconds, his eyes were strange and unfocused. Then they sharpened.

"We're too low on the mountain," Nate said. "At this altitude, we won't intercept them until it's too late. We've got to start climbing and stay on a bead to the southeast until we see a granite ridge. The way we're going now would lead us beneath that ridge. We need to be above it.

"There are fourteen of them approaching the ridge. Four have broken off and are heading to a group of boulders closer to the ranch and below the ridge. Axel is behind all of them on an ATV."

Geronimo was speechless. Then his eyes widened, and he stood and looked straight up into the air. The peregrine was a tiny dot in the darkening sky.

"My God," Geronimo whispered. "You're seeing the battlefield through the eyes of your falcon."

Nate didn't deny it. He rubbed his eyes, as if emerging from a trance, then rose again to his feet. He gestured to the southeast through the trees. "That way," he said. "We need to keep up the pace. We've got to be above them by the time it gets dark."

Geronimo said to Nate, "You've got to explain to me what just happened. That is an entire level beyond *yarak*."

"What do you think I was doing all those months by myself in the canyon?" Nate asked.

B-Lazy-U Ranch Interlude

The New Centurion Banquet

THE EVENING WAS cooling when Allison carried a large tray of cocktails down a gravel path to deliver to a group of Centurions and their wives, who lounged in lawn chairs on the manicured grass lawn of the B-Lazy-U. The gravel pathway was bordered with luminaria consisting of sand-weighted brown paper bags containing candles. It wasn't yet dark enough to *need* the luminaria to see, yet she walked both carefully and briskly with the tray balanced on her right palm. She steadied it with her left hand.

When Allison reached the group of Centurions who'd made the order, she carefully dispensed the cocktails from the outside of the tray first to keep it all balanced. The secretary of defense snatched his double bourbon on the rocks eagerly and drained half of it. His wife sipped from the rim of a pink cosmopolitan.

"I'll order another one now," the man grunted while flashing a boxy smile. "Keep 'em coming."

Then, under the tray and out of her view, Allison felt a small wad of cash get stuffed almost roughly into the top of her jeans. When she flinched, the secretary waggled his eyebrows at her.

"Floyd, don't startle her," the secretary's wife admonished.

"Aw, she loves it," he responded. "Who doesn't like a little extra cash?"

At that moment, the lights flashed on above the empty stage at the top of the lawn. Background music—something very classical, martial, and ancient-sounding with piercing horns—thundered from massive speakers stationed at either side of the stage.

Allison delivered the last of the drinks, took several more orders, and glanced over her shoulder as she turned to go back to the lodge. A Centurion dressed in armor and a metal helmet adorned with a bright red comb on top strode to the microphone. He was flanked on both sides by two other uniformed Centurions carrying standards aloft.

"Greetings, Centurions," the speaker announced. "As your Imperial Legate, I welcome all of you to the annual Centurions banquet and the hallowed initiation rite of our three newest members. But first, let us honor the memory of those honored members who have passed since we were last together . . ."

ALLISON APPROACHED THE bar and stood next to Peaches Tyrell, who was reading out a list of orders to the two bartenders, who were manically in the process of filling them.

"This'll be the last call until the initiation ceremony is over," she told Allison. "Some of 'em may try and order more, but it's going to get too dark to see along those gravel pathways. Plus, some of 'em get angry when we block their view of the stage while we deliver drinks."

"Got it," Allison said. "How long will the ceremony last?"

"Half hour, forty-five minutes," Peaches said. "Then they'll all get invited to come back in here for the rest of the night. That's when things will really get wild."

Yes, Allison said to herself. *That's when things will really get wild.*

Rather than call out each order to the bartenders, Allison detached the top page of her notebook and handed it over the bar.

"I'll be back in five minutes," she said.

"We'll be ready for you," the nearest bartender promised.

Allison rushed ahead of Peaches as she was headed back to the lawn so she could open the door for her. Peaches could balance a full tray of drinks with grace, Allison thought.

"Thank you, honey," Peaches said as she passed Allison at the open door.

"My pleasure," Allison replied. Thinking: *You're going to be spared if I have anything to do with it.*

ALLISON FOLLOWED PEACHES outside and then turned sharply to her left and walked the length of the wooden porch. As she did, she dug the folded cash from the top of her jeans. The secretary had given her five dollars made up of single ones. She whispered, "Cheapskate" to herself.

Before going out through the opening at the end of the porch, she glanced around to see if anyone was watching her movements. There was no one on the porch, and all of the Centurions had their backs to her out on the lawn. They were glued to the speech of the Imperial Legate.

"... I would now like to introduce our camp prefect, who will present to you a short biography of our new Centurions before they appear here after their torchlight march down the mountain . . ."

ALLISON ENTERED THE hidden vegetable cellar and felt around on the shelving for a headlamp she'd stashed there the day before. It was completely dark inside until she clicked it on and secured it to her forehead.

She approached the three boxes marked with "X's" in the back and used a box cutter to unseal them. All were filled to the top with canned vegetables and canned fruit cocktail.

Allison emptied the first box on the floor of the cellar to see that it was entirely filled with the cans. Then she spilled the second one out. The top row was, in fact, fruit cocktail. But beneath the containers was a large, misshapen plastic bundle of bubble wrap. She lifted it out and was surprised how heavy it was.

Then, using the box cutter, she sliced through the bubble wrap to reveal two matte-black .40 Glock 23 semiautomatic handguns. She lifted each one up and inspected them in the beam of her headlamp. She looked carefully at the squared-off back of the receivers to confirm that each of the weapons had been converted as promised.

They had. Devices known as "Glock switches," which had been manufactured illegally by a 3D printer, had been installed on each weapon. The Glock switch was designed to bypass the trigger bar and turn the weapon into a continuous-fire submachine pistol. Also in the package were four long thirty-one-round magazines filled with hollow-point .40 rounds.

Allison fitted the magazines into the grips of the pistols and snapped them into place. Then she stood and aimed them at the back of the cellar wall, one in each hand.

The guns were heavy due to the weight of the extended magazines, but she had no problem holding them steady. As they were fired like a machine gun in manic bursts, they'd become much lighter very quickly.

She racked rounds into both, then lowered the weapons and laid them on the top of the third, unopened box, where she could find them and snatch them up in seconds. She laid the two extra magazines next to the pistols. Those, she'd jam into the back pockets of her jeans for quick access after the first sixty-two rounds had been emptied on the crowd.

She stepped back and looked at her phone. She'd been gone four minutes and knew she needed to get back to the bar quickly to get her full tray and deliver it.

Allison held out her hands and looked at them in the full light of her headlamp. They were trembling, and she hoped they wouldn't fail her. She took a deep breath to calm herself, but it didn't really work.

Was she actually going to do this? she asked herself. Was it really the right thing? Would it change anything at all, despite what Axel assured her?

Then she recalled Abbey Gate. Her friends were dead, while the men outside in lawn chairs sipping cocktails had simply moved on to the next war.

As ALLISON HALF walked, half jogged across the porch toward the bar door, she heard what she thought must be errant popping sounds up on the dark side of the mountain. She recalled that Peaches had mentioned something about fireworks accompanying the graduation of the new Centurions.

Someone had jumped the gun on the fireworks display, she assumed.

A few of the Centurions apparently thought the same thing because they laughed out loud. The camp prefect on the stage paused for a moment and grinned and said, "Somebody up there is a little quick on the trigger tonight," which produced a smattering of applause.

CHAPTER TWENTY-THREE

JOE WAS FOLLOWING the recently trodden path down from the summit in the near-dark when he heard what he recognized instantly as distant gunshots farther down the mountain. He stopped for a moment to listen. The popping continued, but it was punctuated with several throaty *BOOM*s that were unmistakable concussions from a .454 Casull.

It was getting dark, so he fitted his headlamp over his hat, turned it on, and picked up his pace.

There was no doubt that the people who had inhabited Summit had used the same trail he was on. He saw distinctive boot prints where the soil was soft, as well as three parallel knobby tire tracks from an ATV. He had no idea how long it would take for him to get to the ridge he'd seen on the aerial photo in the lobby, but judging from the sound of the gunshots, the ridge was still several miles away. He knew from experience that it was all but impossible to judge the distance of gunshots in the mountains, where their sound could carry for miles and bounce around and echo across the terrain.

Joe took a deep breath before trudging on. His hope had been to somehow get to the B-Lazy-U before the gunmen did. Now he knew he was too late.

HE'D LEFT EISELE at Summit with Henry two hours before. He'd also left his Glock with Eisele, after telling the man to not hesitate to use deadly force to defend himself if any of Soledad's people came back unexpectedly. They'd located two handheld radios in the comms room and Joe took one and kept the satellite phone. That way, Eisele could communicate with him if necessary as Joe marched up and over the mountain toward the ranch.

Before departing, Joe had called Kany in Warm Springs to explain the situation. She'd been absolutely stunned to hear what he had to say.

"Call off the search," Joe had said. "At this point we no longer need it. But let Sheriff Haswell know what's going on and ask him to put out the word to every LEO in a hundred-mile radius that they need to get here as fast as they can. We need bodies that are armed and briefed on the situation, and we need them there fast. I don't know if we can prevent what's about to happen, but we have to try. Do you have any contacts on the ranch itself?"

She'd said, "I've met the manager and I know a couple of the fishing guides. Do you want me to call them and warn them?"

Joe hadn't responded immediately because he wanted to think it through. Would alerting the ranch management create a panic and make the situation worse? Would they even believe her? He wasn't sure.

Then he'd said, "Yup, let them know and make sure the head

Centurion, whoever that is, is fully briefed. They may have an emergency plan of some kind in place. Let's hope so, at least."

Kany said, "I'm calling them now," and had disconnected the call.

The new satellite phone lit up several minutes later. "They didn't pick up," she'd said. "I tried the business office first, and then the cell number I have for the manager. They're probably busy with the ceremony I told you about, and cell phone coverage is bad out there. But I can keep trying."

"Keep trying," Joe had said. "I'll contact the governor."

Which he had. As usual, Ann Byrnes had taken the call, since it came from a number she didn't recognize, so she could screen it.

"I found Mark," Joe had said. "He's injured but alive. Spike Rankin was murdered by a pack of domestic terrorists who are about to unleash hell on the Centurion confab at the B-Lazy-U Ranch."

For the first time since he'd met her, Byrnes was speechless.

Finally, she said, "We got a call an hour ago from the supervisor of the Wyoming FBI office. He said he'd talked to an agent out of D.C. who is on the ground there. This agent, Rick Orr, claimed the same thing you just told me. They're in the process of putting together an attack team and they requested the use of three of our National Guard helicopters. The governor was skeptical, but he authorized their use."

"When will they get here?" Joe had asked.

"I don't know," she'd said. "At least a couple of hours, I'd guess."

"I hope that's not too late."

"Joe, the governor will be *so* grateful to hear that Mark is okay. Maybe he can move back into the mansion now."

Joe had grunted before disconnecting the call. Rulon moving back in with his wife and reconciling with his daughter was now the last thing on his mind.

Marybeth had answered on the first ring.

"I'm okay and I found Mark Eisele alive," Joe had said. "But now I've got much bigger problems."

"You need to find Nate," Marybeth had responded. "He's down there, you know."

Joe hadn't been surprised that his wife's first thought was to team up with Nate. That was *always* her first response.

And now, after hearing the heavy *BOOMS* farther down the mountain, he surmised that finding Nate might be in the cards after all.

A HALF HOUR before, Nate and Geronimo had covered enough terrain that they were in sight of the ridge. They could see it from the steep side of an adjoining slope through a gap in the heavy timber.

The granite outcropping was horizontal and pale against the dark timber of the next mountain. It stretched for nearly a mile across the face of the slope. Geronimo dug a pair of binoculars from his pack and steadied himself by leaning into a cedar trunk.

After twenty seconds, he said, "I see movement."

"What do you see?" asked Nate.

"Not much. But a couple of them have walked behind an open crack in the rock. They're all hunkered down behind that wall. I see them wearing combat fatigues and carrying rifles."

"Is Axel with them?"

"I haven't seen him."

Nate said, "I'm glad we got here before they attacked. But I have a feeling it could happen at any minute."

Geronimo lowered the binoculars. "We need to outflank 'em," he said. "Get behind them before they know we're here."

Nate nodded in agreement, then sank quickly into a cross-legged sitting position. He closed his eyes.

Geronimo now knew better than to say anything or interrupt his friend. Instead, he watched him in silence and then tilted his head skyward. The peregrine was doing a lazy loop far above them, a black speck moving across a fading cumulus cloud.

After a moment, Nate said, "The bulk of them are behind the ridge, but a few of them are out ahead, moving down toward the ranch. I'm guessing they're the professionals. Soledad would want his best people out front, and I don't blame him."

"So how do we do this?"

Nate said, "We circle around behind them, like you said. I'll come down from their right, and you come down from their left, and we move on them from two different directions in a pincer movement. If we do it right, they'll be trapped with their backs to the rock wall."

Geronimo nodded.

"We communicate with hand signals so they can't hear us," Nate said. "And we fire different weapons at intervals so they'll think there are a lot more of us than there are." Then: "I want Axel myself."

"Maybe," Geronimo said. "But if I get him in my sights first I won't hesitate to kill him dead. And I won't leave him lying there to bleed out like I did before. I want him extinguished this time."

Rather than argue, Nate unslung his Ranch Rifle and racked a round from the fifteen-round magazine into the chamber. Out of habit, he also checked to make sure all five rounds in the cylinder of his .454 were filled.

"After we take them out," Nate said, "we need to hustle down the mountain after those vets. They're creeping down through the trees, so if we go all-out we should be able to engage them."

"I told you I don't like the idea of killing my brothers," Geronimo said.

"You've made that clear. I don't want to do it, either. Maybe we can convince them to turn around and go home."

"Do you think that's possible?"

Nate shrugged. "I hope it's possible. But either way, after we've engaged the vets we need to book it to the ranch itself. Soledad has to have a couple of infiltrators down there. Whoever they are, they might be able to pull off the operation practically on their own if we don't stop them."

FIFTEEN MINUTES BEFORE Allison and Joe heard gunshots, Nate and Geronimo had approached the ridge from the side. They'd advanced taking cover from tree trunk to tree trunk, being careful not to expose themselves to anyone who might be looking in their direction. They moved stealthily, leapfrogging each other across the slope. While one moved, the other peered carefully around his tree for movement on the top of the ridge or through cracks in the rock wall.

When they reached the northern edge of the ridge near a field of loose scree, they paused for a moment and Nate nodded to

Geronimo, meaning it was go time. Geronimo nodded back, and he cut straight up the mountainside until he vanished in the shadow-darkened trees. For such a big man, Nate thought, Geronimo Jones could move like a cat.

Nate approached their position in a low crouch, careful to keep a large boulder between him and the activists. When he reached the boulder, he pressed his back against it and held his rifle at port arms.

He gave Geronimo time to climb the hillside and loop around to the south. While he waited, he could hear the militants on the other side of the rock wall. He heard snatches of low talk and several scratchy radio transmissions. Several higher voices confirmed that at least some of the militants were women. Nate guessed that the person on the other end of those transmissions was Axel. But he couldn't yet see him or sense where Axel was in relation to his ground force.

Other than the occasional murmuring from the other side of the wall, it was remarkably still and quiet. The evening had cooled at least twenty degrees since they'd set out, and it felt like fall in the high mountains. The air was thin, and every sound carried.

Someone, a male, said, "Look. What kind of bird is that?"

Nate looked straight up into the darkening sky to see his peregrine soaring above the mountain. The bird had caught a current that flowed north to south at a lower elevation than before, and the raptor was close enough that Nate could see its light-colored, mottled breast.

"Where is Axel?" he whispered to the peregrine.

But he received no answer, because all at once four things happened almost simultaneously. First, there was the throaty roar of a two-stroke engine starting up, followed by several rifle shots. Then there were three rapid-fire shotgun blasts. Then a scream.

Geronimo had begun the assault, and Nate scrambled into place by quickly climbing through the scree to a position above and to the left of the ridge. As he cleared the scree, he saw three camo-clothed figures to his right twenty yards away. They were turned with their backs to the wall, and one was pointing up the timbered slope to where he apparently thought the shots had come from.

Nate had hoped the militants would all be bunched together in a pack, but that wasn't the case. There were groups of two, three, and four along the length of the wall. The closest group of three raised their rifles and two of them fired wildly uphill. He could see now that it was two men and a woman. They hadn't spotted him because they were looking the other way, up and to the right.

He heard Geronimo's semiautomatic shotgun bark rapidly three more times. Geronimo was apparently going after a group of four militants farther down the wall. Nate saw two of them fall immediately, and one scramble into a crack between boulders.

Since the three closest to Nate were all standing side by side away from him, he aimed his rifle at the head of the closest one, a lanky white male with dreadlocks, and shot him. When the man dropped away, Nate's front sight was already trained on the male farthest away in the group, because he was taller than the female in the middle.

Nate fired and that man cried out and fell, leaving the woman.

She was small, with pink hair and terrified eyes. Nate shifted his aim to a spot on the bridge of her nose. She looked to be in her midtwenties and her face was all sharp angles. But instead of the woman in front of him, he saw the face of Bethany in bed in that Sublette County vacation home, and couldn't make himself pull the trigger.

Only when she snarled at him and swung her rifle up in his direction did he squeeze off another round. She fell on top of the third militant.

It was chaos. The remaining activists were shooting up into the trees as fast as they could fire their semiautomatic rifles. It was now dark enough that muzzle flashes popped and lingered for a moment in his vision. But they were firing wildly, blindly.

Geronimo had apparently put aside his shotgun and was now going after them with both of his 1911 .45s. Nate could see the heavy rounds smacking and sparking against the granite wall. The militant who had slipped between the boulders a moment before screamed when he was hit, and he tumbled out onto the dirt.

Through it all, Nate could clearly make out a furious monologue coming from a radio clipped to the uniform of one of the three militants he had taken out. It was Axel, screaming at them to *"Get down behind cover. Don't fire blindly, you idiots! Pick a target and squeeze the trigger. Stop panicking! You assholes are completely useless!"*

The pincer movement Nate and Geronimo had applied had worked almost perfectly, Nate thought. Geronimo had wiped out the four militants on the southern end of the wall, and he had cleared the three on the north side.

That left three in the middle—two men and another woman. They had huddled together after throwing down their weapons.

"We give up," one of the males shouted, his voice cracking. "We give up. We're not armed anymore."

He stepped away from the other two and raised his hands high into the air.

As he did so, there was a sharp *crack* of a rifle from somewhere up above them in the trees, and the man in the process of surrendering was hit and fell straight back into his comrades. Nate ducked down, knowing the shot hadn't come from Geronimo.

Twenty yards ahead of him, the two surviving activists broke their embrace and bolted across a clearing away from the wall into thick brush. They did so holding their arms over their heads, as if that gesture could ward off bullets. There was another *crack*, but the shooter missed, and the round smacked into the scree and threw sparks.

"*Fucking useless morons*," Axel Soledad screamed from the shadows.

Then the two-stroke engine whined as he rode away.

Geronimo appeared from behind a boulder to Nate's left. He'd holstered his .45s, but held his combat shotgun loose and ready at his side.

"That was Axel," Geronimo said. "He killed one of his own and tried for another one. Then he took off like the coward he is."

Nate didn't say anything. The wild cacophony of gunshots still rang in his ears, and his nostrils were filled with the sharp odors of gunpowder, dust, and blood.

Geronimo looked at the carnage around them and shook his head sadly. He said, "It's just a bunch of stupid kids. When I saw what they looked like, I hesitated. But one of 'em saw *me* and started blasting away, so I shot back."

"I heard the sequence," Nate said. "You had no choice."

Geronimo said, "It's a good thing for me that they couldn't hit what they were aiming at. In fact, they didn't even know what they were doing. They had no training to fall back on when things got crazy. And two of 'em got away, but I'm fine with that."

"Agreed," Nate said. "They aren't worth chasing down. But we're not done."

And with that, Geronimo quickly reloaded his shotgun and slapped fresh magazines into the grips of his .45s. Then he broke into a run down the mountain.

GERONIMO MOVED WITH such speed and stealth that he nearly ran into the professionals in the dark. The four of them had crept down the slope and had positioned themselves within sight of the lights of the B-Lazy-U below, as if they were awaiting some kind of signal to move out. Their broad backs were to him.

The scene on the valley floor was otherworldly, Geronimo thought. He could see scores of dull, orange-colored luminary candles far below, set up in lines to mark pathways through the grass lawn. The luminaria threw off just enough light that he could make out groups of onlookers in lawn chairs or sitting on blankets.

Between where he was and the lawn below, three figures dressed as Roman centurions wound their way down an S curve of a mountain path toward a stage that had been set up at the end of the lawn. They were carrying sputtering torches. As they marched, thunderous classical music blared from speakers.

The vets seemed to be entranced with the goings-on in front of them, until Geronimo raised his shotgun and said, "Gentleman, this is over. Lower your weapons, turn around, and get face down in the dirt."

The four of them froze.

After a beat, one of the vets slowly turned his head. His white skin was darkened with camo face paint that reflected the low lights from below. He had a quizzical expression on his face.

"Who are you?" the man asked.

Geronimo said, "Geronimo Jones, at your service. I'm the guy who really doesn't want to shoot up my brothers at the moment. But it's your choice how this goes down."

The man next to the vet who'd turned his head said, "Sergeant, he has the drop on us."

"Did you engage those hippies up on the mountain?" Sergeant asked Geronimo. "We heard the fight going on, but we couldn't get any intel."

"Axel didn't tell you we took out your second wave?" Geronimo said. "How very like Axel."

Geronimo noted that the four of them were wearing tactical armored vests and carrying AR-15s and combat shotguns much like his own. If they turned on him, it could get very dicey, he thought.

He heard footfalls thump behind him, and he knew it was Nate without turning around. A second later, Nate stood next to him, breathing heavily from his run down the slope. All four of the vets had now stood up and turned around to look at them.

"Do what he says, boys," Nate said.

The four vets exchanged glances. One of them cursed under his breath. Then, one by one, they laid their rifles aside and drew their sidearms out of their holsters and dropped the weapons in front of them.

"The worst of the worst are down there on that lawn," the man called Sergeant said. "They'll continue to get our brothers and sisters crippled and killed in more shithole countries if someone doesn't stop them."

Nate said, "We're sympathetic to your cause, but we're not going to let you finish your mission."

"Some of us are more sympathetic than others," Geronimo said with a side-eye glance toward Nate. Then, to the vets: "We're going to zip-tie your hands and feet together for now and keep you out of the action. I'd appreciate your cooperation."

Afterward, Nate turned to Geronimo and said, "You've got this."

"Where are you off to?" Geronimo asked. "Do you know where Axel is?"

"Not at the moment."

"Then what are you . . ."

But Nate was gone, running down the rest of the mountain toward the ranch.

ALLISON EMERGED FROM the vegetable cellar with a fully automatic Glock pistol in each hand. She looked both ways, then started walking toward the lodge. She kept in the shadows as she did so.

On the stage, the three new Centurions handed their torches to other similarly clad members and stood to face the crowd on the lawn. The Imperial Legate stepped to the microphone and announced, "Please help us welcome our newest Centurions" to applause from the people on the lawn. "After the initiation oaths are complete, please join us in the lodge to celebrate the membership of our three newest warriors."

Allison approached the side door of the lodge when she heard a *snick-snick* metallic sound from the darkness to her right. A man appeared with mean eyes, a blond ponytail, and a massive revolver in his hand aimed at her. He'd just cocked it.

"Allison Anthony," he said. "Don't take another step."

"Who are you?" she asked.

"It doesn't matter," he said. "Drop the weapons and tell me where Axel Soledad is."

At that moment, the fireworks behind the stage erupted as the ceremony reached completion. The night sky lit up with rockets and exploding multicolored shells. Psychedelic colors pulsed across the lawn and the ranch buildings.

"Double-A?" someone called. "What's going on?"

It was Marshall Bissett. He'd returned from duty at the front gate to take his place inside for when the celebrants crowded into the lodge. Like Allison, he carried two modified Glocks low at his sides.

The blond man didn't hesitate. He swung his gun to the side and shot Bissett with a single shot to the heart. Then the huge muzzle was whipped back around to her, and the cylinder rotated within the movement. It had happened so fast she wasn't able to react, and the sound of the gunshot was muffled by exploding fireworks.

"You killed him," she said.

"I recognized him from before," the man said. "Are there any more of you down here?"

Allison hesitated. Then: "No. But others are coming."

"Not anymore."

And it dawned on her that the "fireworks" she'd heard earlier had been been a mixture of gunfire and pyrotechnics.

"Where's Axel?" the man asked again.

"He's not up there?" she asked, indicating Battle Mountain.

"He ran off when the situation got raggedy."

She was confused. *Axel ran away?*

"How did you know my name?" she asked.

"I met people who care about you, and that's why I'm going to let you walk away from this. But first you need to drop the weapons."

She looked over to see that the Centurions were making their way from the lawn to the lodge. The party was about to begin.

"I know what happened in Afghanistan," the man said. "I understand. But you've been manipulated by Axel into doing this. He's good at that."

She stared deep into the eyes of the man with the revolver. Something about them reminded her of a bird of prey. His eyes were sharp and relentless.

"But . . ."

"There are other ways. You don't have to throw in with Axel. He doesn't deserve you.

"Go home," he said. "Get in your car and go home."

Allison took a deep breath and sighed. Then she let the Glocks slip from her hands into the grass.

"Go," he said. "Don't look back."

She didn't look back.

———

JOE JOGGED DOWN the trail on the mountainside, trying not to exert himself to the point of useless exhaustion. The gunshots had gone silent, but following them there had been the frenetic crackling of a fireworks display that had briefly lit up the sky. He debated whether he should stop and call in what he'd heard and seen, but decided to keep going, keep pushing.

A few minutes later, ahead of him farther down the trail, someone wailed. It was a desperate, plaintive sound and he paused to catch his breath and listen. Seconds later, he noticed a light bobbing through the trunks of the trees ahead of him. A headlamp.

He stepped off the trail and got behind the trunk of an ancient ponderosa pine. He doused his headlamp. The light got brighter in the darkness, and he heard the racked voice of a woman saying, "*Oh my God, oh my God, oh my God . . .*"

Joe wondered if she was actually a believer, or if she had chosen this moment to invoke a higher power.

Then he saw that she wasn't alone. Two figures emerged from the dark timber, staggering back up the trail. The man wore the headlamp, and the woman was with him. They stepped into a small clearing between a wall of trees and where Joe had hidden. For a moment, Joe could catch a glimpse of them coming, starlight on their shoulders. They were about thirty yards away.

"*Oh my God, oh my God, oh my God . . .*"

The high-pitched whine of an engine revving cut through the stillness, and suddenly the two figures were illuminated by a single headlamp coming up behind them. Joe saw the man pause and turn toward the sound, but the woman broke into a panicked run toward the ponderosa.

It happened fast: The ATV with Axel Soledad behind the handlebars burst from the timber and bore down on the man with the headlamp. Joe saw a flash of steel in the starlight as the ATV roared next to the male activist and the blade was plunged into his side as if Soledad were performing a joust. The activist fell away, clutching his side and howling.

Joe stepped out from behind the tree just as Soledad rammed into the back of the fleeing woman and ran her over with the knobby tires of the ATV. After she was down, he hit the brakes and paused for a moment, the exhaust of the tailpipe curling up pink-colored in the rear of the vehicle due to its brake light. It was obvious that Soledad was planning to back up over her.

"Axel, freeze," Joe shouted as he raised his shotgun. He was bathed in the white of the ATV headlamp.

Soledad looked up, puzzled. He'd obviously not seen Joe until that moment.

"Turn it off and stand down," Joe barked. "You're under arrest."

Soledad glared at Joe; his twisted scowl illuminated by his gauge lights. He wasn't happy.

Joe shouldered his shotgun and took a step forward. He needed to be wary of the blade Soledad had just used on the activist, so he moved to Soledad's left a little.

Then Soledad leaned forward on the seat and gripped the handlebars and accelerated toward Joe with shocking speed.

As Joe dived for the cover of the trunk again, he held the shotgun out with one hand and pulled the trigger in the direction of the oncoming ATV. He hit the ground at the same time the machine smashed into the tree on the other side, rocking it and sending a shower of pine needles and a few broken branches earthward. Because he'd been pressed against the trunk itself, the impact of the collision sent shock waves through Joe, as if he'd been hit directly.

With a mouthful of dirt and covered by a carpet of dislodged pine needles, Joe raised himself to his hands and knees and peered around the base of the trunk. The ATV was wrapped around it, the engine dead and hissing. But there was no rider.

Joe scrambled back and located his shotgun. He listened for the sound of Soledad staggering around, but he heard nothing over the hissing.

Joe got to his feet and twisted his headlamp on. Ten feet behind the ATV, Axel Soledad lay on his back with his arms askew. His bloody blade was next to him in the meadow grass.

There was a baseball-sized hole from the shotgun blast in Soledad's tactical vest where his heart would have been.

Joe quickly checked on the two people Soledad had injured. The male was crying and rolling from side to side in the grass. The woman was unconscious or dead.

"Stay still," Joe said to the injured man. "I'll call for help."

The man stopped rolling and turned his face to him. There was terror in his eyes, and Joe realized the wounded man was looking at something over Joe's shoulder.

Joe wheeled around to see that Soledad was struggling to his feet with his crutches. The shotgun blast had stunned him, but the body armor he wore had saved his life.

Before Joe could react, a sudden *BOOM* sounded from the

darkness of the trees and the left side of Soledad's head vanished. Then he collapsed into a heap like a broken doll.

Nate stepped out of the timber holding his revolver in front of him in a two-handed grip.

"Are you okay, Joe?"

"Yup."

"We got him," Nate said. "We finally got that son of a bitch."

JOE SQUATTED DOWN and placed the back of his hand up to Soledad's lips. No breath. Axel Soledad was dead.

Joe sat down in the meadow with his shotgun across his lap. He leaned back and locked his elbows and threw back his head to the night sky. He felt equal parts stunned, triumphant, and sickened.

Then he heard the sound of helicopters approaching from the eastern sky.

PART SEVEN

"Free! You cannot know what freedom means till
you have seen a peregrine loosed into the warm
spring sky to roam at will through all the far
provinces of light."

—J. A. Baker, *The Peregrine*

CHAPTER TWENTY-FOUR

CONGRATULATIONS," GOVERNOR RULON said wryly from behind his desk. "You've helped preserve our military-industrial complex for years to come. And very, very few people will ever know what you did."

It was two days after the battle on Battle Mountain, and Joe squirmed uncomfortably in his chair. He was in the governor's private office in Cheyenne, along with Geronimo, Susan Kany, and Mark Eisele. Ann Byrnes hovered on the side, half sitting on a credenza and clutching her cell phone.

Joe had spent the last forty-eight hours being shuffled from Game and Fish headquarters to the state FBI office to a windowless soundproofed room in the basement of the federal building filled with anonymous men in suits and military uniforms. He'd told them all what he'd experienced so many times that he was sick of the sound of his own voice. And he was so ready to get back home that he'd almost left the engine running in his pickup.

"You were wise not to volunteer anything to those people,"

Rulon said to Geronimo. "The less you say to the feds, the more likely you'll stay out of prison."

"I learned from the best, sir," Geronimo said.

Rulon smiled at that.

"What do you mean, no one will ever know?" Eisele asked his father-in-law. Eisele's arm was in a clean white sling and Joe noted that he leaned to the side in his chair to avoid putting pressure on his other wound.

"No one in power wants the public to know what almost happened here or how easy it was to get to them. Those Centurions have more collective power and connections than any group you can imagine," Rulon said. "What happened here will never show up in the national media, which they own. Maybe we'll hear a few rumors from fringe websites down the road, but for the most part, it'll be buried into a black hole.

"Of course," Rulon said, stabbing the air with his index finger, "*I* know what happened. I can keep that information in my back pocket and use it when I'm negotiating with the feds. It's an enormous gift, from a political standpoint."

As he said it, Joe noted that Ann Byrnes looked away.

"What about those vets we found on the scene?" Geronimo asked. "I'd hate to hear that something happened to them, sir."

"I like how you call me sir, but you can relax. This isn't Colorado. As for your vets, into the black hole they go," Rulon said with a shrug. "Federal custody, I imagine."

Eisele asked, "What about all the bodies? Those activists . . ."

"Black hole," Rulon said.

"At least Allison got back with her family," Geronimo said to Eisele.

"I'm glad for that," Eisele responded. "I think she saved my life."

"Which I'm grateful for as well," Rulon mused. "It meant I could move back into the mansion.

"You all did well," Rulon said to the three of them. "I'm proud of you. Especially you, Joe. I'm sorry what happened to poor Spike Rankin, but you found my son-in-law."

Rulon turned to Joe. "I hear you've got another sheriff problem in Twelve Sleep County."

"Yes, we do. Or did," Joe said. "Apparently after he was cut loose, Bishop cleaned out his office and his home and no one knows where he is."

"Probably for the best," Rulon said. Joe agreed.

"Are you headed back to Colorado now?" Rulon asked Geronimo.

"Yes, sir. My family just returned. I'm anxious to see them."

"Good for you, although we could use a few more like you up here in God's country. You might want to think about that."

"I will, sir."

Rulon grinned and clapped his hands sharply. The meeting was over.

"Oh," he asked Joe. "Where is the third musketeer, anyway?"

"He's back in Saddlestring," Joe said. "He's getting reacquainted with his daughter."

ACKNOWLEDGMENTS

The author would like to thank the people who provided help, expertise, and information for this novel.

All of the epigraphs came from a single work, which is *The Peregrine* by J. A. Baker. *The Peregrine*, first published in London in 1967, is a closely observed and extraordinary nonfiction classic about nature, falcons, and obsession. Also cited: *Kabul: The Untold Story* by Jerry Dunleavy and James Hasson (Center Street, 2023).

There is no community called "Warm Springs" in Wyoming. Similarly, there is no actual annual gathering of a group known as the Centurions.

Special kudos to my first readers, Laurie Box, Molly Box Mc-Carty, Becky Box Reif, and Roxanne Box Woods.

A tip of the hat to Molly Box and Prairie Sage Creative for cjbox.net, merchandise design, and social media assistance.

It's a sincere pleasure to work with professionals at Putnam, including the legendary Neil Nyren, Daphne Durham, Ivan Held, Alexis Welby, Ashley McClay, and Katie Grinch.

And thanks once again to our agent and friend, Ann Rittenberg.

Yarak!